W9-BNS-844

The Widow's War

The Widow's War

Sally Gunning

wm
WILLIAM MORROW
An Imprint of HarperCollins*Publishers*

This book is a work of fiction. The characters, incidents, and dialogue are drawn from the author's imagination and are not to be construed as real. Any resemblance to actual events or persons, living or dead, is entirely coincidental.

FIRST EDITION

Designed by Sarah Maya Gubkin

Printed on acid-free paper

Library of Congress Cataloging-in-Publication Data

Gunning, Sally.
The widow's war : a novel / Sally Gunning.—1st ed.
p. cm.
ISBN-13: 978-0-06-079157-5
ISBN-10: 0-06-079157-8 (alk. paper)
1. Massachusetts—History—Colonial period, ca. 1600–1775—Fiction. 2. Marginality, Social—Fiction. 3. Self-realization—Fiction. 4. Cape Cod (Mass.)—Fiction. 5. Whaling—Fiction. 6. Widows—Fiction. I. Title.
PS3607.U548W53 2006
813'.54—dc22 2005047939

06 07 08 09 10 JTC/RRD 10 9 8 7 6 5 4 3 2

For the widows

Now one of the most essential branches of English liberty is the freedom of one's house. A man's house is his castle; and whilst he is quiet, he [should be] as secure in his house as a prince in his castle.

Are not women born as free as men? Would it not be infamous to assert that the ladies are all slaves by nature?

—James Otis (1725–1783)

Our happiness depends on ourselves, on the calm and equal state of our own minds and not on the versatile conduct of others.

A state of war has ever been unfavorable to virtue.

—Mercy Otis Warren (1728–1814)

Acknowledgments

Many thanks to the following people who either helped me ferret out key bits of historical information or pointed me in the right direction: Suzanne Foster and Teresa Lamperti at the Brewster Historical Society; Jim Brown at the Harwich Historical Society; Mary Cicchio at the Nickerson Room, Cape Cod Community College; Fred Dunford at the Cape Cod Museum of Natural History; Marjorie Jones at the Yarmouth Historical Society; Ernest Rohdenburg III and Joseph Nickerson at the Chatham Historical Society; and Nancy Thacher Reid.

Special thanks to my agent, Andrea Cirillo, for hanging in there through my various flights of fancy and for finding the widow such a good home; to my editor, Jennifer Brehl, for the enthusiasm and care she has devoted to the project; to Mimi and Warren McConchie, for the maps, the mill area information, and the millpond tour; to art director Barbara Levine for all her hard work on the jacket; to Kathleen Remillard, Adult Services Librarian, Brewster Ladies Library, who first enthused with me about the project and then tracked down the resources that made it happen; to Ellen St. Sure, who came up with historical answers before I could get out the questions and proofed the manuscript as well; and to my cousin Bob Thomson, who provided much of the family genealogy that grounded me in time and place.

My heartfelt gratitude goes out once again to my family of readers who advised and encouraged along the way: Jan Carlson, Diane Carlson, Nancy Carlson, Doris Fisher, John Leaning, Carol Appleton, and Betty de Jongh. My thanks also to the members of the various writers' gatherings at Brewster Ladies Library.

And for my husband, Tom, a swollen heart full of thanks, one for each time he read the manuscript, and one more for always supporting the limb as I crept along.

I take sole credit for all errors.

The

Widow's

War

I

January 2, 1761

Lyddie Berry heard the clatter of the geese and knew something was coming—Cousin Betsey, Grandson Nate, another wolf, or, knowing those fool birds, a good gust of wind—but when she heard the door snap hard against the clapboards she discounted all four of them; she whirled with the wind already in her skirts to see the Indian, Sam Cowett, just ducking beneath the lintel. He had the height and width to crowd a room, and the black eyes—what was it about a pair of eyes you couldn't see through? She took a step back and was sorry she'd done it, but he'd not have noticed; already he'd looked past her, calling into the empty doorway behind, "Blackfish in the bay!" The words had been known to clear every man out of town meeting, so Lyddie wasn't surprised to hear the instant echo of Edward's boots or see the great sweep of arm that took up his coat and cap along with his breakfast. The bread went to pocket and the beer to mouth; he set back the mug and smiled at her; never mind it was a smile full of whales, not wife—she answered it, or would have if he'd stayed to see it—he was gone before her skirts had settled.

Lyddie ate her bread and drained her beer and stepped into her day, scouring down the pewter, building up the fire for the wash, shaving the soap into the kettle. At the first trip to the well she looked up at the trees and noted the wind, coming up brisk but constant in direction; by the fourth trip it had turned fickle, angling in first from the north, then the east, then the west, sometimes in a great gust and sometimes in a whisper. She went back inside and pounded out the shirts and shifts, tossing them into the pot to boil, all the while listening to the wind. She descended the ladder into the cellar to fetch the vegetables for the stew, and even there in the hollow dark she caught the echo; she climbed out and chopped turnips and listened, put the salt fish to soak and listened, trimmed and set the candles and listened, smoothed the bed feathers and listened. Once she'd hung the stew pot, poked the fire, and stirred up the clothes, she grabbed her cloak and cap off the peg and went out.

The winter had begun mild, and the ruts were deep and soft in the landing road; Lyddie was muddied to the tops of her boots by the time she took the rise at Robbin's hill and saw the ash-colored bay spotted all over with boats and foam. She leaned into the wind and soon had a clear view of the beach, blackened as far as her eye could see, by the whales, driven ashore by the men's oars beating against the water. It was a rich sight and one not seen in the bay for some years; Lyddie stood on the bluff wrapped tight in her cloak and gloried in the view, but she made no peace with the wind. It worried her around the ears, it heeled over the boats and slapped them back; it herded the waves far up the beach and left them to die among the whales. She looked for Edward's whaleboat, but they all looked the same, although she thought she picked out the great shape of the Indian. At length she gave up and let the wind push and pull her home.

On her return she put out her midday dinner of the stew and bread and beer. They'd finished the old loaf at breakfast, and she set out the new one with her usual satisfaction at the symmetry of its shape, the tight seal of the crust blocking out the petrifying air. She had only one moment of unease, that she should waste a fresh cut into a new loaf without Edward home to share, but the minute she'd heard the word *blackfish* she'd expected to take the midday meal alone, and it didn't trouble her long, wouldn't have troubled her, if it weren't for that wind. She hastened through the meal and put away the remains, wrapping the bread in the cloth with care. She washed her plate, hung the clothes in front of the fire, swept up the pieces of bark and dried leaves and pine needles that trailed everywhere on the heels of the firewood, scoured the floor with sand, watched the darkness lie down, and listened to the wind.

When was it that the sense of trouble grew to fear, the fear to certainty? When she sat down to another solitary supper of bread and beer and pickled cucumber? When she heard the second sounding of the geese? Or had she known that morning when she stepped outside and felt the wind? Might as well say she knew it when Edward took his first whaling trip to the Canada River, or when they married, or when, as a young girl, she stood on the beach and watched Edward bring about his father's boat in the Point of Rock channel. Whatever its begetting, when Edward's cousin Shubael Hopkins and his wife, Betsey, came through the door, they brought her no new grief, but an old acquaintance.

Shubael spoke. Lyddie heard that Edward's boat had gone over, that the four men with him had been fished out alive, that they had searched till dark but had found no sign of Edward; after that Lyddie heard nothing until she realized there was nothing to hear, that the three of them now stood in silence, that the candle had lost an inch of height.

She looked at Shubael. His coat was crusted with salt, his hair glued dark and wet below his cap.

"You were near when it happened?"

He dropped his eyes, shook his head. " 'Twas Sam Cowett got there first. He recovered them. All but—"

"How many hours past?"

Husband and wife exchanged a glance. " 'Twould be four, now. With the cold, and the heaviness of the sea—"

Lyddie waved away the remainder of his words. Every wife in the village knew a man didn't survive four hours in a winter sea. She felt her cousins' expectation heavy in the air around her. They would have her weep or rail, but she felt no inclination to do either. She felt nothing but lightness and calm; her oldest fear had befallen her, and now it was over.

Cousin Betsey stepped up to Lyddie, wrapped her in her arms, and pulled her into her splayed bosom. "Take heart, Cousin, take heart in God's plan. Edward's at a greater place; he's answered the call made direct to him to come away; let us pray for your dear husband's soul to find a quick safe route to his Master." She dropped to her knees, bending her head. Lyddie looked at her cousin's malleable neck, the thinning hair tucked into her cap, the dry lips moving in easy prayer—this cousin who had borne and raised eight healthy children, whose own husband still lived and breathed beside her—and felt her calmness leave her. Her hands wouldn't fold in prayer. They itched to reach out and slap Betsey's mouth closed. Who was she to hasten Edward away, to hand him over to God without a minute's quarrel? The Reverend Dunne had promised that God could breathe eternal life into all men if it so pleased him; if he could breathe the great fire of eternal life into Edward, why not the small, flickering blaze of this earthly one? Lyddie had given over four small children to that other life; surely it was no great thing to ask God to return to her the sustaining warmth and hardness of her husband's flesh.

Lyddie had found her prayer. She dipped her head and clasped her hands. The outer door flew open; the candle flame shot high; Lyddie spun around and saw her one living child, her daughter Mehitable, start across the room toward her. Nineteen, Lyddie thought, the girl is nineteen and a girl no longer, Lyddie's age at the time of her marriage and now three months into her own. Mehitable possessed Lyddie's own high color and tall, strong body, but as Lyddie watched her daughter approach the girl seemed to fade and shrink, as if she'd walked into her mother's past, or her own future. Lyddie dropped her head and closed her eyes, but her prayer now read as what it was: a childish effort to move back instead of forward; it would protect neither Edward nor her daughter. Lyddie reached for the other prayer, Cousin Betsey's, but that one seemed as childish as the other. Why attempt to direct a God who did only as it pleased him?

2

Lyddie opened her eyes to black, shifted her head against the bolster, and saw a pale gray square of window in a wall that shouldn't have one. She shifted in the bed and felt a rush of cold that should have been a warm body positioned between her and the door. She closed her eyes to block out the window but was unable to block out the cold or the sound of the wind carping against her raw edges. She looked around in the rising light, recognizing the room now as the cold one in the northeast corner of her son-in-law Nathan Clarke's house. Someone had packed her small trunk for her; she saw it against the wall jammed in between the chest and side chair. She pushed through her usual series of aches, threw back the bed rug, and searched out the night jar. Yesterday's clothes lay across the trunk lid; she hurried the quilted petticoat and under vest over her shift, fastened the tapes, pulled on the wool dress and stockings, pushed into her shoes, and hunted around for her shawl.

Something clattered behind her; she turned to find a young girl, thickly bundled in blue wool, picking a knitting pin off the floor. Mehitable's stepchildren were all pale-haired and pale-eyed; Jane at thirteen had just turned womanish, young Nate at twelve was now studying with his tutor for Harvard; there followed a lengthy gap during which Nathan Clarke had wasted some years on a barren, consumptive wife before he was able to lay her in the ground and find another, that wife barely working in this child, the five-year-old Bethiah, before retiring to lie beside her predecessor and make way for Mehitable.

Bethiah lifted an anemic, heart-shaped face and coughed. "Mama says do you want to take breakfast with us."

"Thank you, child. Tell Mama I'll be along."

The girl stayed where she was. "Mama says Grandpapa's drowned. She says you live with us now. She says you're to have this room for yourself and your own part of the hearth and your own day to use the oven. Mama bakes Friday. What's to be your day to bake?"

"Not Friday, then."

The girl cantered away. Lyddie went to the washstand and splashed her face and hands. She picked up her hairpins and twisted her hair around her fingers; she had to do it three times before she could jam the pins home. She found her shawl and pulled it tight, already trembling with the cold, or not the cold. She breathed in, breathed out, and walked into the keeping room.

All were seated at table except for the Negro, Hassey, who was busy crossing and recrossing the floor with mugs and plates. Lyddie sat down on the bench where young Nate made room, and Jane handed her the platter of bread.

"Well, Mother," Nathan said, "you appear to have come through this ordeal unharmed. I'm told every man and boy returned alive from yesterday's excursion except for one and that one is, of course, our dear father. I have no words for such cruel luck. I've been at the shore and I may tell you the whales lie so thick I might walk to Rock Harbor on their backs. I can't begin to calculate our take—I had two boats and ten men in it. I hear the price of oil is excellent."

Nathan finished his bread, pushed back his chair, and pulled his waistcoat taut over his belly. "Come, Nate, we've Father's stock to gather."

The rest of the table broke up with them, each with her chore to do: Mehitable to the cellar, Jane to the stairs, Bethiah to the dishes, Hassey to the cows and chickens. Lyddie looked through the window at the tops of the trees; the wind had come onshore now; the tide would be near high, too. She collected her hat and cloak and went out.

Lyddie stood a minute in the King's road and looked around, stunned that so little of the outside world had changed. The houses squatted low and gray in either direction along the road, their roofs peaked sharply against the wind; to the west the waterwheel at the mill roared around in its usual frenzy, and the horses outside the tavern did their perpetual snort and shuffle. Lyddie set off down the King's road east, moving at a good pace, and soon the cold outside seemed hardly worse than that inside; she didn't slow until she reached the landing road and turned down it. As she passed Edward's house she heard sounds of the two Nathans in the barn, but she didn't look or stop; she pushed on until she reached the bay, now gone from ash to slate, the beach a checkerboard of black and red, now the butchering of the whales had begun. As Lyddie stepped onto the sand a few of the men's heads lifted like a ripple of wind through salt hay, but Lyddie turned her back on them and walked with the wind, westward along the sand, her eyes on the wrack line. None of the men carving up the blubber troubled her; they knew what she was after: not a living, breathing man, but proof of a dead one.

Lyddie walked the shore as far as the mill creek, then turned along the creek itself until hard peat turned to swamp, but she found nothing of Edward except the water that had suffocated him. She stood with her back against the wind and looked at the water, wondering what it was like, drowning, finding nothing in her life to bring her close to it until she turned around and the wind tore down her throat, snatching her breath. She tucked her chin and faced down the wind. This time, as she approached the bloody carcasses, she saw that a second phase of activity had begun; the try pots had been hauled from the try yard, and a handful of men and boys ran back and forth stacking firewood under the great kettles and lobbing thick chunks of blubber into the pots to boil down, while the old men stood by with their long-handled dippers, ready to skim off the oil. One of the men laid down his dipper and started toward her: Edward's cousin Shubael Hopkins. Lyddie had had enough words from Shubael; she reached the track to the landing road before Shubael could hail her and turned down it.

This time Lyddie snuck a look at Edward's house and barn as she passed: the same gray salted shingles, the same heavy planked door, the same windows tucked up under the eaves, but the whole of it now seemed webbed in a strange new deadness. She hurried past onto the King's road until Nathan Clarke's house came into view, a grander thing than the others along the road, defying the wind for a full two stories.

Nathan Clarke was about to receive a visitor: a long, gangly, rusty-haired gentleman had just swung his leg over the rump of an equally long and gangly bay horse. Putting man with horse, Lyddie came to the name: Ebenezer Freeman, Cousin Betsey's brother, late of the village of Satucket and now practicing law in the town of Barnstable. Lyddie had come to know the lawyer around the edges of meetings with her husband or in accidental intercepts of his visits to his sister; she pushed herself up the drive and caught him just as he finished tying his horse inside the barn.

Years of riding the court circuit in hard weather had given the once-clean planes and angles of the lawyer's face a cobbled-together look; when he saw Lyddie his features disrupted themselves further.

"Widow Berry! I'm just come from my sister's. I was there last night when Shubael . . . I wish to say—" He stopped and looked away. "I do not . . . I'm sorry, I cannot—" He brought his eyes back. "Here, let me take you in out of the wind."

He reached for her arm. She pulled it away. Why must they all move so fast? From barn to house, from house to house, from wife to widow. She looked through the open barn door at Eben Freeman's horse lipping hay off the ground; behind the horse stood a neat row of Nathan's livestock: a pair of bays and a black, three cows. . . . She looked again. The black horse, the smaller cow, were Edward's.

She turned to the lawyer. "You called me widow just now. Am I assumed so before the law?"

"Not now, no."

"When, then?"

He paused. "You will be officially widowed when either your husband's remains are returned to you or a court of law declares him dead."

"You made up his will, did you not?"

Again, the pause.

"We need wait for no court here, Mr. Freeman. My husband is dead. I would know my situation."

"Very well, then. In your husband's will he gives you your standard 'widow's thirds.' Mr. Clarke, as your nearest male relative, receives title to all property while you, as Edward's relict, retain life use of a third of either the physical property itself or a third the interest resulting from its sale, whichever Mr. Clarke deems appropriate, for as long as you remain Edward Berry's widow. Your husband stipulated that you might keep any personal property brought with you to the marriage; he further provided that you receive the use and maintenance of the cow. Your keep and care is to be charged to Mr. Clarke, again, for that period of your life in which you remain widowed. If you should so happen—" He broke off. "Widow Berry, you shiver. Please, come inside with me now."

He took her arm, and this time she let him turn her. Inside the house, the keeping room had grown livelier: Hassey scoured the floor, Mehitable tended a kettle, Jane trimmed and set candles while Bethiah sat at table scraping the mold off a squash.

At the sound of the lawyer's voice Nathan came out of his study. "Freeman! Glad to see you."

"My sympathies, Mr. Clarke. To you and—"

"Yes, yes, we are greatly distraught. I don't see how we'll recover. Now come in here, we've a great deal to discuss on the matter."

He pulled the lawyer into the study and closed the door.

3

The Sabbath broke with a continued heavy wind swirling down the mill valley. The women and girls squeezed into the chaise, while father and son saddled their horses. The water mill stood quiet on the Sabbath, but nothing had quieted the creek, which foamed angrily out of the millpond, over the rocks and down the valley out of sight into the bay. Mehitable guided the chaise past the Smalley house and two more Clarke houses without seeing a living being; at Poverty Lane they overtook a cart full of Perrys and the Sears family on foot, and by the time they caught sight of the meetinghouse the King's road was dotted with walkers and riders from both directions.

Nathan Clarke dismounted in front of the meetinghouse and took charge of the carriage horse; the family spilled out onto the ground. Cousin Betsey came up and offered Lyddie some further words about Edward's great reward at hand; Lyddie managed to receive the blessing and disengage in one turn, but she lost the image of Betsey's soupy eyes only to gain a similar one of the bay beyond. She hurried in. She found Mehitable and the children in their pew, set her hot brick at her feet, and sat down. There were, as usual, near three times the number of women as men at meeting. Would that ratio hold in the life beyond? Lyddie wondered. Was that the reward Cousin Betsey had in mind for Edward?

Linnell Foster brought his infant to the front to be baptized, and Lyddie heard a sharp crack of ice as the Reverend Dunne dipped into the bowl. The babe wailed as cold fingers touched the fragile skull. "Look not to this earth to find your comforts." Those were the first and last of the minister's words that Lyddie heard, but she couldn't have said where her mind had gone for the remaining two hours; she would have said she thought of nothing, felt nothing, but cold.

After the service they stepped out into stinging snow. Nathan Clarke decided they would pass the time before afternoon service at Bangs's Inn across the way and led the family into the road. Lyddie found herself separated from her family by the Gray brothers, Jabez and Roland, who shouted back and forth to each other above the blow.

"Sea won't lay down for a week now."

" 'Twouldn't bother that mad Indian."

"He knows his way in a whaleboat, mad or no."

"Mebbe so, but I'll not crew for him."

"He makes me more per share than any Englishman I know."

"Talk to me about shares when they fish you out of the drink."

"He saved those four, didn't he? I guess I'll not quarrel with him."

"Then I guess you're not Edward Berry."

Edward's name came back at her on the wind like a slap, bringing her up to pace, allowing her to catch up with her family just as they entered the inn. She set her brick in the fire with the others to rewarm, and looked around. The long room was thick with chattering folk likewise sheltering from the storm; the steam rose from their clothes, smoke whirled outward from fire and pipe, Lyddie felt more breathless than she had out in the wind. She took a step toward a nearby door and felt her arm gripped as if by a hawk's claw. She whirled around and discovered that she'd been speared by the old midwife, Granny Hall.

"Take heart, Widow Berry. Your husband sits at God's hand, helping Him look after your children."

"Cannot God tend his dead alone? He should have ample time for the task, as he spends so little of it in care of the living."

Granny Hall blinked. Several people near Lyddie turned around. She could feel the iron band of control that had wrapped her tightly for three days begin to rust at the edges; she slipped out of the old woman's grip and passed through the nearest door into a smaller, empty room. The fire there had been neglected; she moved her skirt aside and got as near as she dared, but the heat failed to reach her face.

A voice cut through the chill—a familiar voice—echoing from the depths of the next room.

"Three good-size chambers below," Nathan said, "plus one smaller, and the pantry, and nice, tight attics above."

"And the woodland?"

"Six acres. And if you want his share in the sloop—"

"What need I of shares in a sloop? I'm after setting up my daughter at housekeeping. Now if you were to offer furnishings—"

"Furnishings! Certainly. But we barter separate on furnishings."

"Very well. For the house and woodland I'll offer three."

"Four."

"Three-twenty."

"Three hundred and eighty pounds, Smalley, and there I rest as if against a wall. What say you?"

"Very well. How long till we settle? The court must declare the death."

" 'Tis no great matter; we've witnesses saw him go down."

"Yes, all right. But I shall want to look the place over."

"Then you shall look it over. Thursday nine suit you?"

"Thursday nine."

The footsteps divided, one pair fading, one sharpening. Lyddie turned, preferring to meet whichever party came her way eye to eye, and as she was tall and Deacon Smalley short, she did so literally. He looked surprised to find her off alone in the empty room but recovered himself with the usual civility.

"Good day to you, Widow Berry."

Lyddie dipped her head. "You were speaking to Mr. Clarke about my husband's house?"

"Ah, so you've heard, and now you must chastise! Very well, I give you my word there'll be no more talk of business on the Sabbath. Will that satisfy?"

"My concern is not the Sabbath, my concern is the house."

"Then you've no concern, Widow Berry. Your son and I have it well in hand. Now I must be off to collect my family. Good day to you, Widow Berry."

Lyddie woke to a clean, pure silence, as if a cloud of nagging insects had suddenly flown off. No more wind, but in its place came the smell of oil from the try pots, seeping through the cracks as insistently as the wind had done in the days previous.

And it was colder. Lyddie used the night jar and hurried into her clothes, pausing when she heard a sharp crack on the outer door. Early for a visitor. She heard hushed voices, heavy feet, shuffling feet, Bethiah's piping, "Who is it? Oh! Who is it? What, Jane? What? 'Tis not! Oh, 'tis not!"

Lyddie heard the rest as if inside a well: Nathan's order for a blanket, the scrape of a chair, the clatter of a bucket, the thud of booted heels on wood. She opened the door and crossed the keeping room to the table, where the family had assembled around the thing that remained of Edward. She reminded herself that this was what she had been hunting on the shore, this proof of him dead, and here was proof beyond testing. His rough work clothes remained intact, but his exposed face and hands had been ravaged by the sea bottom or whatever scavengers still lurked in the frigid water; she had trouble finding her husband under the discolored, misshapen, tattered flesh. Better the sea had kept him.

She felt a not ungentle hand on her elbow. Nathan's.

"Let us pray."

The family dropped to their knees around the table. "Blessed are they who die in the Lord," Nathan said.

The amens rang around her.

4

Lyddie moved through time with a mindless will borne of long practice. People passed in and out, carrying with them the pervasive scent of whale oil, draping Lyddie in piousness; the long, muffled night cracked open with more visits and more prayers, and in the morning the solemn procession marched to the churchyard, after which everyone turned from Lyddie with clandestine relief and went back to their own business.

Nathan Clarke called her into his study that night after his supper. He sat at his desk with his chair turned from her, his waistcoat open over his rounded belly, a pipe in hand and a tumbler at the ready. He twisted a pouched neck in her direction.

"I've good news for you, Mother. Deacon Smalley's made a handsome offer for Father's house and woodland, as well as its furnishings. I should say this will bring you a tidy sum for all your pins and ribbons."

"Some of those furnishings came with me to my marriage."

"No doubt."

"I understand from Mr. Freeman those things remain with me now."

Nathan Clarke had lifted the tumbler but paused without drinking. "Well, indeed, if you desire them. As you're well aware, my wife has, with great goodwill, relinquished the large front chamber for your use, but as I'm sure you've taken note, there's little room elsewhere to displace its current furnishings. Far wiser to sell the bulk of yours to Deacon Smalley and thereby augment your earnings. Now, if you wish to keep the odd candlestick here, a piece of dinnerware there . . . I know you possess a few nice bits and naturally—"

"I have need of a few things, yes."

He took his drink and set the glass down crisply. "Very well, then. Collect them before Thursday nine, so I may strike them off the inventory."

She asked the Negro Jot, Hassey's husband, to take her in the wagon. The smell from the try pots remained strong, and Lyddie's throat tightened against it, tightened again when she saw the house. That look of utter deadness persisted. She pushed open the door, saw the cold hearth, and understood what had seemed so wrong as she stood outside the door: she had seldom seen her chimney without its smoke.

She stepped inside, closed the door behind her, and moved straight to the hearth. Except for the absence of fire, nothing had changed—the pot hung from the crane; trivets, toaster, and iron spider sat on the bricks; Edward's pipe, tongs, and musket hung from their hooks above; her wool wheel and flax wheel sat in their corner. Lyddie took the tinderbox off the shelf, laid the rag on the hearth, and set to work with the flint and steel. It was not her best skill; one day of mortification early in her marriage she'd allowed her fire to go out and had run to the Smalleys to borrow a live coal rather than go through the ordeal with the tinder, but at last she got a spark, and from the spark came a smolder and from the smolder a flame. She scrabbled in the wood box for bits of bark and fed the flame into a decent burn and eased on more wood until the heat set her back on her heels. She sat that way until she warmed, but as soon as the discomfort of the cold was gone she became aware of the greater discomfort of an idle pair of hands.

Lyddie stood and looked around, sorting mentally through her things: the table and chairs, which Edward had made, would have to be left behind for the deacon's daughter, but she would take her iron and copper kettles, old friends through twenty years of marriage, as well as her pewter plates and tankards and spoons. Lyddie knew of mothers and daughters who ignored the custom of keeping their households separate despite sharing a roof, but Mehitable had made no such hint, and Lyddie had not expected it. Unless invited otherwise, Lyddie would take her own meals at her own fire, but as she and her daughter would use the oven on different days and launder on different days they might share the dough trays and bread peel, buckets and washtubs. Lyddie would keep her own milk pans and molds, hoping to find room for them in Mehitable's buttery. After all, Edward had seen that she would have her own cow, knowing full well her pride in her cheeses; in fact, he had himself proudly pushed so many wedges on their callers that Lyddie had once accused him of trying to get rid of it.

Lyddie crossed to the front room. Here there were few things that had come with her to the marriage, but several that she counted among her treasures: a miniature of Edward in a silver frame that he'd commissioned for her in Boston, a favorite candle stand, the cherry tea table, the looking glass Edward had carried home for her all the way from the Carolinas. She would take the miniature, of course, but she could lay no true claim to the stand or table; surely, though, the looking glass could be said to belong to her?

Lyddie approached the glass. It had been weeks since she'd looked at herself, and she was shocked at the change but unable to name its specifics. The twists and falls of hair held the same lone swath of white, the fans at the corners of her eyes hadn't deepened, but cheek and jaw protruded, as if the loss of her old desires and cares had hollowed her, honed her to a new keenness. She must learn to know this woman. She would take the glass.

Lyddie carried the glass through the short hall, past the stairs, into the bedchamber opposite the front room, and there she found most of the things that were indeed lawfully hers. The bed had come with her to her marriage, her own hands had pulled the goose down that filled the bed tick, she'd stitched her eyes blurry on the coverlet and hetcheled the flax and spun the thread and woven the cloth that had made the linen underneath it. Still, Lyddie had no need of bed or tick at Nathan Clarke's; she would take the coverlet and linens and leave the bed for Smalley to buy from her. She piled the bedding into her arms, returned to the keeping room, and spread it on the table. She took the pewter off the hutch and wrapped each plate with care until she realized that as she worked she was listening for sounds from the other room, straining for something to fill the empty air. She stopped working and turned back to the fire. It was still in healthy blaze, but she wanted more—a wild flame, a loud roar, a heat thick enough to choke the deadness around her. She reached for a log but paused before dropping it on the fire, seeing a vision of Edward with ax in hand, out on the woodlot in the bitter wind, but soon enough she came to another vision: Nathan Clarke and Deacon Smalley haggling over the woodpile as they'd haggled over the woodlot, the one growing richer as the other grew warmer, as Edward grew colder, as she grew colder. . . .

Lyddie dropped the log on the fire and sent up a shower of sparks. She reached for another and tossed it on, then another and another.

She pulled back her skirt with one hand and stretched out her other, almost into the flame, and still it felt cold.

The door rattled behind her. In one motion Lyddie pulled the spit from the fire and spun around to find Sam Cowett, the Indian, standing in the doorframe and staring at the spit, held like a lance in front of her.

Lyddie eased the spit to the floor. "Good morning, Mr. Cowett."

The Indian shifted his great shoulders and allowed the door to close behind him. "I saw smoke."

"I've come to pack up my things," she said. "I live with son Clarke now."

The Indian looked around the house. "And who lives here?"

"Perhaps Deacon Smalley's daughter. He meets my son here Thursday nine to discuss the matter." Saying the words cost her. She turned away to jab the fire and collect herself; when she turned back she found the Indian's black eye fixed on her.

The door rattled again; the Indian swung around; Nathan Clarke stepped in. "Hello, Sam," he said.

The Indian brushed past him and out the door without a word, the furrow in his brow deep enough to grow corn.

"I see your neighbor's in his usual fine fettle," Nathan said.

"Because you address him as Sam. He's made it plain all over town: he'd be addressed by his surname like any Englishman."

"Bah! He's too full of rum to notice what he's called."

"I smelled no spirit on him."

"Mark me. He'll have measured his length by sundown."

"Or yours, if you persist in so calling him."

Nathan gazed at her coolly and dropped his eye to her collection. "What need you of two kettles for one little fire? Leave the big one for Smalley. And we've a glass at home. I'll send Jot for you at half the hour."

He left. Lyddie returned the large kettle to the hearth but slid the glass inside the coverlet.

The cold hovered. Nathan ordered that while such weather continued they should keep but one big fire in the evening, so after supper Lyddie huddled with the family around the keeping room blaze. Bethiah worked at hemming an apron and Jane a sleeve; Mehitable sat altering those of Edward's clothes that could be made to fit husband or son, and young Nate sat studying his Latin grammar. Lyddie had suggested she take over the spinning as her contribution to the household tasks and had been shocked to find that her daughter had put away both her wheels; with the low price of English cloth she saw no need to "trudge around in homespun."

So Lyddie sat turning a heel in a stocking until Eben Freeman disrupted them, arriving encased in mittens and muffler. He handed Nathan a letter he had intercepted in Barnstable, and Nathan carted him away to his study.

The fire was hot enough to sear Lyddie's face, and still her back felt as if it had iced over; young Nate left for his bed rugs first, and the minute he was gone Jane set down her sleeve and picked up his grammar, puzzling over the pages. Lyddie had often done the same with her brother's books, but had had such little time with them she had made poor progress, until her marriage. Edward had taught her to keep his accounts in his absence and had read aloud to her on winter evenings as she sewed. She had often taken comfort among his books while he was away and on his return would pepper him with questions.

"My husband had some fine books, Jane," Lyddie said. "They reside now in your father's study. Perhaps he would allow—"

"If you intend to do nothing but play with books," Mehitable cut in, "you might do your sister's hemming for her. I'll get nothing of my own done if I'm jumping up each minute to fix her messes for her."

Bethiah dropped her apron and fled for the stairs. Jane set down the book, picked up the apron, and began to finish the hem herself.

Lyddie held out her hand to Jane. "Here, child, give the apron to me. And your sleeve. 'Tis too cold to sleep alone. Go with your sister."

Jane gave over the two pieces and went happily after Bethiah.

Lyddie turned to her daughter. "Bethiah only wants instruction. Perhaps if I took her in hand—"

"You say I neglect her?"

"I say only that she's lost her mother young, and those early lessons were denied her. As I have time to spare where you do not—"

"I'm able to manage my house, Mother."

"Indeed you are, but for a minute or two, here and there, you might give it over. For example, right now. You sit and shiver and rub your eyes raw. Why don't you go to your bed and leave me the sewing?"

"I've the men to tend."

"I'm able to carry a jug yet."

Mehitable got up. "There's fresh tart in the pantry if they wish it." She departed, her face a lovely, tight mask.

Lyddie finished off the apron and Jane's sleeve, then picked up a waistcoat of Edward's that Mehitable had been altering for Nate. Lyddie raised her needle but had some trouble seeing the seam; when she had last touched her needle to that cloth Edward had been sitting beside her, reading to her from Richardson. She set the piece down and turned to prompt the fire. She was still staring blindly into the flame when Nathan called from the other room for more cider.

The men sat close on either side of the fire, angled toward the blaze, the empty cider pitcher on the table at Nathan's elbow. As

Lyddie entered the room the lawyer's face did its odd creasing and he looked about to speak, but Nathan waved one hand at the jug and one at the lawyer. "Go on, go on. Who's to challenge the Writs?"

"Our own James Otis. From Barnstable."

"Otis! And will he be able to put a stop to this nonsense? Why, they want to search for smuggled goods anywhere, anytime, without cause or evidence! What the devil! If we're forced to pay duty on every barrel of French molasses—"

Lyddie picked up the pitcher and left the room. She went into the pantry and located the cider barrel; as soon as she removed the bung the tiny room filled with the sweet scent of fermentation. She filled the pitcher and returned to the study.

The two men were still at James Otis.

"I don't know," Nathan was saying. "I hear strange talk of him. He would free the slaves. I don't mean he would do like some others and abolish the import of any new slaves, he would actually *set free* all slaves, right here, right now. Will you think on the carnage?" Nathan held up his pitcher, and Lyddie filled it. She crossed to Freeman's chair, and he held up his mug; she wasn't sure, but she thought he winked at her as he did it.

"Yes, he would free the slaves," Freeman said. "And he would not enslave our women, either. He declares them born as free as we are; he would give them education and suffrage alongside us."

Yes, he had winked, she was sure of it. She left the room as Nathan burst out in a stream of vitriol against James Otis, freed slaves, voting women, unlawful search and unlawful duties, mixing them up with one another until he couldn't find his own tongue in the middle of it.

5

At a quarter to the hour of nine on Thursday Mr. Clarke left to meet Deacon Smalley at the house. Mehitable was in bed with a stomach gripe, Hassey had gone out to kill a chicken for dinner, Nate was at his tutor, Jane worked a crust, and Lyddie and Bethiah were making soap, Bethiah leaching the ash with boiled water and Lyddie mixing it with the winter's collection of grease. When Mehitable called out from her chamber Lyddie's hands were the easiest freed, and so she was first to the chamber door. She found Mehitable curled under two rugs, her face pale and damp, her hair tangled, her cap missing.

"Have you taken a vomit?" Lyddie asked. "A little violet root will induce—"

"I know well enough how to induce a vomit, Mother. I would have a mint tea, if you would tell Jane—"

"I'll get it."

"Send Jane, please. I've some other instruction for her."

Lyddie returned to the kitchen. The mint tea barely covered the bottom of the canister. She directed Jane to brew up the remains, returned to her room for her cloak and boots, and set off for the store.

The minute she stepped outside Lyddie was choked by the smell from the try pots. She had once welcomed the foul odor as a sign of unexpected bounty, but not now; by the time she reached Sears's store she felt as ill as Mehitable. She selected her tea and took it to Caleb Sears to mark it off the account. When she saw him write it in the ledger under Edward Berry she corrected him.

"I'm sorry," he said. "It goes to Mr. Clarke, now?"

"Yes, to Mr. Clarke."

It was a little thing, but it unsettled her, and when she left the store she turned wrong, moving a dozen rods past the Clarke house before it struck her. Did she think she was going back to her old house, then, one last look before Smalley took possession?

And why not?

Lyddie kept going, turning left at the landing road, leaving off the muddy ruts for the sandy track and the general for the familiar. Here the shadblow cracked by the wind, there the old wall, next Edward's fence, and there, or was it? Yes, the chimney and roof and there the barn; from the distance she could even see the horse tied in front and think it was Edward's chestnut darkened with sweat from a lengthy ride, and the sound of an ax ringing out in the woodlot could well have been made by Edward as he set up next winter's wood to season over summer.

Lyddie shook herself to earth. The horse was a bay, not a damp chestnut, and no doubt Smalley's. But if the horse was so easily explained, the sound of the ax wasn't. She moved around the far side of the house until she had a clear view of the woodlot. The pitch pines, used for a quick start or a bright light, had lost their north side to the wind, and gave the lot an appearance of tilting away from the sea; the oaks, used for steadier, slower heat, were more evenly grown, but in disparate heights: those that had recently shot up from the old stumps and those that had been growing at least a decade and a half and were again ready for cutting.

The Indian stood in front of one of the adolescent oaks. Lyddie watched him swing the ax up and bring it down in one long, smooth motion, gouging a thick yellow chip out of the trunk, the slap of ax almost but not quite drowning out whatever it was that Nathan was shouting at him. Lyddie caught the words *devil* and *trespass* and *constable,* but none of them disturbed the Indian's stroke, and at length Smalley turned away and strode toward the barn so that Nathan was forced to turn and trot after him, still shouting.

"Hold! Smalley! You're not put off by such a trifle, are you? I'll have it sorted by morning. He likes to make trouble; you know that as well as anyone."

Smalley stopped by his horse. "He says he's got deed to the wood."

"And so have I got deed to it. And we'll soon see whose deed holds up."

"You'll have it in writing?"

"I bloody well will," Nathan said. "*In* blood, if I have to." He thrust a hand at Smalley, who shook it, but Lyddie noticed Smalley's upper body leaned away, like the pines, as if he would commit no more than he had to.

Eben Freeman arrived again, not long after supper. He had barely shaken off his hat and coat and greeted Mehitable and Lyddie when Nathan Clarke appeared and swept him into the study, barking over his shoulder at the nearest pair of hands, which happened to be Bethiah's, for cakes and cider.

The men were not long out of sight when Nathan Clarke's first outburst traveled through the door, left open by Bethiah.

"Thieving, bloody cannibal!"

Eben Freeman responded in normal tones, but used to the courtroom, his voice carried to the keeping room with little trouble. "There was no thieving," he said. "Sachemas, Cowett's great-grandfather, made a gift of the piece to Edward Berry's great-grandfather."

"There you have it, then! He gave it. And once the will's proved, it's mine."

"Yes, he gave it, but he kept for himself and his heirs the right to cut wood for fence or fire on the woodlot. It's all there in the deed. And as Sam Cowett is son and heir of Paumecowett, who was son and heir of Sachemas, he's well within his right to cut wood on that lot. Therein lies the problem."

"Too bloody right it's a problem! So what's your solution?"

Silence. "If you're asking me for a legal opinion—"

"I'm asking you how to get rid of that bloody Indian!"

More silence.

"You might inquire if Mr. Cowett would be willing to sell you his wood rights," said Freeman at last.

"What? Give him hard money for something I already own? Are you daft?"

"Then perhaps you'd prefer to sell the lot to Mr. Cowett outright."

"And get what for a house with no woodlot? You're getting dafter by the minute."

"Then divide it with him."

"Which is the same as giving it to him!"

"Or you might maintain the status quo, and sell the house and woodlot with the deed restriction. I can recall of no instance when it posed a problem for your father-in-law."

"We're not dealing with my father-in-law now, we're dealing with that bloody old woman Smalley! He near shed his skin when he saw that Indian. No, I want you to run Cowett off that lot and sew it up in whatever legal jargon you have to. Do you understand me, Freeman?"

Again, silence. Lyddie had a vision of Eben Freeman uncrossing a pair of long, jackknifed legs, carefully wrapping his fingers around his mug, and draining the remnants.

"I believe I do understand you, Clarke. Let me make sure you understand me, or at least the reason for my presence here. I was legal representative to Edward Berry, and, I like to think, a friend to him, and as such have made a point to be on hand at the settlement of his estate. I'll see the will proved; I'll see you take lawful possession and the widow settled. I'm in no way free to undertake any additional representation on your behalf in the matter thus described as relates to the Indian. Now, if that remains the only subject left to discuss between us, I'll say good evening."

If Nathan said good night to the lawyer, Lyddie didn't hear it. The next audible sound from him was a shout for Bethiah to refresh the pitcher.

Bethiah leaped to her feet, but so did Jane, no doubt in a well-practiced shoring up of sisterly defenses, and Lyddie waited alone, thinking something in the way of courtesy was now due Eben Freeman. He emerged from the front room, attempting an adjustment to his features that did little to improve them.

"We had no trouble with the Indian over the woodlot," she said.

He raised an eyebrow.

"I overheard your conversation, Mr. Freeman. I find it best to admit such things at the beginning."

Freeman's features improved. "A safe policy, Widow Berry. So your husband acknowledged the Indian's right to the wood, did he?"

"I don't know if he did or didn't. In my life I never saw the Indian cut within sight of our house."

"Indeed? Then I find it curious that he did so today."

"Perhaps he wished to make known his claim."

"Perhaps. Finding land held in common is a rare thing, nowadays."

"Why so?"

"Well, with so few Indians remaining in the village . . . Only look at their sad little nation at the pond—" Freeman either shivered with the cold or shook himself off the topic. His eye came to rest on her.

"You're well, Widow Berry? You're comfortable?"

"I'm well."

Had he noticed she'd only answered half his question? He started to say something that began with a *when*, changed it to an *if*, and then left it off entirely.

6

February arrived and with it more bone-cracking cold; first the well froze, then the clock, next the ink, and finally the bay, in great chunks that separated on the ebb and crashed together on the flow to forge rooftops of ice all along the shoreline.

Sam Cowett sat under Nathan Clarke's skin like a wood tick. Smalley would not commit about the house; in desperation Nathan decided to take the advice offered him by Freeman and make the Indian an offer for the wood rights.

Lyddie had just ventured into the keeping room with a pair of stockings for Mehitable and been met with a stiff thank-you when Nathan burst into the room.

"Well, Mother," Nathan said, "what do you have to say for your neighbor now? He will sell no wood rights, nor will he divide, nor will he engage in civil converse on the matter. I've a good mind to talk to the constable. 'Tis not to be borne! If a man can't sell his own lawful property—"

"You might sell it to someone other than Deacon Smalley," Mehitable said. "Mr. Dillingham's daughter is to be married soon."

"Dillingham's a damned Quaker, that's what he is, and he's already cost me dear. The town's now voted to exempt them from paying the soldier's bounty, in honor of their peaceable principles! I said at meeting, ' 'Tis my principle not to pay any man's share but my own, what say you to that principle?' And Smalley—by God, it was Smalley—stood up and said—"

Bethiah, who had been cutting up pumpkin, gave out a screech.

"God's breath!" Nathan shouted. "May I not have a minute within doors without all this noise rising to the ceiling?"

Lyddie rushed over, a step ahead of Mehitable. The child had cut her finger, but not deeply. Lyddie took her to the bucket, washed and wrapped the wound, and settled her in front of the fire with some yarn to unravel, the girl's already pale face now the color of watered milk. When Lyddie's first boy had sickened he'd turned just such a color. Edward had left a pale boy and gone to the Carolinas after spermaceti; he'd come home with his casks full of blubber to find his child dead in the ground. He'd shed no tears, voiced no despair, was all concern for Lyddie's sorrow only, until one evening after supper he'd gone out to meet his cousin and was gone so long Lyddie had walked out to the King's road to look for him. She had found him in the churchyard, staring down at the fresh-mounded dirt.

She walked up to him and stood beside him, silent.

"I have some trouble reconciling it," he said.

"As do I."

"Yes, and I wished to help you in it. Now I do naught but hinder."

" 'Tis a task best tried together."

He took her arm and pulled it through his, pinning it fiercely to his side, anchoring her fingers in his. After a while, they walked home together.

Lyddie pushed her dead children back into the dark recesses where she had kept them for so many years, much as she had kept their old beds under the eaves in the attic. Soon, very soon now, she must find a place to push Edward. On Tuesday Lyddie had almost joined Cousin Betsey's lament over the impending departure of the whale men for the Canada River until it struck her she was now spared this small grief on account of the greater. On Friday Lyddie woke from a doze to the smell of Nathan's pipe, and in that sweet, thick minute before full consciousness thought, "Edward's home." Sunday at meeting, when James and Betsy Lincoln stood up to confess to the sin of fornication after giving birth to a six-month child, Lyddie's mind had trailed off after memories of that thing she would no longer be knowing.

Nathan's voice hit a high note and pulled Lyddie back to the present. He was now listing the sins of those less peaceable Quakers who used to charge into meeting to denounce the standing order's religious practices. Lyddie had heard this particular rant before and knew it to go on some minutes; she finished cutting up Bethiah's pumpkin, collected her cap and cloak and muffler, and moved toward the door.

"Where are you going?" Mehitable asked.

"To walk."

Lyddie couldn't wonder at the look her daughter gave her; such idle behavior would have seemed strange in good weather. She left the house, steering carefully away from the landing road, past the water mill and Winslow's fulling mill, just rebuilt after the old one had mysteriously burned down in the middle of the night. She cut south along the creek, seeking shelter from the wind, continuing without thought until the ground became smooth under her feet and she realized she had wandered onto the worn depression of the Indian trail that circumvented the millpond. It had been years since Lyddie had walked so far; she looked ahead and saw a pair of huts covered in marsh grass with anemic streams of smoke rising from holes in the roofs; she began to turn around, but Eben Freeman's words about the sad little nation came back to her. Why did some Indians like Sam Cowett move successfully into the mainstream of English village life and some stay here in poverty, among their brethren?

Her curiosity took her forward. The millpond stretched frosted hard before her, and two young boys chipped at the edge. An old woman stepped out of the nearest *wetu;* as she lifted the flap Lyddie saw an English table and chairs inside. In the distance a small hive of women scraped a carcass that hung from a tree, another pair pounded a skin on the ground. Two small children chased a pig between the huts. She saw only one man, either very old or very crippled, hobbling into view with a basket of firewood slung over his shoulder.

Lyddie turned around and slipped back through the trees.

When Lyddie reached the house she found that Eben Freeman had just delivered some more papers and letters from Boston and now stood at the door under bombardment by Nathan's favorite diatribe: Mr. Winslow's usurping of the millstream. Lyddie greeted both men and went inside, where she found the *Boston Gazette* lying on the table. She picked it up and went to the fire. In a minute the lawyer joined her there.

"You're interested in the newspapers, Widow Berry?"

"I've not the wit to comprehend all that I find in them. But I am interested, yes. I see your friend Otis named in it."

"He's your friend as well, Widow Berry."

"Mine!"

"He would say you've all the wit but not the education for the paper. He has a sister, Mercy, a rare creature; her father sent her with her brothers to their tutor. And James brought home his Harvard books to share with her. He's now seen firsthand what an educated woman might accomplish and would spread the practice further."

"And what has Miss Otis accomplished?"

"She's Mrs. Warren now. And I believe she writes poems on the seasons."

"And what does her husband say when he's served a poem for his dinner?"

Freeman's face did that thing she'd come to recognize as a smile. "He claps for her."

"Then there's your rare creature."

"Please. Don't mistake me. When I said Mrs. Warren was a rare creature, I referred not to any great rarity in her cleverness, but to—" He paused.

"But to the fact she has three such men around her?"

"I . . . Perhaps . . . well, yes. Indeed."

"And don't mistake *me*, Mr. Freeman. I'm lost in admiration of them all: both the brother and the sister, and the father who sent his daughter to the tutor, as well as Mr. Warren, who claps for her."

"Ah! Now I must do something to add myself to your list. Perhaps if you made a poem and I clapped for you—"

"We'd all be better served if I made your dinner and you clapped for Mr. Otis."

"If Mr. Otis does what he's set out to do in his challenge of the Writs, we'll all clap for him."

"Except, perhaps, the members of Parliament?"

"Widow Berry, you underestimate your own wit. Perhaps you should make Mr. Otis's speech for him."

The notion made Lyddie smile, and as the muscles around her mouth pulled back stiffly, she thought, Have I lost this, too, my talent for laughter? Or was it Edward who had found all the amusement in their life? Perhaps so, but if so, he would certainly have found it in this: his wife talking writs and Parliament with Ebenezer Freeman.

7

Mehitable came to Lyddie's room in rare smiles and invited her mother to join the family at dinner. Nathan, too, appeared in peace, so much so that when his discourse on the price of barrels in Satucket versus Boston ran down, Lyddie decided to interject a question.

"I walked to the Indian village today. They're greatly dwindled in number. Are they gone away someplace?"

"They're gone where all weak people go," Nathan answered.

"I know of their great trouble with disease, but surely that touches both sexes. I saw no men in the village."

" 'Tis more than just disease that has reduced them to this pathetic gaggle of women and children. 'Tis our war with the French."

"Do you mean to say the men have all been killed in this war?"

"Killed or crippled."

"But why so many Indians and not Englishmen? Surely our own men fight in the war in greater number."

"Not in such great number as compared to their total population. If the Indians have five men in their village they risk all five in such manner."

"Why so?"

"What else might they succeed at?"

"You call death and dismemberment success?"

Nathan laid down his knife and studied her. "Is there some purpose to your questioning?"

"None whatever."

Bethiah let out a burst of air that stood for her odd version of a laugh and was rewarded with a cuff to the cheek; but the cuff was followed with a tousle of her braid, and, "Very well, Mother, as the alternative appears to be naught but discussion on whether the reverend looks best with his wig or without, I shall take this opportunity to educate you on our Indian brethren. It so happens these people live in a land that has become greatly populated with Englishmen. You will note, please, we did not conquer or capture these lands but bought them at fair value. Oh, you will hear all manner of talk: we took this piece for a cow or this one for a kettle, and yes, the old sachem sold this very parcel we sit on for a cow, but the next month it was sold again for five pounds, and I ask you, what was the worth of the cow? *Six* pounds! And as to the kettle, which held the greater value at the time, ten acres of woodland out of hundreds of acres of forest or a thing made nowhere on this continent, shipped to us all the way from England? And what did I pay old Sequattom for our meadowlands? One hundred ten pounds for a paltry forty acres—"

"Then whence comes the trouble?"

"Well, Mother, if you'd stop your constant interruption I might tell you whence it comes. Here, on the one hand, you have an Englishman who would own a stable piece of land and keep on it and farm it; on the other hand, you have an Indian who might plant a field in one place in summer, then move to the woodland to hunt in winter, then find a fresh field the next year, etc., etc. But suddenly the Indian finds that in his greed for cows and kettles and English silver he's sold away so much land there's not enough left for this old way of living. Now in such case the Englishman might say, very well, I'm unable to live by my old methods, let me put them aside and try living by this new one, but this the Indian will not do. He calls farming woman's work; the man's work is the hunt; and if he can't hunt his deer and bear and fox, he'll hunt his fellow man. 'Tis an instinct in him. So he goes to war for the English, and not only does he get a respectable wage, he gets a steady ration of rum in the bargain. And there, my dear Mother, we come to yet another cause of the Indian's dissipated condition. Look at your *Mr.* Cowett and you have it in a nutshell."

"Mr. Cowett served in our army?"

Nathan laughed. "Mr. Cowett would not go to the aid of his own mother, let alone his king. I reference the man in regard to his habit of drink, not in any fondness for the military. When they were out drumming up men for the attack on Nova Scotia he hid his boat in the Point of Rock channel."

"As did half the men in this town, as I recall, including your brother."

Nathan slapped the table. "And so would I have done after what happened to Louisburg! Hundreds of Cape Cod men giving over their living to march to Canada, carrying their whaleboats with them, capturing the fort with much blood and pain only to have it turned back to the French in the next treaty. And now what do we have? Those bloody French setting out from that same bloody fort, pirating our coast from sunup to sundown, costing me a bloody fortune! And if that's not enough to bear we have these bloody Writs come down on us—"

Mehitable stood up with the pudding and refilled her husband's bowl, a tactic that proved successful only in diverting her husband's fire in her direction. "What are you doing, you bloody woman? Did I ask for more pudding? I'm done with eating. Fetch me the rum." He pushed away from the table and retreated to his study.

Mehitable got up and took the rum bottle off the shelf, casting a look at her mother that was not what Lyddie would have called dutiful.

It was some weeks before Lyddie was again asked to join the family table.

One night in early March Nathan called Lyddie into the study.

"Mother, I've been going over the accounts, and I'm appalled at our tally at Sears's store. My wife can answer for but half the total; she informs me you've done a good deal of shopping there."

"I purchase my foodstuffs there, yes."

"I skip over food, although it does seem that tea and sugar are used to excess in this household. I refer to three charges made to the account this week for which my wife takes no credit: pins, shoe buckles, almond oil. These are yours?"

"They are."

"I don't mean to be petty; indeed, a woman needs her pins. I might ask what she needs with new shoe buckles every week or two, and I'm quite certain my wife has almond oil in the pantry, as I used it for a sore tooth not a month ago—"

"Teeth are the very devil, are they not?" said a voice behind Lyddie.

She turned and saw Eben Freeman just canting his long frame against the doorjamb.

"Good evening, Widow Berry."

"Good evening." Lyddie turned back to her son. "If you'll excuse me."

"Yes, yes, but have a care. When I sell the bloody house you'll have your pin money and you may spend it as you like, but until such time—"

Freeman straightened. "As Edward Berry's legal representative I might point out that you are charged with his widow's keep and care."

"She's got her keep and care, Freeman. She wants for nothing."

"Did I not just hear evidence to the contrary? Something of shoe buckles, was it?"

"Shoe buckles! Do you see her limping around on a stocking? I've settled her husband's debts; I don't need to put down half a fortune at Sears's store every month as well."

"I recall no extraordinary debt when the will was proved," Freeman said.

"Would you call me a liar?"

"Here, now. We need no such words—"

"I should say we do, since if I'm not, you're one."

Lyddie heard a sharp click from the lawyer's direction, but she couldn't decide if it came from his teeth or his heels. "I make it a practice in life to speak with utmost fairness of everyone," he said quietly, "and in that vein I would be pleased if you'd not toss around your own words unwisely."

"Ah! So now you call me a fool!"

"In four decades of life I've never been so big a fool as to call another man one. And I believe if you gave thought to the matter at hand you would conclude that dispensing a few shillings per month to your widowed mother in advance of the sale of the property would in no way compromise your long-admired talent for economy."

To Lyddie's great surprise this speech seemed to mollify her son-in-law. "Very well then, Freeman. Now, what's your business? Mother, you will excuse us."

She would have done, but the lawyer stayed her with a finger on her sleeve. "My business is twofold, Clarke, and one of those I'm sure will interest the Widow Berry. But let's settle yours first." He reached in his pocket with his free hand and withdrew two envelopes, handing one to Nathan. "I served on the committee of arbiters to determine the shares in the oil profits and these are yours." He handed Nathan the second envelope. "And these are Edward Berry's." As Edward's profits had been earned at such a great cost to Lyddie herself, she had some curiosity to know the tally; she watched closely as Nathan opened the envelope and counted down: fifteen pounds eight shillings.

"And as to the second piece of business," Freeman said, "it concerns a friend of the widow's: Mr. James Otis."

Nathan looked first at the lawyer and then at his mother-in-law with astonishment. "*Her* friend?"

Freeman winked at Lyddie. "A new one, but nevertheless, I believe, a friend. His speech before the superior court regarding the Writs of Assistance has set the town on its end. As the widow has some interest in matters of Parliament I thought she would like to hear—"

"Matters of Parliament! What the devil are you on about? Leave her be and get on to it. I've not had a paper in a month, nor an informed letter, nor a decent conversation. What of this speech?"

"Otis spoke above four hours, but in my life I never heard such learned discourse, nor such passion, nor boldness, nor wit. He was a flame of fire. He began by declaring such things as natural laws—"

"Natural laws! What the devil are natural laws?"

"Laws that are written in a man's heart. And he put those laws above any laws made by any Parliament. He found basis for this rule of natural law in old Saxon law, the Magna Carta, and the English

Constitution; among these natural laws he claimed a man's right to his life, his liberty, and his property. He declared it a man's natural right to sit as secure in his house as any prince in his castle."

"Well, there's Otis for you, off chasing castles. I'd like to know what castles have to do with it."

"They have to do with a man's right to live safe from interference by immoral, illegal search and seizure, put in place by an immoral, illegal, man-made law of Parliament. And Otis made his case, Clarke; you'll not find a man in the chamber who'll deny it. He then went on to define the power of the court in such a way that it could not prevail unless it declared itself supreme and Parliament irrelevant. Oh, it was a pretty piece of work. I assure you, even his opponent stood lost in admiration of it."

"Ah! Then the matter was defeated."

"It was not. The court chose to confer with England before issuing an opinion. The matter was postponed to the next term and the session closed without a verdict."

There Nathan launched into his view of the court and the great lot of thieves and wastrels that sat on it. Freeman apparently decided that the best way to stem that particular tide was to bring on another wave of equal proportion; he then mentioned that Otis used the occasion of his speech to put forth his plan to free the slaves. There Lyddie excused herself and continued through to the keeping room, but Nathan's voice gusted so loudly after her that Mehitable looked up in alarm. "What in heaven can it be now?"

Lyddie attempted to form a short answer but found her mind too clouded for it; she needed time and quiet to wrap her wits around all that Freeman had just described. The little she could grasp seemed so large and awful and magnificent that she would have felt sure she'd misconstrued it if Freeman himself hadn't appeared to stand in such awe of it. Lyddie lifted her shoulders to indicate her own puzzlement to Mehitable and stepped quietly out into the dark.

Lyddie hadn't yet untangled her mind when the door opened behind her and Freeman stepped through it. He'd taken the first few strides toward the road when he saw her standing by the barn and diverted.

"Widow Berry! What on earth are you doing out here?"

"Thinking. And having no great success at it. But I'm glad enough to have this chance to thank you for your help in regard to my funds."

"Do not, please. I was not useful."

"You saved me a much-needed pair of shoe buckles."

"I should have wrung his neck for them. And if it had stopped his speech an hour, I'd have considered myself well paid into the bargain." He took a deep breath. "I beg your pardon, Widow Berry."

"You needn't."

He reached for his pocket. "Widow Berry, if you would please allow me . . . until your husband's affairs are settled . . . a small loan—"

"Thank you, Mr. Freeman, but I cannot."

He paused, hand halfway in and halfway out, but at length he returned it to his pocket.

"Very well, then. Good night." He turned away.

"Mr. Freeman?"

He turned back.

"In his speech, did Mr. Otis mention the women?"

"He did not. I think the rumbling over the Negroes may have discouraged him."

"May I ask another question of you, Mr. Freeman?"

"You may ask me anything at any time, Widow Berry."

"My husband met with you a month after our daughter's marriage. Was it to change his will?"

"It was."

"In the one before, how did he leave me?"

"With life use of his house and lands entire, with title to his cousin Shubael."

House and lands entire. And then Lyddie's daughter had married Nathan Clarke, and her husband had rewritten his will, and along with it Lyddie's life.

"What were Edward's words to you, Mr. Freeman?" she burst out. "Why did he make such a change? Why didn't he do under Nathan as he'd done under Shubael?"

"And leave you a woman alone when you now had a son's fine roof for shelter?"

"Woman alone! How many months in the year was I alone? In spring my husband sailed for Carolina and in summer for Canada, in fall he went to Boston for weeks at a time, in '44 he was pressed into service alongside a man-of-war and gone three months without warning. Do you think I don't know how to be a woman alone? Do you think " She stopped. She breathed in and out.

Freeman cleared his throat. "When your husband made out his new will he expressed great relief to me that in the event of misfortune, you would now be secure in the bosom of your son's family."

In. Out. "Yes," Lyddie said. "Yes, of course he did. I thank you for your time, Mr. Freeman, and I'll take no more of it. Good night."

"Widow Berry."

"No, no. Excuse me, please. Thank you for telling me of Mr. Otis, it was most interesting. Good night."

The lawyer said good night again. He appeared to have come on foot the three miles from his sister's; he stepped out into the dark, and Lyddie watched him fade to nothing. She stayed where she was, thinking again of this curious man, James Otis. Had he caused this thing that burned in her? Would he at least understand it? Would his sister, or father, or sister's husband? No, none of them. Because they still sat secure in their homes as so many princes in their castles. But

Edward. Must she now say the same of Edward, of the man with whom she had come to share every strength as well as every weakness? Lyddie looked up at the sky, moonless and star-pocked. Oh, Edward, she thought, how could you possess such knowledge of my flesh and so little of my spirit?

8

When Solomon Paine died, he dictated in his will not only which shrubs his widow might use to dry her laundry and in which part of the meadow she might graze her cow, but also that a new entrance be built to his house so his widow might come and go in private. At the time Lyddie thought Mr. Paine had taken it a step too far, but now she saw his sense. Whenever Lyddie happened to stop on her way through the keeping room to aide Bethiah with a stitch or Jane with the washtub, Mehitable's face took on a pink, slapped appearance. When Lyddie delivered a new pair of stockings or a pile of mending she got a tight-lipped "Thank you, you needn't." If she happened to be passing through when Nathan began to rail about the price of hay or Bethiah's cough or the color of his toast, Mehitable looked at Lyddie as if her mother had just jammed a knitting pin up under his coattail. But in truth, Nathan did seem to launch into some sort of tirade whenever Lyddie was present, and after a time she decided that the best aid she could offer the household was to keep out of it.

She took to walking. Most days she traveled along the sheltered path beside the creek, looking for early scouts among the alewives as they worked their way up the stream from the bay to spawn in the millpond above. But one day, after the wind had died down and the sun had actually stayed out long enough to give off a little heat, she turned the other way, toward Edward's house.

The grass remained a close, brown mat, the buds on the shadblow still curled tight, dried leaves and sticks filling the garden. Lyddie took several steps into the yard, thinking to clear away the debris, but stopped. Why bother? She returned to the road and kept walking, not the way she'd come, but forward, northward, past the woodlot, toward the landing. Ahead of her lay the Cowett house, and if Lyddie hadn't seen Rebecca Cowett hanging her wash on the shrubs outside the door she might have thought it was any Englishman's squat gray frame house. In dress, too, the woman might have been English, if one didn't notice black hair and eyes in a town full of blond and blue.

Lyddie paused as Rebecca Cowett hurried across the ground between them.

"Widow Berry," she said. "I wish to tell you my great sorrow at the death of your husband. My own husband greatly laments his failure to save him; I could not console him. I told him, God weighs things according to his own scale."

"Indeed," Lyddie said.

"Indeed, yes. But that was not how my husband answered. He said God must fill his scales with earth on one side and water on the other, as together the four men saved weren't worth the one lost."

Lyddie searched for some word of response but could dredge up nothing.

In turn, the Indian searched her face. "Forgive me if I've offended you, Widow Berry. I was raised a good Christian, but I'm afraid the same cannot be said for my husband. I should not have repeated his words, even to you. Good day and God bless you." She returned to her laundry.

Lyddie's first thought was to follow the woman and say something to assure her that no offense had been taken, but on second thought she realized she didn't want to. A small angry coal burned in her gut, like the bile at the end of a vomit. Why *hadn't* the Indian saved Edward? What little amount of extra trouble or cold could it have cost him to save five instead of four, or, if only four, why not Edward first and then three others, any three others, of the rest of them?

She walked on at a hard pace, unaware of her direction until she came to the water. It stretched out calm and thick like lead, its fickleness making the coal inside her burn harder. Why couldn't the whales have swarmed to shore on this day, not the other?

Lyddie strode to the lip of the wet and stared out across it. She wondered what Edward had thought of as he went down. Lyddie? The whales? The boat? The Indian who wouldn't save him? She corrected herself. The Indian who *couldn't* save him. The molten water turned to silver at the edge and ran up the sand toward Lyddie's feet; she backed up and it backed up, rustling, whispering, mocking her.

Lyddie made her way back to the landing road, and this time when she came to the door of her husband's house she went in. She walked directly to the front room, sat down in Edward's chair, closed her eyes, and tried to feel the old warmth of his flesh through her skirt. She felt nothing but hard, cool wood. She got up and went to his desk, spreading her hands flat on the burnished surface, but all was coolness there as well. She reached out and touched Edward's pen, opened the drawer, and found nothing but her own journal. Of course, Nathan would have taken away Edward's papers, just as, of course, he would leave behind Lyddie's worthless drivel.

Lyddie opened the book.

Thursday 1 January. A still, mild weather; so far we are lucky. The fox got two more hens. Edward went out hunting it but got nothing. Have finished his coat and begun the waistcoat. Edward calls it too fine for plain living and would save it for Ned Crowe's wedding.

Lyddie remembered the rest of their conversation on that day, the part that hadn't gotten into her journal. They had discussed Ned Crowe, and Edward's assertion that it was imperative for all lusty young men to marry as soon as they were able, "in order to save wear and tear on that poor whore at the tavern."

"And what of the lusty young women?" Lyddie had asked, and Edward had answered, "You make a fair point. As they offer no such accommodation for the fair sex at the tavern, I shall take it on myself to visit them each in turn," and Lyddie had said . . . What had she said? She couldn't remember. But it had made Edward tip his head back and shout a great laugh at the ceiling.

Lyddie picked up Edward's pen, inked it, and wrote:

Friday 2 January. Edward drowned this day.

She reinked the pen, drew a line across the page, and closed the book. She stood up and tucked it under arm but paused at the stoop. The journal was not a part of her life as it was now; it was part of the life she had lived in this house. She went to the pantry, pulled up the cellar hatch, and backed down the ladder.

Nathan had been as thorough below as he had been above: the entire winter store of peas and beans was gone, as were the salt meat and fish, the casks of Indian meal, the rounds of cheese and tubs of butter, all barrels of beer and jugs of cider. Some mushy apples and molded potatoes and squash had been left behind. Lyddie picked up the shingle she used to use to scrape the shelves clean, scratched a hole in the dirt floor, laid the book in, and covered it over.

Lyddie walked to the water the next day and the next, without understanding why she did it, unless it was to count each day how the water lay, calm versus stormy, as if in the final tally she might comprehend something of God's workings. The third day she saw the Indian woman out turning over her garden, and Lyddie forced herself to stop out of penance for her previous discourteous thinking.

"Good morning!" she called across the field.

Rebecca Cowett set down her spade and hurried over. "Good morning, Widow Berry." She appeared about to say more, but didn't.

"You've set yourself hard work," Lyddie said.

"My boy used to help with the turning, until he came old enough to go with his father."

"How old is your boy now?" Lyddie asked.

"I don't know, Widow Berry. I don't know if he's living or dead. He went to Nantucket for a berth twenty-one months ago, and I've not heard from him since. Mr. Scotto Chase heard a boy went off the rigging at Hatteras—"

"There are many boys, Mrs. Cowett."

"Not here in our little corner, are there, Widow Berry? I lost one to distemper and one at Annapolis; this boy was my last child, as your daughter Clarke is yours, but you have grandchildren, which I do not. Of course, you have an added sorrow now, which I do not." She stopped. "I shouldn't delay you in your errand."

Lyddie was gratified the Indian didn't ask what the errand was. She said good-bye, moved down the road to the water, and watched the lip run serenely up the beach as her mind churned over the bizarre collection of facts she'd just received. She hadn't known about the Indian boy; she was surprised the woman knew so much about Lyddie's children. Lyddie wasn't sure she liked the idea; she was quite sure she didn't like the other woman's efforts to match their sorrows.

9

By the next week Rebecca Cowett's length of ground appeared refreshed and readied for planting. Lyddie walked by it on her way to the landing but caught no sight of the Indian. On her return she found the woman just entering her house, and Lyddie called out a greeting. Rebecca Cowett answered back, and then, with some hesitation, she added, "Will you stop for tea?"

Lyddie found in herself a curiosity to see the inside of the Indian's house. She stepped up, and when Rebecca Cowett opened the door Lyddie saw nothing inside but what she might have taken pride in herself: a well-made table and chairs, a neatly banked fire, several gleaming copper utensils, freshly whitewashed walls, and sanded floor.

"I've just finished the spring clean," Rebecca Cowett said. "I could enjoy a cup of tea myself. Please, Widow Berry, sit."

But somewhere between the last minute and that minute a heaviness overtook Lyddie; it felt wrong to be there. "No," she said. "I'm not able to stay. I just wished to say—" What? "I heard Seth Cobb is back from the south and I wondered if he had news of your son?"

"He had none."

"I'm sorry, then. I'm very sorry. Good morning, Mrs. Cowett." She hurried out and away from the Indian's house, struggling against the heavy feeling, unable to put a name to it, in her struggle not thinking where she was going and finding herself on the path to her old door. But once she realized her location she continued forward, pushing open her door, and there it all came clear.

In the ordinary course of events this was the time of year in which Lyddie would have done what Rebecca Cowett had just done: reordered her house after the winter's abuse. Instead, she now stood facing sooted walls, salt-filmed glass, dirty hearth, dusty webs, and piles of seed husk and mouse droppings in all corners. She thought of Deacon Smalley looking on such a sight and Lyddie's face burned with shame.

That night Lyddie approached her son as he left his supper table. "What news of Deacon Smalley?" she asked.

"The devil take Smalley. I'm on to Ned Crowe now. He means to marry in a month. He comes to view on Friday."

"I saw the house today. It stands badly neglected. If you would allow me—"

Nathan turned on his wife. "What the devil is this? Have you not looked to the house?"

"Please," Lyddie said. "Allow me to tend it. If I took Jane we'd be done in a morning."

"Jane?" Mehitable cut in. "You would take Jane, and tomorrow my day to bake?"

"Well, then, perhaps Bethiah."

The younger girl's face lifted.

"Yes, yes," Nathan said. "Let her cough somewhere else for half a day, thank you. Just see that it's done by Friday."

They packed a chicken pie and set out with the sun. The girl spoke little until they approached the house and Lyddie saw the tall form of the Indian ahead of them, making his way toward the shore; something must have triggered his awareness of their presence because he stopped and turned. Bethiah drew back. Lyddie fought her own instinct and kept her feet square in the road, even lifted a hand in greeting, but if it was returned she couldn't tell. He moved off.

"Oh, my!" Bethiah said. "What a fearsome thing he is! Mama says to keep away from him. But he's so close to your house, Grandmama! Dare we go down?"

"He's well past. He won't hurt you. Move along, now."

The girl skipped to catch up, her tongue at last shaken loose. "Nate says that the Indian's the best whale man in Satucket. He says he's so strong that he pulls the whales instead of the whales pulling him. He says Papa doesn't like him. I asked Nate why Papa didn't like him and he said it's because he does as he pleases. I should like to do as I please. Mama says no one does as he pleases, but I said what of the Indian, and she said one Indian does not make the rule. I said who does make the rule and she said God and Papa. I think God or Papa should have told the Indian the rule, don't you, Grandmama?"

"Here we are," Lyddie said. "Get the rake from the barn. You may start by raking the seaweed away from the foundation."

"Why do we put seaweed around the house, Grandmama?"

"To keep out the cold."

"Then why do we rake it away now?"

"To keep away the rot."

The girl bobbed off toward the barn, craning her neck for one last look at the Indian before he went around the turn.

Lyddie drew water, went inside, and tucked up her skirt. She decided to begin with the cellar. She knocked down what cobwebs had managed to foil the round design of the cellar, collected the bits of molded food, and scraped the shelves clean. Back upstairs she cleaned the glass and had just begun to wash down the walls when Bethiah came in, wild-eyed. The Indian. The Indian was coming. She dashed behind Lyddie and caught hold of the band of her apron.

The door rattled under a hard pair of knuckles, and Lyddie stepped forward to open it, dragging the girl behind, her own heart accelerating. Which of us feeds the other? she wondered. And just what was it they feared in this Indian? His sheer power and size? His darkness? The fact that "Papa doesn't like him"? Or was it that he "did as he pleased," fearing neither God nor Nathan?

He stood filling the doorway. "You're back now?"

"No, we're cleaning. The house is to be sold, as I told you. Mr. Crowe comes to look on Friday. This is my granddaughter Bethiah."

The Indian moved his eyes without haste from Lyddie to the girl, but they didn't linger. It seemed to give Bethiah courage to be so quickly dismissed; her grip on the apron band lessened. "My wife spoke to you," he said.

"Yes."

"About your husband."

"A little, yes."

"I had him. A good grip. He was alive. I felt him take hold."

"Yes. All right."

"It tore."

"What?"

"The coat tore."

"All right. Yes."

"He was in my hands and then he was under."

"Yes, Mr. Cowett. I understand. And I do thank you."

He didn't move. "Ned Crowe," he said, as if he were the subject all along. "Ned Crowe looks to live here?"

"We have good hope of him," Lyddie said. "Deacon Smalley proved a disappointment, but things are looking up now."

Silence.

Would he never go? Or look away? In the end he did both together, in one graceful swing of his shoulders, and Lyddie's "Good morning" struck at his back.

She was surprised when he stopped, turned, and offered a half-bow in answer.

"Oh, *my*," Bethiah said.

10

Lyddie snapped out of a nightmare about Edward in the well—Lyddie reaching for his coat sleeve and his arm coming off with the sleeve to hang limp in her hand—but it wasn't the dream that had woken her, it was sound, a whole series of sounds: doors, voices, feet. She heard Nathan shout, "What the devil! Sister!" She slid to her feet, pulled her shawl around her, and felt her way to the keeping room.

Nathan stood at the door with a single candle held high, ushering in his brother Silas's wife, along with her five children. The candlelight touched down here and there as they filed by, lighting up first a gold head and then a pair of pale eyes and then another, and another, until at the end of the line came the shadowed hills and valleys of the mother's worn-out face.

"I'm so sorry, Brother, so sorry to trouble you, 'tis Silas, mad drunk, come at me with a knife this time, and I didn't know where to go at this hour. Have you room? Just for this night? He'll be right as rain come morning."

"Room! Good God, woman, look at the lot of you, I'm not an inn! There now, the whole house is up. Go on, go on, Nathan; you girls, back to bed with you. Ah! And now here's my wife, and she just asleep after thrashing me about for hours."

Lyddie stepped forward and cupped the two nearest girls' shoulders. "These two might sleep with me and keep me warm." She looked to Mehitable but saw nothing in her eye but the hard gleam of a reflected candle.

"Bethiah and I might share with Aunt Patience and our littlest cousin," Jane said. "And Nate could take the two boys in with him. What say you, Father?"

"Oh, yes, yes, yes. All right. Move along, now, all of you. But I'll ask you to make no habit of this, Sister."

Mehitable spun around and returned to her room, leaving her children to deal with their respective charges. Lyddie guided her two young guests to her room. "What an adventure to be out in the dead of night," she said. "Tell me, did you see any stars?"

They recounted the positions of the Seven Sisters, the Dipper, the Great Hunter, and by the time they were through they were settled under the blankets. They were quickly asleep, but Lyddie lay awake, reminded of the comfort of another warm body in her bed, until she took a sharp blow from a small elbow.

Silas Clarke arrived the next day to collect his family, his head slung low between his shoulders, but if he was expecting reprimand from his brother he received none that Lyddie heard; in fact, the matter was not discussed again until the next day, the Sabbath.

The Reverend Dunne's sermon addressed God's call, not to the righteous but to the sinners, the reverend declaring this call encompassed every one of them, for a sin in the heart was as great as a sin in the flesh. He concluded with a sweeping promise of redemption that tired Lyddie to the core, but it brought Deliverance Smith to her feet to confess her grievous sin of drunkenness and bad language.

Once outside Bethiah asked, "Why didn't Uncle Silas get up and confess his drunkenness, Papa?"

"Because a man may take his drink," Nathan answered. "Our sister makes too much of it, disturbing my peaceful home at the slightest suggestion."

"I'd not call a kitchen knife a suggestion," Lyddie said.

Nathan turned to glare at her before herding his family to the left, toward the inn. Lyddie turned right.

Mehitable called after her. "Mother! Where are you going?"

"Home. I've a great headache coming."

Untruths did not sit well with Lyddie. As soon as she reached her room she went down on her knees to make herself right with God, but all the old words eluded her. She couldn't beg forgiveness for her own actions until she forgave God his, and there it festered, until God in his infinite justice delivered the headache she'd feigned to avoid his sermon. But neither feigned nor real headache saved her; as soon as Nathan came home he took pains to seek her out, inquire solicitously after her health, and then quote the bulk of the reverend's message, ending with a flourish: he who neglects God in this life will face his eternal wrath hereafter.

11

Lyddie continued her walks to the water, although for what reason she couldn't say, as they did little to comfort her. If the sea lay calm she felt angry; if it roiled she felt despair; if it fell in a place between she felt unsettled and on edge, but still it drew her. On a day of rough seas she found her boots caught in the wash, and instead of moving back she moved forward, until her hem was caught and the water began to pull at her. At the feel of the pull she leaped back, but not before she got drenched to her thighs, and as her luck would run, on the walk home she ran into Eben Freeman just exiting the Cowett house.

"Widow Berry! What on earth has happened to you? Did you fall?"

"I forgot to mind my feet, is all. You were visiting the Cowetts?"

"On a matter of business. I'm sorry, but you make me ask . . . others have mentioned . . . you walk often to the water?"

"Now and then. I'm surprised to see you here."

"I've been much in town. Or do you mean here, at Cowett's? I've some business with him." The lawyer smiled. "In fact, Widow Berry, the business has to do with you."

"Me?"

"He's agreed to divide the woodlot."

Lyddie stopped walking, the better to think what she was feeling, and although several of her emotions remained clouded she was able to identify strong curiosity among them. "What persuaded him?"

"I haven't the least idea. But you'll have your shoe buckles soon, now."

"How soon?"

"Quite soon. We pass the papers on the woodlot first, of course, but then we move right on to the house sale."

"You say 'we'?"

"I should say 'we' for the first part only. Once the woodlot is divided it's on to Esquire Doane and nothing to do with me."

"Or me."

"You enter the second part only, Widow Berry. You'll be required to sign over your dower rights to the property. Now watch where you step or you'll wet the rest of you. And as we come again to the subject, I wonder, might you not think of a safer place to walk than the shore? Especially in such weather?"

"I might."

He peered at her a moment. "Widow Berry, if you would excuse me . . . If I might say only . . . I, too, have lost a partner in life, and I believe I know something of the circumstance in which—"

"Excuse me, Mr. Freeman, but you know nothing of my own particular circumstance. You may have lost a wife, but you did not lose your home of twenty years, nor the right to manage your affairs."

"I . . . Indeed. But consider, Widow Berry. A lone woman—"

"Does not turn overnight into a witless fool. Must I remind you again of the many months I managed alone while Edward was at sea?"

"I beg your pardon. I did not mean—"

Lyddie exhaled with violence. "No, I beg yours, Mr. Freeman. It appears this is not a good day for me to attempt sociability. I'll say good-bye." She pushed her legs hard and drew away from him. He could have easily caught her up; she considered it a sign of some understanding that he didn't attempt to do so. But before she made the distance too great he appeared to change his mind and came running.

"Widow Berry, I would have you know, I'm acquainted with your skill at management. Your husband often boasted of it. But a woman temporarily alone and a woman widowed . . . it's quite different."

"In the law, yes."

"In the law and in life. But in either case, please remember, if you should ever have need, I am at your service."

Lyddie had no time for the necessary thank-you. Deacon Smalley had just rounded the turn, and Lyddie had no interest in witnessing any of his joy over the sale of Edward's house. She decided to reverse direction and continue her walk. She took a long loop, and by the time she reached the Clarke house her skirt was nearly dry, but Eben Freeman was only just stepping up the path ahead of her. As it happened, Nathan was just coming down, and Lyddie had no stomach for an encounter with either of them; she stepped into the lee of the barn, thinking they would go directly to Nathan's study and she could slip inside without notice, but where the men crossed in the path they stopped.

The conversation began with some back and forth about the weather: the wind would blow off in a day; no, it would take two, as it was in the main from the north; no, it was east all afternoon;

at which point Freeman cut it off with, "And how fares Mrs. Clarke?"

"She fares well."

"And the Widow Berry?"

"Ah! And to what end do you ask that question?"

"To what end! To the end of determining how she fares. To the end of adding a small note of pleasantry to an otherwise dry conversation."

"Hah! Very well, then. Allow me to inform you that the Widow Berry fares nicely. Very nicely, indeed. She keeps herself neat, she remains fit, there are those who yet consider her handsome; I've no doubt she'll stay but briefly in my stable."

"You appear to mistake me, Mr. Clarke. I inquire after your mother-in-law, not your horse."

"My horse! Hah-hah! Very clever, Freeman. But let me assure you, my horse would cost you a good deal more, and without certain benefits. You've been a single man a long time now, Freeman, some would say too long a time—"

"I've a devoted sister waiting dinner for me, and I cannot linger," Freeman said. "I've stopped here on my way only to tell you that Sam Cowett has decided to divide the woodlot."

"What the devil! What's turned him?"

"That was not for me to determine. I've also run into Smalley and took the liberty of telling him the news. He would indeed like to purchase. I do not represent him, you understand, but as I was coming this way I agreed to pass on the communication."

"Well, well, the bearer of good news on all fronts. I thank you, Freeman. Come in and take a dram to celebrate."

"No, thank you. I must be off. My regards to—"

"Rest assured, I'll inform the Widow Berry of your deep regard."

"I meant to say Mrs. Clarke. But you may of course pass them to the widow as well."

It was little consolation for Lyddie to learn that at the age of thirty-nine she could still blush like a virgin.

The next day Lyddie picked another route to walk. She crossed the road to the mill and continued along the creek, but had gone some distance before she became aware of her surroundings, and once she did, she was astonished. The maple and cherry had popped out in pink knobs, and green spikes glittered among the brown mat of grass. She stepped over a log, peered into the water, and soon enough she saw the gray-green shadows of the first alewives. It was April. They had shed March at last, and she had barely noticed. Lyddie stood in a trance, watching the fish, wondering how much of the world she had missed in her preoccupation with her own circumstances. She had spent too many days like those herring, struggling against the stream. The fish heading upstream were not destined to lay their eggs, no matter how they hurried; many men lay in wait to net and salt and dry them and pack them into barrels to feed the slaves in the West Indies. But the herring going downstream were free to pass at will, as it was believed among the fishermen that the downstream fish were poison. So why not turn and let her own poisoned soul float in the direction that would cause the least trouble to everyone?

When Lyddie got home she found Mehitable out among the chickens collecting eggs. With spring came so much more work; surely Mehitable would have some for Lyddie. She approached Mehitable with fresh eagerness.

In the bright light of day Mehitable's skin looked pale and tightly drawn, the veins showing clearly at the temples. Lyddie felt the old drop of fear in her chest. The skin was such a thin thing to protect the life's blood; so many ills could stop the vital flow from within and without it. Lyddie went up and removed the basket from Mehitable's arm. "Let me take on this chore, Daughter. And perhaps the buttery."

Mehitable smiled more easily than she had in some time, and for a minute Lyddie thought they'd come at last to a peaceful blending. "I've finished with the eggs, Mother, and Jane's at the buttery. But there is an errand you could do for me. Cousin Betsey is short on eggs for her pudding. Take her this basket. Stay to dine. She asked it specifically. She says Mr. Freeman is in need of fresh conversation."

"If it's fresh conversation he's after, you'd best send Jane and leave me the buttery."

"No, no, I don't think so." Again, the smile.

So, thought Lyddie, they all work to empty the stable together. She drew a shallow breath and exhaled evenly, slowly.

"I refuse you only this, Daughter," she said, "and for reasons I can't at this moment explain. But I beg you, ask me to aid you in some other way. I've no fondness for idle hands."

Mehitable's face closed up. "Well, then, you'd best return to your stockings."

12

Lyddie was tightening her bed ropes when she heard several male voices in the study, and soon after, a call for her to attend. She dropped her bed key and hurried in to find five men standing around the table in a sweep of grayed and balding heads that dipped and smiled at her like gone-to-seed dandelions. She knew Deacon Smalley and Griffith and Eldred, the two neighbors on Clarke's side of the millstream feud; the last man was introduced to her as Esquire Doane. As soon as greetings were dispensed they looked in unison at the table. A paper lay on it. Lyddie had never seen the paper before, but she knew what it contained the same way she had known the faces of each of her children before they were born.

" 'Tis all arranged, Mother," Nathan said. "Deacon Smalley takes it all off our hands. We wait on nothing but your signature." He dipped the pen and extended it to Lyddie, but her step flagged, as if a stone wall surrounded the table.

"Mother," her son said a second time, more sharply, which was a mistake; his tone planted Lyddie's feet hard on the ground.

"Widow Berry?" Mr. Doane said more kindly. "You do understand the law requires you to sign?"

Lyddie stepped forward, read the paper, and saw it was as she had suspected.

> *I, Lydia Berry, relict of Edward Berry, relinquish all dower rights to the dwelling house and buildings on the parcel of land, said land being bounded westerly and northerly by the public road, southerly by that lot belonging to Theophilus Smalley, and easterly by that lot belonging to the Indian Sam Cowett . . .*

The Indian Sam Cowett, who had caused her to be here, by dividing the woodlot, and thereby indirectly creating this paper. An odd thought popped into Lyddie's head. What would James Otis say of Sam Cowett? Was obeying only those laws written on your heart the same as doing as you pleased? And did Sam Cowett actually do only as he pleased? Could anyone?

"Come, Doane," Nathan said. "She's no experience with legal documents; show her the place to sign."

Doane stepped forward. "Here, Widow Berry. You affix your name here, and Mr. Eldred and Mr. Griffith bear witness to it."

"And you, Mr. Doane? Do you sign as well?"

"No, no, I'm here only as Mr. Clarke's legal representative."

And Lyddie's unbiddable thoughts flew off again, this time to Eben Freeman. *In law and in life . . . I am at your service.* Dear God, did she dare? And what would it get her? Nothing but time, a few more minutes or hours or days before she was forced to put that pen to that paper. She lifted her eyes to meet her son-in-law's. "And where is my legal representative?"

"Good God, Mother, what need you with a legal representative?"

"Did not you just say it? I've no experience with legal documents. Best send for Mr. Freeman."

"Nonsense, Mother, 'tis all just formality. Tell her, Doane."

Esquire Doane smiled at Lyddie. "Perhaps your son has neglected to explain it to you in such a way that you may have a full understanding. Let me do so now. If you wish to have your funds, you must sign your consent to the sale. There, I think that says it most simply."

"Very simply, Mr. Doane. Wouldn't you even say perhaps too simply? By 'funds' I take you to mean in this case my widow's thirds, or the profits on one-third the sum received from the sale?"

"Exactly, Mother," Nathan said. "Now let's get on, shall we?"

"And if the house were not sold, I should retain life use of one-third the property?"

Nathan smiled. "And what use could you possibly make of a third the property?"

"The same use I made of it before. Shall we send for Mr. Freeman now?"

"Good God, you can't be serious."

"I think we'd best send for Freeman," said Doane, and from there the conversation moved around Lyddie as a storm circles its eye.

Clarke: "I'll not waste my time in this!"
Smalley: "I would have us address any legal problems that might arise, now versus later."
Doane: "There are no legal problems; get her attorney here and he'll assure her of it."
Clarke: "I want this done now!"
Eldred: "I doubt Freeman's even in town."

> Smalley: "No, no, he's at his brother's house yet."
> Doane: "Go ahead, Clarke, send one of your servants for him and get this over with."
> Clarke: "First I take time out of my business and now I must take it out of my household as well?"
> Doane: "If you prefer to schedule this meeting for another date—"
> Clarke: "And pay for your time double? Time I shouldn't have had to pay for at all if Freeman hadn't been such an old woman over taking on a little extra paper?"
> Doane: "Indeed? In that case—"
> Clarke: "Oh, the devil take it! Jot! Where the devil is Jot? Jot! Go to Shubael Hopkins and fetch us back Freeman. Tell him the Widow Berry wants him; that should set him running."

There followed a span of time during which none appeared willing to approach Lyddie except the lawyer Doane, but Lyddie was sorry he bothered, for otherwise she might have excused herself from the room. Lawyer Doane chattered on about the differences in the weathers between Satucket and Boston, the likelihood of rain, and the condition of the roads, until Jot returned with Eben Freeman.

Lyddie had not really expected him to come, but she was glad, very glad to see him. He was the tallest, if leanest, man in the room, and adding him to Lyddie's side of the table went a good way to correcting the imbalance.

Doane gave a brief summation, during which Freeman controlled his features well, shooting only one look at Lyddie for confirmation.

As soon as Doane ceased speaking, Nathan Clarke took it up. "If you think to make mountains out of molehills, Freeman, you'll find yourself in want of earth to move around. This is nothing but a lack of understanding."

"I've noticed no lack in the widow's understanding," Freeman said. "By the condition of her husband's will she's perfectly within her right to retain her use of a third the property, in addition to her keep and care—"

"Which keep and care she will receive, once she puts pen to paper."

"Which keep and care she will receive *whether or not* she puts pen to paper."

Nathan gave a crusted laugh. "Very well, Freeman, how do you see your client managing her property?"

"If she were to set up her fire in the easterly corner of the keeping room hearth, and keep a table and chair and cupboard at that end, and put her bed in the southeast chamber, and take charge of the pantry, as well as a corner of the barn for keeping of her cow, I think she would be well within the strictures of the will and the laws of the colony."

"Indeed. And who shall muck out the cow's corner and harvest its hay and chop her wood? Does she think herself rich enough to hire out such chores?"

"She thinks you rich enough, Mr. Clarke. You're charged by her husband's will to keep her in comfort. Now in the case of the Widow Howland, 'comfort' was determined by the court at forty cords of wood a year, eight bushels of Indian meal, two of rye, eighty pounds of beef, fifty of pork—"

"Mr. Doane," Nathan said, "pray, put a stop to this nonsense."

Mr. Doane gazed at Mr. Freeman. "I make the eighty pounds of beef to be high. In the case of the Widow Selew—"

"Hang the Widow Selew!" Nathan said. "What care I about the Widow Selew? 'Tis all mad chatter, Mr. Doane, I assure you. Do you imagine a woman of her age would give over such easy life under my roof to live alone in squalor?"

"Squalor?" Lyddie said. "You think your wife's parents lived a life of squalor? You may keep your chaise and your silver porridge bowls and your servants. You may even keep your eighty pounds of beef. I'll take the wood and the hay and the meal and my third of the house to live in."

Freeman's head whipped around, his features at last unbridled. "A minute," he said. "Gentlemen, you will excuse us a minute," and without ceremony he grasped Lyddie's arm, drew her from the study and into her room, closing the door behind them.

"My dear madam," he said, "what are you about?"

"I'm about governing my life, Mr. Freeman."

"When I spoke just now . . . but surely you knew? I spoke to give pause, to perhaps achieve some small addition to your keep and care. I in no way recommend a course of separation from this household. Why, it would be madness."

"Very well, then, call me mad. But take no blame on yourself; you didn't invent this idea, in fact, you've done nothing but shown me a way to remove several obstacles. With ample wood and grain—"

"No, no, no. The law is one thing; the other is the practicality of the situation. Do you think for a minute that by casting yourself outside your son's care—"

"He must care for me wherever I am. Did you not just say so?"

They stood and stared across the foot of space between them, like two people who had just met by surprise in the road, one come from a wedding and one from a funeral. Standing so close, Lyddie noticed that the lawyer's queue was caught up in his collar. He'd ridden out in such haste he hadn't settled his coat on his shoulders; he'd taken a good piece out of his day on her behalf; she owed him a great debt that she had no means to repay. She could do nothing for him but reach up and lay flat his queue, but the simple gesture loosed another flood of emotion across his features; as she removed her hand he caught it in his own long fingers.

"Widow Berry. Lydia. You see? I say your given name, speaking to you now as a husband would if he were present. As your husband would. He talked of what he wished for you, what he felt was best for you—"

"And you agreed with him? That my best happiness lay in my son Clarke's home?"

The eyes flickered away.

Nathan Clarke shoved open the door. "All right now, you've had your little chat. Come, Mother, and sign the paper. Doane must be off to Barnstable this hour."

"I shall be glad to sign a paper," Lyddie said. "As long as it's one written up to the specification just now outlined by my lawyer."

Lyddie might as well have stuck Nathan with her knitting pin. She had some trouble believing that her own son-in-law would say such things, not only to her, but also to Eben Freeman. It drove all the visitors from the house in quick order, except Eben Freeman, whose presence did nothing for Lyddie but draw half the venom. Even Mehitable's soft tones served as nothing but kindling, although she did manage to entice her husband out of their presence, if not out of their hearing.

" 'Tis done!" Nathan roared from the next room. "Over! Finished! I'll not have her in front of my eyes! I'll not have her at my table! She'll find out what kindness she's forfeited! Let her sleep in the barn with the bloody cow if she wishes!"

Eben Freeman cleared his throat. "I wonder if you might like to dine with my sister and me. She's often suggested it."

Lyddie accepted.

Betsey greeted her cousin with the kind of welcome Lyddie recognized as that of a woman whose husband had just left for a season on the Canada River. Eben Freeman attempted to portray the events of the morning in the lightest possible manner, but Betsey's eyes immediately turned the size and color of pewter porringers.

"You'll stay the night," she decided. "Let the man cool. We'll send Eben back with a message so they won't fret about you."

It seemed like a good idea to Lyddie. No doubt it seemed a better one to Mehitable; when Eben Freeman returned he carried a sack for Lyddie in which her daughter had packed two skirts, two shifts, one gown, her hair comb, her letter book, and four pairs of stockings, both winter and summer.

13

Lyddie slept poorly. The room she'd been given smelled like paper and ink and horse and tobacco and sweat-dampened broadcloth; she began to suspect she'd been put to bed in the room Eben Freeman used while visiting his sister. The Hopkinses had two girls only left at home, but had in addition taken in an old woman called Aunt Goss, no living person's aunt as far as anyone knew, but called so by Eben Freeman, who had been great childhood friends with her son. Aunt Goss's husband had gone out of Nantucket on a whaler and not come back—it had been rumored he lived in the Azores with a mistress—and her one son had been gored by a bull and died some years previous. When Aunt Goss had become enfeebled, Eben Freeman had made arrangement with his sister and her husband to keep her at his charge. Aunt Goss lived in the tiny northeast bedroom, while Shubael and Betsey occupied the southwest one and Lyddie the southeast.

Which left Freeman where, up in one of the old beds on the boys' side of the attics?

The suspicion seemed confirmed at breakfast when the table had to be cleared of several thick wallets of paper, and the thought that Lyddie had disrupted a second household made her dull. The conversation moved around the table with no great help from the others; the two girls fetched and carried in dragging silence; Aunt Goss seemed at best blind and deaf, and at the worst witless; she dropped her shriveled face as close to her plate as she could and picked at the same crust of bread with knotted fingers; Betsey chattered into the air on a variety of subjects that could interest no one but herself; Freeman ate with a steady concentration and an occasional indiscriminate "indeed," or a nod of the head in his sister's direction.

As Betsey wrapped the bread in a cloth Lyddie said, "Thank you for your hospitality, Cousin. I'll be off as soon as I get my things together."

"Off?" Freeman said. "I don't know that I call that wise. Best you keep my sister company in my absence. I leave for Barnstable this minute."

"Barnstable!" Betsey said. "What's this news? And when was I to be told of it?"

Freeman attempted to signal his sister with a lifted finger, which Lyddie caught, but Betsey didn't. Even Aunt Goss raised her head and looked back and forth between them like a small brown sparrow hunting seeds.

"Did I not say it yesterday?" Freeman said. "I'm sure I said it yesterday. I distinctly recall asking you what you wished me to bring you from Barnstable as my way of thanking you for your kind hospitality."

"Hospitality! What a word between family! You fuss over me too much and I've often said it. Perhaps some small trifle; last time you gave handkerchiefs, did you not? Very nice. You know my taste; I'm much more simple-minded than some others in our village. Have you seen Mrs. Smalley's hair comb? Far too grand for me. But if you're off to Barnstable, let me give you a package for Henry." She left the room.

Freeman glanced at Aunt Goss, whose chin had dropped to her chest as if she were sleeping. He turned to Lyddie. "I've some trouble understanding my sister," he said. "For instance, this gift. Common sense suggests a repeat of the handkerchiefs; instinct, however, directs me to the hair comb."

"I think you understand your sister very well."

"My wife was of a different nature. In some ways, you remind me of her. What you mean to say, you say."

"And what I'd better not say as well."

He smiled. "A small price to pay for the larger principle."

Betsey came back with her parcel. Eben Freeman took it and stood. "Good-bye, Sister. Good-bye, girls. Good-bye, Widow Berry." He glanced at Aunt Goss. Her mouth lay open, but her eyes had closed. Nonetheless, he stepped over to her and touched his lips to her temple. The eyes never opened, but Lyddie noticed the gnarled hand lifted just far enough to pat Freeman's. He turned back to Lyddie. "Enjoy your visit."

As soon as he was gone Betsey started up again. It was hard, very hard, to be left alone with an old woman and two sickly girls, her husband and sons all gone, not a single male relation left in the village. She'd understood her brother had had a good deal of business with Winslow over the millstream, and she'd looked forward to his having a nice, long stay in Satucket, but now he was gone to Barnstable. She hoped he remembered to stop at her son's and deliver her package. Henry's wife had served Betsey a turned leg of mutton on her last trip to Barnstable and she'd been determined not to say a thing about it, but when it appeared again the second day . . .

Lyddie stood. "I must be off," she said.

"Off! Whatever are you saying? Did you not hear what Brother told you? You're to stay here, he said. He said—"

"I must go, Cousin."

Lyddie went to her room; Betsey followed and fussed around her as she assembled her belongings, but once she saw there was no turning her she gave over and went to fetch a wedge of cheese and loaf of bread for Mehitable in exchange for the eggs she'd delivered.

Lyddie left the house with Betsey's voice and Aunt Goss's sparrow eyes, open now, following her closely. She headed straight along the King's road, but at Foster's way she found herself cutting shoreward, thinking to avoid any traffic on the main road, and along with the traffic, any questions. The road was wet but firm and she found the first decent sun of April comforting. She thought of nothing else but the unexpected fineness of the day until she reached the Point of Rock and saw Bangs's sloop in the channel, unloading lumber across the flats. Several men looked up as she passed, raised their arms in greeting, and went back to their business. What was one more housewife on the beach with her sack, collecting sand to scrub her floors? She turned left and strode the track along the sedge ground behind the lip of dune. She made poor time over the rough surface, and after a few rods, with a growing damp under the heavy hair at the back of her neck, she came to another opinion about the sun; by the time she reached Robbin's landing she was dripping under her arms and between her breasts and thighs, but she had managed to come the whole way without speaking to anyone.

Lyddie left the shore for the landing road and continued down it until she reached the Cowett house. She saw Rebecca Cowett setting plants and waved to her but continued without stopping. When she reached her old house she circled it and went straight to the well. The dark, silky water gleamed up at her; she pumped a bucketful, and before the water even touched her lips she could taste the cool sweetness. She drank hard, and when she was through she dipped both hands in the bucket, splashing her face and neck and halfway up her arms. She bent down, removed her shoes and stockings, and dashed water up under her skirt. She stood still until the breeze took hold of the wet spots and she shivered; she sank down and stretched her length on the grass to dry off in the sun. When had she last done such a silly thing as lie in the sun? she wondered. Before she'd become old enough to sew and scrub and cook; before the age of four, then.

Lyddie lay in the grass a long time, not to rest, but to feel her space between the two worlds: the damp earth below, the warm sun above. And in what world might she find Edward now? Lyddie wondered. But as she wondered, she discovered that along with her loss of faith in God she'd also lost faith in his heaven and hell. And had she also lost faith in Edward's soul? No, she decided. He was too much with her. Which left her the problem that if Edward's soul were neither above nor below, where was it? Did he walk the earth? And if he walked the earth, would he walk it here, in this place of his domestic comforts, or would he choose a place of power, such as the deck of a sloop, or the meetinghouse during town meeting, or even the tavern, where, as Edward had once said, ideas were born, along with the bastards? She knew too little of the world of men to say for sure what Edward might choose; she could say only what she might choose in the same instance. But even to say what she might choose didn't answer the question, because Edward's choices were not her choices. Her choices were this house or that house, this man or that man. Or herself, alone.

Alone. The word rang through her head like a promise. This house that was written so deeply on her heart, why must she leave it now? She had Betsey's loaf of bread and a wedge of cheese that would keep her two days, three if she were parsimonious. Betsey would think her at Nathan's; Nathan, if he cared, would think her at Betsey's. Two or three days in her old corner, and she would ask for nothing more.

Something set off a trio of crows. They shot out of the woodlot, beating and screaming at the air. Lyddie sat up. The birds settled in the garden on last year's pumpkin vine, but whatever had spooked them continued to disturb their peace; they retched out their warning until Lyddie began to believe them. She got up, no longer wet, but certainly damp and most certainly stiff. She worked her spine straight and faced the birds. "Be gone!" she shouted.

The birds flew off, rebutting her all the way. Lyddie returned to the dooryard, picked up her sack, and went into the house. A hush as thick as pudding met her. And more damp. She felt a strong desire for tea and looked without hope at the shelf. Little of value remained on it but the odd bits of crockery, the salt box, the worn dough tray, several wooden trenchers and—she saw it without lifting her expectation—her rusted tin tea canister. She pried open the lid and found enough stale leaves for a day or two. She could feel her mouth relax, the corners rise. She went straight to the tinderbox and worked the flint, worked it and worked it without a spark. The fear rose in her. She had crossed her son and her lawyer. She had spurned her cousin. She should never have left Betsey's; she should never have come here.

The rag caught. Lyddie fed it a few sticks from the bottom of the wood box and sat back on her heels, as breathless and sweating as she'd been during the walk. She picked up the bucket and returned to the well. The day had gone the way of most fine April days: one minute all sun and warmth, the next chill and gray. The crows had left their post in the garden; either the danger had not materialized and they had returned to the wood, or whatever it was that had scared them in the first place had now chased them farther away. Lyddie pumped the handle and filled her bucket, feeling the rawness of disuse in her upper arms, and again as she lugged the bucket up the path. Half the bucket went straight to the kettle and the kettle to the fire; the rest went by the door for washing. She was ready for food but decided not to eat; a meal postponed meant a meal saved. She went instead to her old room, the east chamber, the one Eben Freeman had posited as hers under law. She had left nothing on the bed but an old blanket to protect the tick; she'd expected Smalley's daughter and her new husband to sleep on it next, but instead she would sleep on it, in her clothes, under the musty blanket, alone.

Alone. But why did she not feel alone? She pulled the blanket off the bed and carried it outside for a shake and a snap. She draped it over the inkberry bush and went back to inspect the bed tick. It had survived the mice but needed a good fluffing; she wrestled it outside to join the blanket. Next she swept up the mice droppings and dead insects and cobwebs that had collected in the corners, and by then she was starving. The tea was ready; since she had no milk or sugar or even molasses she took it straight, but Betsey's loaf was sweet, and it all went down together in a welcome paste. She cut a thin wedge of cheese and looked around the keeping room, noticing other things that had been removed since her last visit: Edward's pipe and tongs, his musket, the clock. And why not? Those things were Nathan's now. Lyddie was surprised to discover in herself the sense of greatest loss over the musket. Edward had taught her to fire it back in the early days of their marriage, after a band of Iroquois had beaten in the door of his brother's house in Duxbury, and although the Cape Indians had never troubled their English neighbors, Lyddie had shot more than one fox with that musket. She had taken comfort in that musket.

Lyddie finished her meal, scoured her plate and cup, brought in the bed tick and blanket, and stood idle.

In Lyddie's old life there would have been much to do, so much that she wouldn't see the end of it, but now she had no workbox for sewing or knitting, no flour for baking, no soap for washing, no tallow for candle making. Neither had she a garden to tend, a cow to milk, eggs to collect, or husband to feed and clothe.

It grew dark. Lyddie found three candles in the candle box, but as she had no book or handwork she decided not to waste them. She banked the flame, went to her old room, and still in her clothes, got under the old blanket. She was more exhausted than she'd been in months, but instead of sleeping she lay awake, listening to the house.

She'd forgotten it. That creak, was it the shadblow outside the window, or the dried-out ship's knee beam in the attic? And that scratching sound—bullbrier against glass, or mice? In the woods an owl—or was it a dying rabbit?—let out a wild screech, and Lyddie sat up. She swung her feet to the floor and felt the smooth planks that Edward had laid.

"Are you here?" she whispered.

Something answered with a dry rattle that could have been a man's rusty laugh, watery cough, or last year's corn husk.

14

Lyddie came awake with the mourning doves. As she walked to the necessary a lemon-pink band was just pushing up the gray sky on its eastern edge, and the tang of the sand flats caught at her nose. On her return trip to the house she noticed the plum bushes were in bloom and that a number of shoots had cleared the accumulated leaves in the garden.

She blew up the fire, boiled herself some weak tea, and cut a thin slab of bread; after that, for no good reason that she could think of, as she had nothing to put in it, she decided to go out into the garden and clear away the rot. She visited the barn first. It smelled of old dung, musty hay, and something dead, probably a trapped bird or a rodent. Nathan must have had no need of a new shovel or an ax because she found both of Edward's left behind for Smalley to buy, but the only hoe was a broken one, with a bare foot of handle attached; she took it with her, along with an old sack to kneel on.

The minute Lyddie settled down on her knees the crows in the woodlot started up again; well let them, she thought, there'd be no corn for them to scavenge this year, and no flax for her to pull and spin into linen thread, and no cucumber or cabbage or squash or beans or anything else. So why did she bother over this bit of ground?

Lyddie's mind continued to work along that theme, but her fingers paid no attention. They picked away the dead stuff first and then attacked the earth with the broken hoe—the soil came up in thick chunks like molasses candy, and she had to work it loose with her fingers.

Lyddie had worked well past the dinner hour and cleared an eight-foot square of earth when Eben Freeman rode up. He dismounted stiffly; it might have been that or it might have been the lack of his usual effort to disarrange his face that made him appear to have aged since their last visit.

"I've just been to Clarke's in search of you," he said. "My sister said you'd gone back, but the Clarkes were adamant you hadn't."

"And then you came here?"

"I knew full well where you'd be."

"Clever."

"I'm surprised to hear you say so. Having ignored my counsel, having deceived both my sister and myself—"

"I intended to deceive no one, Mr. Freeman."

"And what do you intend to live on?"

"Your sister sent me away with a loaf and cheese for Mehitable, a small theft I hope to make good at a later time, but for now—"

"Do I understand you? You alienate all source of support and hinge your existence on a loaf and a cheese? Or do you count on whatever it is that might sprout by divine intervention out of bare ground?"

He pointed to the earth at Lyddie's feet. She'd been prepared to admit her intention of staying only two or three days, but how, then, to explain the garden? "Did you find your sister's gift in Barnstable?" she asked instead.

By the look he gave her she might have asked him if he'd found the king's jewels in Barnstable. "No, I did not. I was otherwise occupied the short time I was in town, and was in some hurry to return, thinking I might now resolve—" He broke off.

Lyddie dusted her hands and walked toward the house. Freeman followed her.

"I would ask you to dine, but you might guess the menu."

"You can make a joke of this?"

"Yes," Lyddie said, realizing it only as she spoke. "I've dirt on my hands, a catch in my back, and an ache in my stomach, but I feel more like myself than I've felt in months. My one difficulty at the moment is determining how I might repay a loaf and cheese. And I'm well aware I owe you for your recent services."

"You owe me nothing. Your husband compensated me previously for all matters that might arise relating to his estate."

"Very well, then."

"Very well? By now I suspect he would like to strike me dead. To have set you off here alone, at odds with your son—"

"You're not responsible for what I've done, Mr. Freeman, although as such an admirer of Mr. Otis I should think you of all people would understand it."

"I am at a loss to know what Mr. Otis might have to do with this."

"Did he not talk of a man's right to sit as secure in his house as any prince in his castle?"

"A man, yes. A woman is another matter entirely."

"Your Mr. Otis spoke of giving women the same rights as men."

"He also spoke of giving them to the Negro, and yet he doesn't free his own servant. Mr. Otis speaks in theories only. You cannot—"

"Why don't you tell me what I *can* do, Mr. Freeman? If you must continue this conversation, that would be a more useful topic. Am I or am I not allowed by law to be here?"

"You're allowed by *law*, yes. But you must see, you're too clever a woman not to see—"

"That the law will be of little use to me? I do see that, yes."

Freeman's face took on a muddy, slapped appearance. "Excuse me for disturbing you. Good afternoon."

"Good afternoon," Lyddie said. She might have added something else to ease the parting, but her easing skills seemed to have played out along with Edward. She considered it no mean gift that she at least managed to say nothing else until Freeman had remounted his horse and departed.

Lyddie had just finished her much delayed dinner of bread and cheese when she heard another horse. She looked out, identified her son-in-law, and decided to take up a position of strength on the stoop, if for nothing else than to raise herself above him as he approached. It seemed to work. He bounced off the horse and strode up the walk like a deer flushed from the woodlot but slowed as he drew close and came to a full stop with some feet yet left between them.

"Well. 'Tis true, then."

"I don't know. If you mean am I here, then, yes."

"And you think to stay."

"I see no lawful reason why I should not occupy my third of the house."

"While you deny me the sale of my portion? Do you expect me to feed and clothe you at the same time that you take food out of my own family's mouth?"

"I expect nothing which—"

"You expect rightly, then. You're no mother to me or to my wife. As of this date you're cut loose."

He turned and walked back to his horse. Nathan had always chosen leggy beasts, no doubt hoping it would augment his own stature; in fact, it made him appear nothing but what he was: a small man on a big horse.

15

Cut loose. The words hung around Lyddie like so much fog for the rest of that day and through the night, never making their meaning clear until the morning, when she stepped outside and caught sight of the woodpile. From the distance it looked like a pile of chicken bones after a good boiling; she moved closer and saw she might get to October on it, especially if she had no food to cook or clothes to wash. She walked past her cleared patch of garden and thought, I can do that much—plant my garden—and then thought, plant it with what?

Lyddie hadn't sent the thought up as a prayer. It couldn't have been God, then, who sent Rebecca Cowett around the corner of the house with a basket on her arm.

"My husband told me you were back and at your garden," she said. "You start so late, I thought to speed you a little."

And how had her husband known Lyddie was back? Well, the

smoke, of course. But how had he known she was at her garden? Then Lyddie remembered the crows starting up in the woodlot, without any apparent provocation. Did he lurk there and spy? No, she decided. If Sam Cowett wanted to know anything of her plans, he'd have walked up and said "You're back, then," as he'd done the last time.

Rebecca Cowett set the basket on the bare earth. Lyddie looked into it and saw cabbage stumps, tiny squash and cucumber sprouts, young strawberry plants, and a few onion sets. All very nice, but she'd be long starved by the time any of it proved useful.

Wheels rattled on the rough road, and both women looked up. An ox and a cart, with a boy and girl in front. Nate and Bethiah. And Lyddie's trunk. They pulled up to the dooryard and got down; the girl began to unload a pile of linens from the cart, and Nate came toward the women with a paper in his hand.

"Your grandchildren," Rebecca said. "I'll not disturb your visit."

Nate approached and handed Lyddie the folded paper. She opened it.

Mother,

I have sent your belongings to you. I don't know why you have done this thing, but as you have chosen to do it you must understand you are no longer welcome at this house.

Mehitable

"Widow Berry?"

Lyddie looked up. Rebecca Cowett had not moved far; she now retraced her steps and laid a hand on Lyddie's arm. "Is all well, Widow Berry?"

Nate had already gone back to the cart where Bethiah tugged at the trunk, her cheeks for once spotted with color, her wrists like stripped twigs awkwardly bending under the weight. Nate took the handle from her, and she moved around to shove from the other end. Lyddie transferred her eye to the Indian woman. "Yes. Thank you. Good-bye."

Lyddie stepped toward the cart, the Indian woman coming with her. Nate had staggered off toward the house with another load, but Bethiah lingered at the cart, fiddling with Lyddie's workbox. Lyddie moved toward her, and Bethiah knocked over the box, spilling knitting pins and sewing needles and buttons and tape onto the ground. Lyddie and Rebecca Cowett stooped, but Bethiah sidled away to the far side of the cart.

Rebecca Cowett began to chatter as she picked up buttons and put them back in the box: what handsome buttons, she needed buttons for her husband's coat, she never understood how a man could be so hard on a coat; but all the while Lyddie felt the Indian woman's eyes on her, like a black swamp, smothering her.

Lyddie took up the box and headed with it toward the house. Nate passed her in silence, hustled Bethiah into the cart, and drove off.

Lyddie worked in the garden till dusk, setting Rebecca Cowett's plants, sifting the meager fireplace ash around their stems, the crows now encouraged to come back and discuss among themselves their plans for their forthcoming dinner. As Lyddie worked she thought about Mehitable's note. *I don't know why you have done this thing, but as you have chosen to do it* . . . But when had Lyddie ever chosen? What had she ever chosen?

Well, she had chosen Edward. She'd been heavily courted by a second cousin from Truro, who had taken the eight-hour journey on horseback twice each month, but Edward had caught her up on her way to meeting one day, handed her a chestnut burr, and said, "Best keep this near you. 'Tis good for putting on chairs to fend off idiot suitors."

"I've no idiot suitors," Lyddie had snapped back.

"Then you must be one yourself, for he's the surest idiot on earth. No brain, no wit, no anything but chin. Are you fond of chins, then?" And he jutted out his own. It was the kind of chin that finished off the face without a great deal of fanfare, but all through meeting, whenever Lyddie had snuck a look at him, Edward Berry had pushed his chin in the air.

So she had chosen Edward.

Lyddie dusted the garden dirt from her clothes and went inside. The house had cooled, and she thought with relief of the bed linens that had come with the children. She ate some bread, now down to the heel, and drank some water, made up the bed and climbed into it, but again lay sleepless, this time thinking about the children. She had barely come to know them, and now, she imagined, she would know them no better. She might see them at meeting or around town, watching from a distance as Bethiah took on the look of a consumptive and Nate went off to Harvard College; Jane would grow lovelier every day until she married and had her own children, and from there her beauty would unravel as quickly as it had come on. And Mehitable? Mehitable would bear and lose her own children, of course, any number of them, if she survived to do it. Lyddie's chest tightened at the thought of Mehitable in childbed until the very tightness wore her out and she dozed off. She slept and woke, slept and woke, slept and woke, till dawn, but with light came some thought with purpose. She must have food; that was first on the list. And she must return Rebecca Cowett's basket with a proper thanks. And thinking of the two together, she thought she might be able to accomplish both things with one visit.

The trees had leafed around the Indian's house and the interior had grown dim; Rebecca Cowett's hair lay in a long, shining braid down her back; Lyddie felt little of that former sense of an Englishman's home, and her unease held her back—Rebecca Cowett was forced to urge her forward into the room in order to shut the door. She led Lyddie to the table, dropping into the nearest chair and waving Lyddie to the other. Lyddie had by now bent her mind to getting away as quickly as she could; she set the basket on the table but didn't sit down.

"I came to return your basket," she said, "and to say the thanks I hurried through so rudely yesterday. You were most kind, Mrs. Cowett."

Rebecca Cowett dipped her head but remained silent, watching Lyddie, as her husband had watched Lyddie. What did these people hope to find with all this watching, wondered Lyddie, the color of her skin on the inside? Lyddie pushed into her pocket and pulled out the buttons Rebecca Cowett had admired the day before. "You're in need of buttons for a husband's jacket and I am not," she said. "I am, however, in need of flour and butter and yeast and—" She stopped there. The dozen jacket buttons had cost her five shillings, but there were now only eight buttons left. She might fairly ask for a bushel of Indian meal and a pound of butter and her yeast, but not a thing beyond.

The Indian held out her hand and fingered the buttons. "May I ask . . . are you at odds with your family, Widow Berry?"

No, you may not ask. The meager light fell behind Rebecca, making her skin appear even darker. The smell was not the smell of an Englishman's house. Lyddie thought of Eben Freeman's room. She had found the smell of him comforting and familiar, but this smell, a similar mix of tobacco and sweat, but a different sweat, and something like sassafras but not sassafras . . . She needed to get out, but how to do it? Fabrication took too long, especially when the fabricating was done by the inexperienced; the quickest way seemed to be the truth.

"I've come away from my son's house without his express permission," she said.

"I see. And it has angered him?"

"Yes."

The woman stood without further words and moved about kitchen and pantry and cellar, returning with a near-full bushel of Indian meal, a pound of butter, what proved to be a half-dozen dried herring done up in a sack, and several ounces of yeast scraped from the bottom of a beer barrel. She filled the basket that Lyddie had just returned, set it next to the bushel of meal, and sat down heavily in her chair.

"Thank you," Lyddie said. "I'm deeply grateful. Good morning."

She hooked the basket on her arm, heaved up the Indian meal, and gained the door just as it flew inward. She jumped back and missed a collision with Sam Cowett by a hand's width. "Good morning, Mr. Cowett. I've just finished paying a visit to your wife. We've bartered some goods and I'm now off. Good morning."

"Good morning. Or do you want another?"

"Another?"

"Another 'good morning.' You gave up two."

"You may save the other for later. Good morning."

He lifted an eyebrow, and Lyddie flushed. She pushed through the door and into the road as fast as her burdens would allow, listening for laughter behind her, unsure if she heard it.

Once at home she laid the fire in the oven and mixed up her dough. By the time the dough had finished rising the fire had burned down to a nest of bright orange coals; Lyddie held her palm to the oven brick and could count no higher than ten before she had to remove her hand: ready for bread, then. She swept out the coals, dusted the brick with flour, and set the loaves in. In the ordinary way, once the bread was done the pudding would go in, then the pies and cake and custard, each preferring a lesser degree of temperature; the beans would go last to sit the night, and the week's baking would be done. This time, her two loaves were the beginning and the end of the week's work. Lyddie refused to think to the next week, or beyond it.

16

The tea and cheese were gone and the second loaf cut into when Lyddie looked out her window and saw her cousin Betsey approaching. She had the door wide when Betsey reached it, and as Betsey pitched straight into Lyddie's chest Lyddie found herself embracing her cousin more warmly than was her habit.

"Cousin!" Betsey cried. "Do you know how glad I am to see you standing? Your daughter didn't know a thing of your condition, but neither did she seem inclined to come and find out; I said very well, then, if no one else will take the trouble I'll go and see what ails her."

"And why should something ail me?"

"Why, when you weren't at meeting—"

"Today is the Sabbath?"

"Heaven help me! I've got you dead on the ground and all you want is an almanac." She dropped into a chair. "Must I beg for a cup of tea?"

"Begging won't help you. I've nothing but water from the well, and bread and butter."

Betsey's eyebrows, which had been nestled into the puffy flesh above her eyes, shot up under the edge of her cap. "So. 'Tis true, then. He's packed you off with nothing."

"He's not packed me off. I went away of my own will."

"And does he provide?"

"He does not."

"Then 'tis all the same kettle. You must go back, Cousin. At once."

Lyddie stood up. "Would you have that water? A slice of bread? Or perhaps you'd care for some dried herring?"

"Herring! Think you to live like the Indians? Or do you shock me with such a thing in hope of getting me to stock your pantry? And me with Shubael off in Canada, conserving daily against his delay or demise, living in constant state of penury? This is not to say I wouldn't be glad to take you in if you could make your keep, but I can't afford to feed you for nothing. Perhaps if you were to ask your son—"

"I don't ask you to feed me or to house me. I came here because I wished to be here. I'll make my way."

"How?"

As Lyddie had no answer to that she said nothing.

"Oh, I see how you are, Cousin. I know you better than some others. They have in the past disagreed with me, but I've long recognized a stubborn side to your nature. And pride. Pride is a luxury no woman can afford; you must go to your son and ask forgiveness for your intractable behavior. Tell him you will stay with me. In truth, my brother comes so seldom now, and with Shubael away, I'd be glad of the company. I'm quite sure if you asked your son he would provide for you at my home the same as he would have provided for you had you stayed under his roof. My brother puts down fifty pounds a year for Aunt Goss—"

"My son wouldn't pay you fifty shillings."

"Fifty shillings! I can't feed a pig for fifty shillings! What do you think I'm made of?"

"I don't think you're made of anything, Cousin Betsey. You may rest easy. Thank you for coming. And please tell my daughter I'm not ailing."

"Shall we pray before I go? As you missed meeting?"

"I'll tend to my prayers in the usual way. Good-bye, Cousin."

The puffy eyes widened, no doubt in suspicion of Lyddie's usual way of tending to her prayers, but in truth, once Betsey had gone, Lyddie was stabbed with some compunction as she considered the degree of her own neglect. She dropped to her knees and tried to send up an apology for ignoring the Lord's Day, but as she struggled for the proper humble words she was stabbed by something stronger than compunction, which gripped her first in the stomach and then rolled outward through her body until it had melted all the strength from her limbs.

Lyddie was hungry.

She pushed herself unsteadily to her feet and went to the pantry. She unwrapped the cloth that had contained the herring and found one remaining. She picked it up and chewed without pleasure, but after a few minutes the sensation in her stomach eased. She unwrapped the remaining bread and considered. If she baked two loaves once a week . . . She rewrapped the bread. Her cousin was, of course, right. She had little choice but to go to her son and ask forgiveness and hope it would go better than her recent effort with God. Lyddie looked down at the remains of the leathery herring with distaste. How was it, she wondered, that the darker peoples so enjoyed this food? Or did they enjoy it? What choice did the slave have? And as to the Indians, they no doubt went after the fish because it was plentiful and accessible. Because they would rather eat than starve. As Lyddie would rather eat than starve. As she would rather eat herring than beg forgiveness.

Lyddie crossed the road and cut through the thick brush to a lonely stretch of the mill creek. It was not as dark with fish as the upper, more congested part of the stream, but as she waited they came, three or four dusty shadows at a time. Lyddie tucked up her skirt, and gripping the tow sack in one hand, knelt down above one of the calm pockets at the edge of the stream. The first pass netted nothing but weeds, as did the second and third and onward until she stopped counting. She sat back to rest and watched the stream. In the protected pool where she'd wildly plunged her sack the herring circled and zigzagged continuously, but directly in the middle of the current the downstream push was so strong that the fish were brought to a temporary standstill. Lyddie edged onto a rock that jutted out into the stream, waited for just that minute of stasis, and thrust in her hands. They closed around the fish; she brought her hands into the air, but the fish torqued violently and flipped free into the stream. The second fish escaped on its way to the sack; the third she dropped into the pouch of her skirt and wrapped it in its folds until it stopped writhing, then transferred it to the sack. She caught two more, and soaked and exhausted, sat back.

So, she could fish. And come summer she would have cabbage in her garden, and by fall she'd harvest the apples from her orchard and pick the plums that would spring out on the scrubby brush behind her house and by winter she would have stored and dried her squash and pumpkin and beans. Lyddie sat in the quiet wood, for once thinking of what God had provided, not what he'd taken; she felt herself drawn close to prayer until the thought struck her that she was now in a greater state of sin than she had been that morning: she'd been fishing on the Sabbath.

17

The fish shrunk to nothing over the fire and tasted like one of Edward's dirty stockings. If she didn't wish to sink to the true poverty food of clams or lobsters she'd have to sell something. Lyddie walked back and forth from room to room, trying to choose the best thing to give up. Although Mehitable had been meticulous about returning her linens and clothing, she had not sent back the pewter or the looking glass, which left the tea table or the candle stand remaining. She had nearly decided on the table when the door trembled under someone's fist.

"Widow Berry!"

She opened the door to the Indian. Every muscle in his body was clenched, his head and shoulders already half turned, ready to run. "She's in a fit. I'm for the doctor. Will you come?"

Lyddie stood, unmoving, for the space of second. "Come!" he rapped out.

Lyddie caught up some clean linen napkins and went, the Indian already out of sight by the time she reached the road.

She rapped at the Cowett door and swung it open without waiting for an answer. A light smoke hung in the air, leaving the house in an afternoon gloom, which made the scene in the tiny sickroom, the one nearest the keeping room fire, seem half surreal. The woman lay twitching on the bed, her eyes rolled back, her teeth clenched, her muscles rigid, the sheet that covered her slimy with vomit. Lyddie folded down the sheet, rested a hand on the woman's brow, and felt the searing fever. She left the room after cold water, and when she returned from the well she dipped her napkin and began to wipe the woman down.

Gradually the twitching eased; Rebecca Cowett's mouth and eyes relaxed, but the body stayed rigid and the eyes closed.

"Mrs. Cowett?"

She moaned. The chest rose and fell in sharp, shallow gusts. Lyddie found a cup, raised the woman's head, and helped her to drink, then eased her back down, listening to her moan with each movement. Lyddie returned to the keeping room and hunted the shelves for brandy, but found no spirit of any kind. Had the Indian drunk it all? Or in an effort not to drink it had he kept it away? Lyddie sniffed. Something was cooking, something rich and greasy and gamy and delicious. She went to the pot and looked in. Stew. With great chunks of dark meat and beans and potatoes and onions and carrots. Lyddie returned to the bed and sat until Sam Cowett arrived with Dr. Fessey.

The Indian moved to the far side of the bed and knelt down. "Beck," he said. *"Beck."*

Rebecca's eyelids flicked open and then crunched back together as if in pain. Dr. Fessey stepped into the room. He'd attended all of Lyddie's sick children with poor result and she had long harbored ambivalent feelings toward him, but he now looked so gray and shriveled, and he nodded to her with such grave courtesy that she felt the full weight of her previous foolishness. She rose and gave her chair to the doctor. He set his bag on the floor and sat down. He uncovered the patient and set to work listening to her chest, looking in her mouth and ears, palpating her neck and abdomen. Each time Rebecca was touched or moved she moaned, but she kept her eyes closed.

He sat back and looked at Lyddie and then at the Indian. "How long has she been unwell?"

"A few days. No more."

"What's she complained of?"

"Headache. A great headache. Can't bear light or noise. Neck pain. She won't eat. Today she vomited. Then the fits came."

Fessey nodded. "Your wife has brain fever, Mr. Cowett. Naught to do but rest and quiet, but you'll need someone to tend her."

"I'll tend my wife."

The doctor looked skeptically at Lyddie. "Very well, then. I'll leave some laudanum with you. The pain in her head will be severe. Twenty drops to an ounce of brandy, no more. You might try a catnip tea every third hour and an onion poultice to the feet to draw the fever. And fluids only. Do you understand?"

The Indian looked at him. The doctor looked at Lyddie. He reached into his satchel and pulled out a small vial.

"Twenty drops only. Do you understand?"

The Indian made no answer.

The doctor leaned toward Lyddie. "You're a kind woman to come. Before you go, you might look to the poultice." He stood up. "I'll be back tomorrow. Good afternoon, Mr. Cowett. Good afternoon, Widow Berry."

As soon as the doctor left Sam Cowett said, "I've no brandy."

"Nor I," Lyddie said. "Let me tend your wife while you go."

"I'll tend her." He left the bed and reached into a pot on the shelf, pulled out some coins, and handed them to her. He picked up the cloth Lyddie had used and began to bathe his wife's flesh with a practiced intimacy that made Lyddie flush. She hurried out. Once in the yard Lyddie counted out the money—three shillings—more hard cash than she'd held in her hand in some time.

Sears's store was a mile to the east; Lyddie covered the ground on foot as fast as she might have done riding pillion. She stepped into the room and Caleb Sears looked up, then down, then up. After a time he said, "Good evening to you, Widow Berry."

"Good evening," Lyddie said. "I'd like two pints of brandy if you'd be so kind."

Sears didn't move.

"Is there a difficulty?" Lyddie asked.

Sears cleared his throat. "No. I mean to say, yes. I mean to say, there is some difficulty with the account. Your son—"

Lyddie reached in her pocket and dropped the coins on the table. "If my son is unable to settle his account I should be happy to assist him."

"No, no, Widow Berry," Sears said. "I meant only to say . . . There's absolutely no need . . . You said . . . a pint?"

"I said two."

He hurried away and came back with two bottles. He picked one of the coins off the counter and pushed back the others.

When Lyddie returned she found the dirty sheet replaced with a clean one and Cowett sitting with his hands loose at his sides, staring down at his wife.

"It hurts her," he said. He pointed to her head. "I touch her and she twitches."

"Perhaps best to leave her alone." Lyddie fetched a cup and mixed the tincture with the brandy, brought it to the bed, and signaled the Indian to raise his wife's head.

Rebecca's eyes opened and she stared at Lyddie a half second before they closed.

"Here, Beck, drink," Cowett said.

She drank and Cowett eased her back down.

Lyddie went into the keeping room and rooted out a cheesecloth and bowl. She ladled stew over the cloth and strained the liquid into the bowl, trying not to inhale the enticing smell. She returned to the little room and handed the bowl to the Indian, but when he went to take it from her, his hand shook.

"Mr. Cowett," Lyddie said. "Let me feed your wife while you go into the other room and eat some of that stew."

To her surprise, he obeyed. It seemed to Lyddie he stayed gone a long time, but when he returned his hand was steady. Lyddie stood up and removed the change from her pocket. The Indian pointed to it. "Yours."

"No."

" 'Tisn't half a day's nursing."

"No, I cannot."

"Shames you, does it?"

"I can't afford shame, Mr. Cowett. But what little I've done this day I've done as a return on your wife's kindness."

He looked at her. " 'Tis true, then? Clarke's struck you off?"

Lyddie didn't answer. She left the room, climbed into the Cowetts' cellar, and retrieved the last of the winter's store of onions. She sliced them up and laid them out in another of her own napkins, then returned to the patient and bound the napkins to her feet. Sam Cowett never looked up from his wife's face or the bed or the floor, whatever it was that he stared at so hard.

In the morning Lyddie found Rebecca Cowett much the same and her husband much altered, his eyes hollowed, his jaw lumpy, his hair loose, his linen shirt stained with his wife's vomit, or the broth, or the brandy, or all three together. He stood up the minute Lyddie reached the bed and studied her face, as if it would tell him how his wife might do.

"Have you seen change?" she asked.

"Another fit. Less pained." He pointed to the laudanum.

"Does she speak?"

"She mumbles. Moans. She looks at nothing, at me as if I'm nothing."

Lyddie rested a hand on Rebecca's forehead and thought it felt cooler. She felt the sheets. Damp. "She's sweated out some of her fever. If you have fresh linens I'll change them."

Cowett pointed to a six-board chest in the other room. Lyddie opened it and found one set only; someone would need to do a washing. Lyddie wondered if a woman from the Indian village might be got to help out, but the little she'd seen of the Cowetts she'd never seen them with anyone from the Indian nation, and she also remembered his words to the doctor, and to her: "I'll tend her."

Lyddie looked again at Sam Cowett and decided he wouldn't make it many more nights through. "Best you sleep a while and let me tend to your wife," Lyddie said. "You can't afford to sicken yourself."

"And you can't afford another day's kindness. If you stay you take your pay."

Lyddie hesitated. "I would take dinner."

He stared at her, nodded. After a minute he said, "Will she die?"

"Best you ask Dr. Fessey."

"I ask you."

"I don't know."

"She might?"

"She's very ill."

He stood up and walked to the door. "If she looks for me—"

"I'll wake you."

He left the room.

Lyddie waited until she heard the sound of bed ropes strafing and boots hitting the floor, then got up and went into the keeping room.

Stew.

18

The doctor appeared at noon, drawing Sam Cowett with him into the sickroom.

"Widow Berry," the doctor said, as if surprised to see her still there. He looked at his patient, palpated her neck, felt her pulse. He opened one of her eyelids and dropped it closed. "Non compos mentis, eh?"

Lyddie took a quick look at Cowett; his face had gone dark, and he glared at the doctor.

"I don't know if she comprehends," Lyddie said quickly. "She doesn't speak or move except to flinch if we move her. She's had no more fits or vomits. She swallows the tincture."

The doctor peered at Lyddie. "Yes, well, you seem quite in touch with the situation."

"Mr. Cowett has hired me to nurse."

The doctor swung around to the Indian. "Then you've got her in good hands, I'd say, Mr. Cowett. Quite the lucky situation for you. All right, then, everything seems as good as can be expected—"

"Will she die?" Cowett asked.

The doctor drummed the edge of the bed tick several seconds, then shoved his hands between his vest buttons, as if to keep them still. "Well, my good fellow, I'd have to say yes, I expect she will do. I'm sorry to say it, but as you ask, I feel I must. Not a thing for it other than what the good widow's doing; and I wouldn't exactly give her up; we deal with more than what we see in cases like this, you know. The body keeps its secrets; you might say 'tis a good sign the heat has left her, but she's in what we might call a comatose delirium. That we don't take as a good sign. Altogether—"

"How long?"

The doctor leaned over, lifted Rebecca's arm, and dropped it. She screwed up her eyes and flinched. "You see? She responds to pain yet. We may take that as a good sign."

"How long?"

"A week. Maybe two. Ah, well, naught to do but keep up the regimen I described to you and send for me if you need me."

As Sam Cowett said nothing, Lyddie said, "Yes. Thank you."

The doctor motioned to Lyddie. She followed him to the door of the house, and he leaned over, speaking low. "You watch out for yourself, Widow Berry. There's of course not a shred of hope for that poor woman, and when she goes, there's no telling what he'll do. I understand you've managed to complicate things with your son, but if you don't mind my saying, considering that I've known you a long time now—"

"I'll watch out for myself," Lyddie said. "Thank you."

She reentered the sickroom. Sam Cowett sat staring at his wife.

"A week or two."

"Yes."

"I've a boat needs caulking and graving. She's had a hard winter at whaling."

"Then why don't you do it? I'm able to stay, I told you."

"For pay."

"Yes, for pay. Let's not talk that round again. I'm through with kindness, I assure you."

His face did something that reminded her, absurdly, of Eben Freeman.

They settled on meals plus two shillings a day, or its equivalent in goods.

Lyddie would have liked to say that her head was filled with concern for Rebecca Cowett, and that thought did occupy a fair portion of her mind, but the rest of it was filled with food. In addition to the stew she found the remains of a turkey pie and an Indian pudding and milk and dried fish and dried meat and dried pumpkin and pickle and applesauce and a fine, heavy rye loaf and a tub of butter and a whole cheese and a basket of eggs and tea, fresh bohea tea, and a tin of seedcakes. The Indian wolfed down the turkey pie before he left, but Lyddie went back for the stew, spearing out fat chunks of meat and vegetables to conserve the broth for Rebecca, icing a thick slice of dark bread with butter, brewing up a strong pot of tea, finishing all with seedcake and applesauce and counting herself well paid for that day and the next one, too.

The Indian was gone three hours. He returned in the middle of the afternoon to find no change in his wife. He would not return to the shore. He would not try to sleep. He paid Lyddie for the day, by mutual accord, a pound of cheese, one of butter, and a half-dozen eggs.

19

The next day the Indian worked at the shore again, this time through heavy rain. As soon as he got home he retreated to change into dry clothes, then went directly to see his wife. As Lyddie had yet to make her report, and as it was supper hour, she set out a plate with bread and butter and cheese and waited. At first all was silent in the little room, but soon she heard his voice, deep and low and so intimate it took her aback. "Beck? Beck. Wake up, now."

More silence.

He reappeared and looked at the plate. "I said naught about you feeding me."

"I'll not charge you, if that's your worry."

" 'Tis your not charging worries me."

"Very well, then, add this to today's nursing and give me an ounce of tea for all."

He got up, shook two ounces of tea into a napkin and shoved it across the table. "Put down a plate and tell me how she fared."

"I'm sorry, Mr. Cowett, I see no change in her. But she swallows. The worst that can be said—"

"The worst. You say naught of the best. Because the best is the worst. For her to lie there in pain—"

"But she swallows. She takes the tincture. I must tell you, we're near run out of brandy, so if you would like me to stay while you visit the store—"

"No." He returned to the money pot, held out more coins. "You go."

Lyddie felt a hot prick of anger. She was not his servant; it was not her job to fetch and carry for him.

"You go," he said again, and this time she caught it, the fear in him, the doubt, what he might do with a bottle of brandy in his hand.

Lyddie took the coins. Sam Cowett went into the little room and sat beside his wife. Lyddie could see nothing of him but his broad back and hear nothing but his wife's name, over and over, "Beck. Beck. *Beck*," louder and louder.

She left them.

The rain still pelted hard at the ground, but Lyddie moved gratefully through the wet. She felt fevered herself, her skin tight and hot, her mind raw. Would he sit and shout his wife's name all night? she wondered. If it were Edward who lay ill, what would she do? The same, she thought. Or, rather, she knew. Once, when Edward had been out in a storm, she'd stood on the black shore and yelled his name until she'd heard her own foolish voice thrown back to her on the wind. She'd been shocked by the anger in it, as if Edward could have known the weather, or sent a message home, or made as fair a living with his feet on land. When Edward had finally come home she had not wanted to touch his cold, sodden body. Later that night, when Lyddie had shifted in the bed for the hundredth time, Edward had stilled her with the weight of his hand. "My friend," he said, "you bear it all while I'm away, my house and my child and my affairs, but when I return, you may give it over. Let me toss and turn. Go to sleep, now."

"I cannot. You cannot. You cannot so suddenly take up the torch and blow me out like some candle."

Edward rose up on his elbow. "What's this, now?"

"I had to buy a cow because the last one sickened. There's not enough to pay your tax."

"The oil will pay the tax."

"And what if you'd not come back with oil? What if you'd not come back at all?"

"Shubael has his instruction."

"And should I not be told of such instruction?"

"Why trouble your head with thinking on such matters?"

"And what else do you guess troubles it? I must steel myself for you to be gone and then steel myself in case you don't return, and when you come home I must put it all away and—"

"Ah! Now I understand all. You would have me stay gone."

"No," Lyddie said. "But I would perhaps save some worry over your tax if I knew Shubael's instruction."

"Well, now, you might. Indeed, I see now that you might. Mind you, never did I think you sat here worrying over my tax . . . Very well, my friend, in for a penny, in for a pound. From hence we share all tossing and turning. Now then, were I not to return, which would only happen, I promise you, if the vessel I am mastering did not return, Shubael pays your keep out of my shares in his sloop."

"In *Shubael's* sloop!"

"If I and my ship go down, what good are my shares in that? So, I took an additional interest in Shubael's, which interest he inherits on my demise and may then sell in exchange for keeping you and our daughter and whatever other children we might have acquired in the meantime. And as we speak of that, if you plan on tossing and turning yet, why not do so in this direction?"

That night they had started a babe, or perhaps it was the next night, or the next, and then Edward had gone, and the babe had come stillborn, and she'd miscarried three more, and lost three others wellborn, with only Mehitable surviving. Mehitable had been a babe in Lyddie's arms that day on the beach in the storm, and despite the heavy wrappings her fair hair had been plastered dark with rain and her cheeks turned clammy and red with cold; Lyddie had done that to her, and yet Mehitable had lived and thrived and grown up to marry a man who sat warm at his fire and let others do his seafaring for him. No doubt if any of Lyddie's boys had grown up, they would have followed their father to sea, so there was that blessing in it, that Lyddie had none of Rebecca Cowett's pain over a boy gone off the rigging at Hatteras.

Lyddie arrived at the store, purchased the brandy without incident, delivered it to Cowett, who still sat by his wife, but silent now, collected her tea, and set off home. When Lyddie reached her house she saw Eben Freeman's long form huddled just inside the barn door.

He ran out from under cover. "Good Lord, Widow Berry, you're soaked to the bone, and no wonder, you stroll along in this odious rain as if it were the first sun in April." He caught up her provisions and hustled her through her own door. "What prompts you out into this weather?"

Lyddie explained.

"And you nurse her? Why doesn't Cowett call in Granny Hall, or one of the women from the nation for that matter?"

"Mr. Cowett seems content with my services."

"I didn't mean to say . . . It merely strikes me odd that the task falls to you."

"It falls to me because I need to eat." She opened her parcel of tea. "Today's pay. May I offer you some?"

Freeman looked down at the black leaves and up at her. "Do you mean to say—?"

"I've been cut off by my son, as you predicted."

"Predicted! I did not predict it. Not this. Not cut off. This is—" He stopped.

It occurred then to Lyddie that for a man who made his living by the fluidity of his tongue, Freeman's stuck too often. "Tea?" she repeated.

"Yes. Thank you. I—" He looked again at the tea. "I must say, the Indian pays you well. Bohea's at three shillings an ounce now."

Lyddie felt the usual flush to her skin but was unsure if it marked shame or anger. Why shouldn't the Indian pay her well? She moved around, delivering their tea, the conversation going along in fits and starts, in favor of weather over Indians, until the tea was finished and Freeman at last came to the purpose of his visit.

"You're determined to remain here, Widow Berry?"

Lyddie considered and discarded several long answers. "Yes," she said.

"You're within the law, of course—"

"And my son is without it. And we've long established there's naught to be done about it."

"We've established nothing like it. We established there was another course, which it now appears you've definitively rejected, against my counsel and advice. And with *that* established—"

"We may say our good-byes and part with no rancor between us. At least that would be my hope."

The lawyer's face went through an entire series of its convolutions and settled into something new and slightly frightening. He leaned forward in his chair. "And mine would be something other, Widow Berry. I attempted in good faith to carry forward your husband's wishes, but as that is now done with, I look to my own ideas. If I may say, as much as I respected your husband—" He paused. "He would see a better nature in a man than I. I would have spelled out my direction. But now we may amend the situation. I have an idea—"

But Lyddie didn't fully hear the rest, her brain stalled on Freeman's previous sentence. Yes, Edward would have seen a better nature in a man—he would have trusted Nathan with all matters concerning her, as he had once trusted Shubael—and now, as she looked, she found she could not blame him for it. He had done as most men would do. She had confessed her worry over a sick cow, an unpaid tax, and he had tried to spare her more of it.

"Widow Berry?"

"I'm sorry. I was after a stray thought."

"And did you catch it?"

"Perhaps."

"Would you forgive my curiosity if I asked what you think about so intently?"

"Edward."

"Ah. Yes. Of course."

He stood up. "I must go. We'll talk more on this later. Please send Cowett my sincerest wishes for his wife's speedy recovery."

20

Lyddie met the Indian next day and listened to his latest report on the patient, which was little different. The boat was now clean and tight and ready for the cod season; he planned to fish three hours either side of high tide—any longer and the sand flats would either ground him or trap him at sea till the next tide cycle.

Once Cowett had left, Lyddie spooned some milk into Rebecca, gave her the tincture, cleaned her, and changed her linen. Rebecca Cowett's breathing had become so shallow Lyddie could barely detect it. Rebecca never opened her eyes or responded to touch or voice, but Lyddie continued to speak to her, telling her of the weather and the status of her house and garden, things she could report on in full, as she'd now taken over most of the indoor and outdoor chores as well.

Lyddie was outside laying the freshly washed linen on the bushes to bleach when she looked up and saw Cousin Betsey approaching. She led her inside and watched with some amusement as Betsey stepped gingerly over the sill, just as Lyddie had once stepped, while now the Cowett home was as familiar to her as her own.

Betsey had brought a pudding and some pennyroyal and sage brewed in beer, a remedy she insisted had healed all her children's ills in a matter of hours. She peered through the little chamber door at Rebecca Cowett and began. Good Lord. O blessed Lord. Is there hope? I would doubt it. I would greatly doubt it. Does she respond? She does not. Do you see, she pays no notice of my voice or hand. And how sunken she is! Will she eat? She must eat. How long, I wonder? Oh, not long. Not long at all. Although I remember little Stephen Cobb lingered two full weeks with brain fever, and he not half the size of this poor creature.

Lyddie allowed Betsey to run on, asking and answering her own questions, until she dropped into the chair Lyddie set for her.

"You're a good Christian," Betsey said at last. "You're a good Christian to be here."

"I know a better," Lyddie said. She pointed to the sick chamber.

Betsey sniffed. "Well, she may come to meeting, but I wonder, would she nurse you with such care?"

"If my husband paid her as hers pays me."

"Pays you! Well!"

Betsey fell silent, her face a picture of confusion. Many Indian women took work in English homes, or indentured their children in exchange for some education or training, but who ever heard of a white woman working for an Indian?

Betsey had not yet untangled her features when Sam Cowett entered. She leapt up. Lyddie explained about the pudding and was relieved when Sam Cowett thanked her in good grace, without mentioning that his wife took no solids. Betsey in her turn made up a pretty speech about the patient's devout nature, reminded Lyddie not to miss the Sabbath again, and stepped out much more decisively than she'd stepped in.

Lyddie and Sam Cowett exchanged a look and, in an instant of mutual accord, for which Lyddie could find no perfect explanation, broke into smiles. Both smiles were fleeting, but in their short lives they managed to carry away something of the strange and leave behind more of the familiar.

Cowett went to see his wife, and Lyddie went to set out their food. In a little while Cowett reappeared and sat down at the table. Orange firelight colored one side of his face while a greenish purple, late-day glow from the window washed the other; he loomed in front of her like some wild, painted pagan god, and yet the things she noticed most were the long crevasses marking his cheeks, the strained cords in his neck, the way his great shoulders appeared shrunken.

"What news?" he asked.

"None of your wife. Some of your cow. I'm afraid she's run dry. I'll get some milk from Sears's tomorrow."

"Why bother? My wife will die soon enough."

As Lyddie could not contradict that, they sat silent.

"Was it like this before they found him?" Cowett said finally. "Someone dead and not dead? Alive and not alive?"

Edward. He was talking of Edward. But unlike Freeman's recent mention of him, which had forced her inside Edward's mind, this query forced her inside her own.

"Something like," she said. "I knew he was dead, but didn't believe he was dead. Neither did I believe he was alive. I felt . . . relieved when I saw him."

Cowett nodded.

"And dead. I felt dead when I saw him." Lyddie leaned across the table. "Mr. Cowett, your wife is *not* dead. You may talk to her. She doesn't speak or look at you, but who's to say she doesn't hear you?

You might have many things you would say to her, things she would like to hear. I would have had . . . I did have . . . many things—"

"So you speak to your god, and your god whispers in your husband's ear. Is that not the way it works with you?"

Lyddie stood up. "Nothing works with me. Good night." She moved to the door.

"Widow Berry."

She turned.

"There's enough milk in the jug for the morrow. Bring some when you return the day after."

At Lyddie's blank look he laughed. "So. You'd forget your precious Sabbath, would you?"

"But what will you do?"

"As you don't work, I don't work. You may tell them at meeting you've turned me Christian." He laughed again.

21

Lyddie woke in an anxious state, the kind that used to accompany having a sick child in the house. What? she thought. What? And then she remembered. Meeting. She rose and tended to her night jar, gave her face and neck and arms a good wash, took out her best dress and unrolled a fresh pair of stockings. She spent some time combing out her hair and then attempting to contain it with pins, back from her face, up under her cap. She seldom wore a cap, a thing that had troubled her daughter; she felt it a gift to Mehitable that she took such pains setting it down now. When she was finished, Lyddie went out to the well and peered down.

A strange woman looked up at her, defiant and drawn.

Lyddie stepped around the house to the road, the breeze off the water tamping down the delicate heat from the sun. A quail burst from the wood and flew across Lyddie's path, a maneuver designed to draw Lyddie away from the young; Lyddie quickened her pace, and after a time she heard the familiar two-note whistle from behind, the mother's "all safe."

Lyddie pushed on toward the King's road, thinking of Mehitable. What dangers lay ahead for her, and Lyddie not there to deflect them? Lyddie pushed the worry away. Mehitable had little need of her mother now, had never had a great need to begin with. She'd never been troubled by the ill health of her brothers and sisters, had, in fact, never appeared greatly troubled at all. She had moved with sturdy quiet steps through her own little world, and even as she'd grown she had chosen her husband in private, lived her marriage in private, and, Lyddie could only assume, grieved for her father in private. But Lyddie would have to say her daughter seemed content in her choice of husband, as much as the choice had puzzled Lyddie at the time and continued to puzzle her now. Mehitable had barely been alone in his company before she had agreed to the marriage. When Clarke had asked his permission of Edward, Edward had said only, "God bless you and good luck to you," but afterward he'd said to Lyddie, "What think you?"

Lyddie had begun by expressing her concerns over Mehitable's youth, but Edward had said, "Better he gets her before she turns headstrong like you."

When Lyddie failed to laugh he said, "Come, woman, he'll keep her better than I've ever kept you."

When Lyddie still didn't lighten he leaned forward and brushed his lips across her buckled forehead. "There can't be another pair as lucky as we two. If by chance my daughter had managed to learn your good sense, Clarke wouldn't know enough to count his good fortune, as I count it daily with you. Don't fret about it, my old friend. They'll make do."

Make do. Indeed, Mehitable seemed to make do, better than Lyddie could ever have managed with such a man as Nathan Clarke. Had Edward known their daughter best after all?

Lyddie thought ahead to meeting. She would not distress her son-in-law by attempting to sit in the family pew, but still, she would be able to *see* Mehitable; she would be able to form a judgment on her health, if not her state of mind, and with that she would make do.

Lyddie stepped into the King's road and took the rise; she joined the foot traffic funneling toward the door of the meetinghouse, and if she ignored the darting eyes around her and the pockets of silence followed by bursts of excessive greeting, it might have been any Sunday of her life past.

Lyddie entered the meetinghouse and took her seat in the women's gallery, straining her eyes to look over her daughter hungrily. Mehitable's face looked rosy and full, her arms plump and strong under her fine English cambric. In due time Lyddie noticed that others looked her way, that her presence in the women's gallery had been noted and passed along with an elbow jab here or a jerk of the head there. If anyone needed further proof that she and her family were estranged it was there in her separate seat in the gallery. Lyddie felt an odd lightness in her head, or possibly her heart; what did it matter what these people knew or thought? She didn't care. She sat back and let them look, until even her son-in-law turned in his pew on the men's side of the hall. Lyddie dipped her head; he turned away; another ripple went through the crowd.

The Reverend Dunne spoke about the son greeted by the fatted calf; Lyddie stared ahead, all attention, and heard nothing.

Lyddie had hoped to leave the meetinghouse without further offending her family, but a jam at the door held her back while the occupants of the pews moved forward, and as a space fell open to her right, Nathan Clarke pushed through. He looked, he saw, he looked away to Mr. Mayo and made a great business of accepting an invitation to spend the noon hour between sermons at his home; Mehitable came around on the far side of the two men, as did Nate and Jane and the Negro Hassey; only Bethiah's face opened bloomlike at Lyddie's side, but she was pulled quickly away, by which hand Lyddie didn't know.

Lyddie cleared the door and struck out directly west, toward home. The wind blew soft and damp from the south; a sky the color of dirty linen hung low; it would rain soon. Since she'd last been along the road the English lilacs in front of Judah Snow's house and the chestnuts along the road had come into bloom. These were Lyddie's thoughts: the weather, the advancing season; she would not have said the fatted calf cluttered her mind at all, and yet suddenly Edward's little cow popped into her mind and refused to give room. Why? Did the cow stand there blocking the road for the other, more somber thoughts that waited in the lay-by of Lyddie's mind, or did the poor creature worry it might be neglected like the Cowett cow, and run dry? Whatever its purpose, the cow stood square in front of Lyddie's eyes until she was forced to look back instead of ahead, back to the reverend's fatted calf, back to her daughter's glowing cheek, back to Bethiah's puzzled eyes, back to Nathan Clarke's noon respite at Mayo's.

And there Lyddie saw the creature's plan as if it had been spoken aloud. The cow would have dropped her calf by now; in fact, the calf would have been put to grass by now; the calf was of course Nathan's property, as was the cow, but the *use* of the cow was Lyddie's, as was enough winter hay for its maintenance, by decree of Edward's will. And twice a day now, Jane would be emptying the cow's freshened udders of the milk that was Lyddie's own. But here sat a stretch of time where the Clarkes would be either at Mayo's or at meeting and the rest of the town would be either at meeting or sheltering indoors out of the rain, which had just begun to scatter its small, dark coins in the pale dust of the road.

22

The Negro Jot was just leaving the barn when Lyddie approached. She'd thought to arrive unnoticed and lead the cow away, but she'd forgotten about Jot and the fact that his Christian leanings were more haphazard than his partner's.

"Good afternoon, Jot."

" 'Noon."

"I've come to collect my cow."

Jot's black forehead erupted in ridges. "Mr. Clarke's at meeting."

"Yes, I've just seen him."

"He knows about this cow, then?"

Lyddie considered the various degrees of truth she might use and settled on, "He knows I'm to have the cow, yes."

Jot ran his hands down his homespun breeches. The rain had not yet picked up in any impressive degree, and he seemed happy to linger. It was all Lyddie's rush.

"I won't keep you from your work," she said.

" 'Tis Sabbath."

"Yes, Jot, it is, and I certainly wouldn't have undertaken such a task today, while Mr. Clarke was out, if he were happier with my presence here."

This Jot understood. His forehead smoothed. "You want to take it now, then?"

"Now."

Jot swung around and reentered the barn. He returned with a length of rope and set off for the meadow in the quickening rain. When he returned, Edward's little cow trailed peaceably behind. He held out the rope to Lyddie, but she hesitated, suddenly foreseeing a situation where Jot would take the blame for her actions.

"I'd best go in and leave my son a note," she said, and before Jot could respond one way or another, she ducked inside.

The house was as the house was on any other Sabbath: the people gone, the fire banked down, any unnecessary household work put away. Lyddie stepped into the keeping room, and the first thing her eye fixed on was her own pewter tankard. Which was worse, she wondered, the half or the whole? She decided that in this case they were equal. She took up the tankard and hunted around for her plates and spoons but was forced to admit she would not be able to manage her kettle. She found a pair of flour sacks in the pantry and stuffed her belongings into them, then strode to her son's study and sat at his desk to search out paper and pen, but the sight of something familiar waylaid her: the old pocketbook in which Edward had kept his important papers. Lyddie stretched out her fingers and touched the worn leather; it felt thick yet; she removed it from the pigeonhole, unfolded it, and withdrew the first paper inside.

> *Know all men by these presents that I Sachemus, sachem of Satucket, for and in consideration of that great love and respect which I bore to my ancient and much respected and kind friend, Jonathan Berry, to whom I am many ways engaged for many kindnesses received, freely and absolutely give all that my parcel of land commonly called the old Indian field, next Satucket river on the easterly side thereof excepting and reserving only for myself and my children and their children and the longest liver of us the right to harvest wood for fence and fuel. In witness thereof I have hereunto set my hand and seal.*

Below the words *Sachem of Satucket* sat a simple mark that looked like a *V*, and the names of the two witnesses to it, *Stephen Paige* and *Willyium Freeman*, with the date of October 13, 1676. But a further note followed:

> *The within and above said Sachemus appeared this 8th of January, 1679, and acknowledged these presents to be his act and deed . . . and that he gave the above mentioned lands freely to the above said, a great while ago and was greatly sorry that his good friend Jonathan Berry had been troubled by it.*
> *Before Thomas Freeman, Asst.*

Jonathan Berry. Edward's great-grandfather. Lyddie's eye traveled back to the primitive *V*. The old sachem would not, of course, have written the formal document himself. Neither did she imagine he would have been familiar with its legal language. But surely the document would have been explained to him before he signed it; surely he must have understood the nature of a gift or he would have stood in expectation of recompense. And wasn't the addendum further proof of his intention? Some question had arisen over the ownership of the land, and the sachem had taken the great trouble to return to court and testify that the earlier gift had been genuine. But why had he given away the land at all?

Lyddie returned the paper to its pocketbook, the pocketbook to its pigeonhole. She removed a sheet of paper from the drawer and inked the pen.

Mr. Clarke,

In an effort not to disturb you I have taken advantage of this time to lay claim to my property. In addition to a few items my daughter has overlooked returning to me I have collected my husband's cow, whose use and maintenance were deeded to me in his will. As to the maintenance there specified, I will expect delivery of the winter hay come fall.

Yours sincerely, Lydia H. Berry

She returned outside. Jot stood with the cow just inside the barn. Lyddie handed him the sacks, and he affixed them without question across the cow's withers.

"I've left my son a letter explaining my action," she said. "In it I make no mention of your presence. It is indeed possible you were off chasing my husband's mare; she's been known to leap a fence or two."

It took him no more than a second. He nodded. Lyddie led the cow out of the barn. The rain had begun to take itself up with some seriousness. The cow trod along behind her in erratic stops and starts, coming to a halt every time the kitchenware clanked together inside the sack. Lyddie soon learned that if she turned around and leaned into the rope the beast planted her feet and went nowhere, but if Lyddie stayed facing straight ahead as if the halt had been of her own devising, the cow soon stepped out on her own.

Lyddie had the good fortune to run into no one along the King's road, but at the intersection with the landing road her luck turned. An old, wasted man limped toward her; once he got close she realized it was no old man at all but Nathan's brother, Silas Clarke, the so-called limp more a list from the usual cause. He drew himself up as straight as he was able and withdrew his hat.

"Good afternoon, madam."

"Good afternoon, Mr. Clarke."

"I say, what have you got trailing?"

"A cow."

"A cow! You say a cow?"

"I say so, yes."

"And what's it got toting? Some meal, is it? Been to the mill, have you?"

Lyddie made a noncommittal bend of the head.

"Well, now! A cow. And a sack of meal. And may I inquire as to how your family is faring?"

"They're well. And yours?"

"Ah, 'tis a sad thing about my family. It seems they've run out on me again. I woke up some time ago and found them gone."

"I believe I saw them at meeting."

"At meeting! Well, now! 'Tis the Sabbath already? I declare, it would appear we have one every two days in this village. I find that very taxing. Well, then, may I inquire as to how your own family is faring?"

"They're well, Mr. Clarke, as we've established. Now if you would excuse me—"

"And your husband off to sea, no doubt? Or has he given it up? Did I not hear something—?"

"He's given it up. Excuse me, please; you see my cow is pulling."

"Well, then, let me assist you, Mrs. Berry. Has your husband taken up dairying over the sea, then? 'Tis all very well to give up the sea, but if one gives up the sea, one must do something else, like dairying. Here, now, let me help you." Silas Clarke wrenched the rope from Lyddie's hands and began to tug the animal in an easterly direction while the cow backed west and Lyddie came in from the north, attempting to regain control. It was all too much for the poor cow. She began to buck and hop until the sacks sprung open and pewter went flying in all the directions along the road.

Silas dropped the rope and stared. "Here, now, I thought you said 'meal'! Did you not say 'meal'? I don't call this meal. I don't call it anything like. Why, these are *dishes.* And look here, why, I call this a fine, big tankard. A very fine tankard. Just lying here in the road! I call that very fortunate." And he wandered off in the wrong direction, or, rather, the right one, assuming he was headed for the tavern.

Unfortunately for Lyddie, the cow decided to trot off after him, and more unfortunately, Lyddie was unable to catch her up until she herself had reached the tavern, where she drew an audience of the two Grays, the tavern keeper Elkanah Thacher, and three strangers whom she identified by their clothes as mariners. Lyddie's wet and muddy form dancing after the cow set the strangers off into hoots, but the Gray brothers shuffled out from under the eaves and came around on the two sides of the cow so that Lyddie could move in and grab her halter.

Lyddie thanked them, set off down the road, collected the remains of her wares, and trudged home. She deposited the cow in the barn, went inside, blew up the fire for tea, took up the bucket, and went back out to the well. The first two buckets went to the cow, but the third went to the kettle; by then every scrap of cloth covering her body was soaked through. She unfastened her skirt tapes and let the skirt fall to the floor, then peeled off her shift, pulling on a loose flannel gown better suited to winter. She padded back to the fire and hung the wet clothes from the beam.

The tea tasted like gold. She cut and buttered a square of corn bread she'd made with the Indian meal and reveled in a guilty flush of contentment until she thought, Why guilty? Not the cow, certainly, and not Jot, or Silas, or the men at the tavern . . . She looked again at the bread and came to it: today had been her first in many without an Indian in it.

23

Lyddie woke to the smell of the try yards and thought of Edward, not alive, but dead, and the heavy air that had followed his drowning for weeks afterward. She ate a quick breakfast, milked the cow, and staked her in the meadow, pleased to be able to set off for Cowett's with a fresh pail of milk for Rebecca. As she drew nearer the water she noticed a mast just topping the stunted growth between her and the landing, and her chest lurched reflexively as of old; was the ship Edward's? Was he safe in it?

Sam Cowett had the news: it was Seth Cobb's schooner, in from his second trip south, with all barrels full of blubber and half his original seamen, the other half having run into trouble with the law at Charlestown. Lyddie told the Indian she suspected she had met the replacement crew the day before in front of the tavern and attempted to make a humorous story out of the cow, but Sam Cowett didn't seem amused by it. After he left she went to Rebecca's room with a cup of milk and a spoon. She lifted the woman's head in her usual way, but as she spooned in the milk it ran out across her cheek. She propped Rebecca's head straighter and tried again; the white runnel traveled straight down her chin. Three more attempts and she gave it up and began to do what she'd advised Sam Cowett to do—she talked to her. About Edward.

"He was no very big man," she said, "not near the size of your husband. But he could lift my linen chest, or me, or our children's coffins. He carried them alone to the churchyard. Always, afterward, he'd want to make another, or perhaps that's where he took his comfort. Whenever he would go to sea I would crave that same comfort, so much sometimes it frightened me."

But no, she wouldn't tell Rebecca about that. She tried to think of other things, but it seemed to come back each time to the same thing, all the way back to the very first, before they were married, the day he'd put her up on the pillion behind him and ridden out to Eastham to tell his brother they'd published their names and would be married the next month. All the way there she'd felt his hard back beneath his coat and smelled his sweat and salt and listened to the rumble of his voice coming through his shoulder blades where she'd pressed her face, and she'd thought, this will be my husband. All my happiness in life will depend on the nature of this man. Have I made fair judge of him?

When they got to Eastham the brother and his family had all gone off somewhere. They checked in the barn and found the wagon out and the horse stall empty, but something about the total emptiness of the barn, or the yeasty smell of damp hay and animal, or the memory of their own physical closeness on the ride over, or perhaps just the sheer power of the commitment they'd just made to each other, pulled them toward each other until they were too close to look and it became all touch and feel. One minute they were standing there perfectly ordered and the next they were all skirts up and breeches down. At first Lyddie thought Edward must have got it wrong because nothing happened but some pain and an odd kind of numbness, but then he gave a shiver and a low shout and the numbness started to go away and she grabbed hold of him so he wouldn't go away and soon after that there was nothing wrong at all.

There were, of course, those times during their long marriage when Edward was neither coming nor going, and Lyddie wasn't rushing between sick child and burned bread, where they took their time with each other's pleasure, but ever since that day in the barn the rush-and-tumble times always quickened Lyddie as nothing else could do.

Lyddie balled up Rebecca Cowett's dirty linens and carried them out of the room. She took a minute to step outside and let the breeze sweep through her hair like fingers.

A sin in the heart was *not* as great as a sin in the flesh, she thought, and someone should tell the Reverend Dunne so.

The Indian came in staggering with fatigue and looked down at the wasted, twitching form on the bed, at Lyddie making one last futile effort to dribble some milk into her.

"She'll not swallow," Lyddie said.

He walked out. Lyddie cleaned up Rebecca and straightened her linens. When Cowett returned he looked only at Lyddie. "How long?"

"Since this morning. She took no—"

"How long till she dies? I want to know how long till she dies."

Lyddie studied the woman in the bed, her accentuated bones, her thin skin. She thought of her last boy, who, had he lived, would be the age of young Nate. He had died at five of the putrid malignant sore throat. He had stopped eating on Monday, and each day thereafter she had run her fingers along his ribs and told herself that they were no more visible than the day before, that his breath was no shallower, until the following Sabbath he'd taken one gulping breath and no more, but he was a boy, a little boy . . .

"I don't know, Mr. Cowett. Not long."

The Indian left the room for the table where Lyddie had set out his food. He pushed it aside and set down two cups. He took down the brandy bottle and poured a measured dose in each.

I should go, Lyddie thought.

He picked up his cup and nodded at hers. He drank, keeping his free hand firm around the bottle.

Lyddie stood in silence, watching the hand on the bottle. When the fingers whitened she said, "She needs you yet."

"She needs nothing."

"You'd leave her lie in her own filth?"

"You can tend her."

"Not through all the night."

"You're afraid of their talk?"

She thought, I'm afraid of you, and then suddenly she wasn't. The hand that gripped the bottle gripped it to keep it on the table, not to lift it. She picked up her cup and took a sip, and it felt like a warm hand on a cold heart. She reached for the bottle, and he slid it across. She barely tipped it against the cup and then set it on the floor, out of sight and out of reach.

The Indian's hand lay in a tight fist a minute longer and then the fingers splayed, stretched, released. "I've naught," he said. "Naught but that woman."

"You have yourself, Mr. Cowett. And you have your neighbor, as you need her. And you may yet have a son who lives."

"Is this how you count for yourself? You make your assets at three? Yourself, your neighbor, your daughter?"

Lyddie began to answer yes, but something in the darkening air made her loath to cloud it further with untruth. "I've come to count on myself, yes," she said. "And I found when I was in need I could count on my neighbor. As my daughter has requested that I keep away from her house, I count on nothing from that quarter."

"As I count nothing for my son's life."

"So that puts us even."

"No, Widow Berry. I'm ahead in the neighbor."

Lyddie said good night and moved to the door.

He called after her. "Take the bottle, Widow Berry."

Lyddie walked home via the road, circumventing the wood, unsure of her footing in the half-light. The quail piped her along half the distance and then a mournful pigeon took up the beat: *poor Beck, poor Beck*. The breeze carried the cold off the water; she ducked gratefully through her own door and found Nathan Clarke sitting at her table.

He looked up at her and then down at the brandy bottle. "So the Indian pays you in his usual coin, I see. And yet it leaves you short enough that you must take to stealing cows."

"Stealing? No."

" 'Tis the big joke at the tavern, my mother-in-law and her cow. Did it please you to make a spectacle of yourself and a laughingstock of me before all the town?"

"You may thank your brother for the spectacle and yourself for whatever laughter you collect. I did naught but claim what's mine by right."

"So you blame my brother. You aren't satisfied with ruining his happy home?"

"I, ruin!"

"His wife's in my parlor now and will not go home whilst he remains there. I made to send her off, and she cried and blubbed until my own children took it up. You've convinced them their cousins are to be murdered in their sleep."

"Well, you have my room now; you may use it for those poor five children."

Nathan leapt out of the chair. "*Your* room! This is the way you speak now, is it, everything yours? It's nothing yours, not the room, nor the house, nor the bloody cow, nor the food you so freely take from my own four children to feed my brother's five!"

"Well, then, you might send the children home with their mother and keep your brother Silas with you, as you hold such little objection to his charging about with knives."

Nathan stood up and leaned into her. "You'll be sorry you began this. You may send your lawyer to badger me all you wish and it will change nothing in the matter. This house is mine, that house is mine, the cow is *mine*—"

"And mine to use. As is one-third of this house. In truth, Mr. Clarke, I marvel you should want me back in yours, or that a man of your means would so miss one little cow that he—"

"The devil take the cow! But, by God, you will not deny me my own property, I don't care how many threats Freeman sends me!"

He strode out. Lyddie exhaled a great gust, dropped her shoulders, and immediately reined them up again. The cow. She rushed to the door, but Nathan had gone straight to his horse and, after a series of one-footed hops, managed to get himself astride. He wheeled and saw her standing in the door. Lyddie raised a hand in a wave. He spurred the horse hard and yanked the reins at the same time so the poor creature had no choice but to travel in a circle until his master had gained some control of himself and, by extension, the horse. As he rode off Lyddie was finally able to work the knots from her flesh until she thought of her daughter, waiting for the man at the other end, and a rich, dark fear enveloped her. What might one brother learn from the other? Would Nathan Clarke arrive home so incensed by the mother he would take revenge on the daughter? Or his own children? Jane and Nate might know enough to keep out of his way, but Bethiah had been born without a shell, and she was the one who would test him soonest with her cough and her clumsiness and her foolish chatter . . . And there Lyddie pulled up short.

Four, he'd said. His own four children. What a fool she was. The lingering winter gripe, the new fullness in Mehitable's face and arms. Her daughter was with child and, if Lyddie counted from the winter gripe, well advanced in it.

24

Lyddie dreamed of her dead children. She woke the next morning and pushed the images away with age-old practice, only to come up against one of the cow. Her son would not leave the situation lie; for her to keep the beast unattended in the meadow asked to lose it. She got up, emptied her night jar, washed and dressed and took some tea and bread and butter. She went out to the barn and milked the cow, this time pouring the milk into her own milk pans in the buttery and covering them with the cloths. To be back at cheese making seemed to Lyddie like the world come right side up for the first time in a very long while.

In the end she brought the cow with her to Cowett's and set her out with his. She went to the door and knocked. No one answered. She pushed open the door with all her old fears back in place. There had been another bottle of brandy at one time.

"Hello!" she called.

Silence.

She looked in on Rebecca and found her face strained and her body twitching. Please, God, end it soon, Lyddie thought, and then realized she'd just made her first prayer since Edward's death.

Lyddie left the room and heard a grunt from the south chamber. She stepped nearer the door and saw a naked calf, a long, glistening thigh, a buttock. She stepped back.

"Mr. Cowett!" she called.

She heard the scuffle of corn husks under him, the creak of ropes. She drew nearer the door and saw that he had pulled a blanket over him and sat up, his eyes glassy. She would have left him to sleep it off if it weren't for the woman in the next room.

"Mr. Cowett? Are you ill?"

He spoke in a rasp. "Aye."

"Well, then, I'll tend your wife and leave you to recover."

She had cleaned and dressed the wife by the time the husband appeared in the doorway. He had clothed himself in a linen shirt worn thin with washing and a pair of faded breeches. He clutched the doorframe and looked down at the twitching woman.

"It started in the night. I sat by her but could do nothing to ease it. To watch such a thing—" He broke off with a spasm of coughing.

Lyddie swung around. The Indian's face and that part of his chest exposed through the open neck of the shirt gleamed with sweat. "Mr. Cowett? You *are* ill?"

"I said." His voice grated like a bound saw.

Lyddie stepped forward and put a hand to his forehead. "You're fevered. Is it your throat?"

He nodded. Coughed.

And chest.

"Mr. Cowett," she said, "you've watched your wife night after night and worked day after day. You've tired yourself till you've sickened. You need to rest now. Go back to your bed."

He looked out the window, gauging the sun. "I've a crew waiting at the landing."

"I'd be happy to take them a message. You can't fish today. You're weak; do you see how you stand?"

Indeed, he leaned hard against the doorjamb, and when he attempted to stand away he staggered. Lyddie approached and took his arm. He let her lead him into the keeping room but not beyond. He dropped into a chair.

"What message do you send?" Lyddie asked him.

He looked at the sun again. "Tell Jabez Gray. Tell him to fetch his useless brother and take him out with them. Tell him to tell his brother I'll come after him with an oar if he refuses."

"I'll tell him to fetch his brother."

"With an oar. You tell him."

Lyddie went to the well for water, filled the smallest kettle, and set it over the fire. She stirred up the coals, fed in fresh wood, and went out to Rebecca's herb garden, where she dug a geranium root, pulled up several young onions, and picked a handful of mint, yarrow, verbena, catnip, and sage.

She went back inside, put the root and the herbs in the kettle to boil, set the onions aside for a poultice, and left for the shore.

The little cow lifted her head as Lyddie passed and went back to her hay. Lyddie followed the landing road to the water, which lay as slick and white as glass. Cobb's schooner had not yet finished its unloading and lay at anchor, waiting for the tide to drop again. She spied Jabez Gray and the three remaining crew members, Simeon Cooke and two Indians, milling about the boat, looking alternately at the sun and then out over the dead water.

Lyddie delivered her message, minus the part about the oar, and

Jabez Gray turned with her to go after his brother. She heard the other men rumbling behind her as she walked off, her own name and Sam Cowett's; no doubt Jabez Gray heard it, too, as he abruptly set off into some Cousin Betsey–type chatter.

"So now, Widow Berry, how do you fare these days? I'd say things are looking well with you. Me, I'm fair to medium, I'd have to say, fair to medium. We need a wind. Too much or too little, that's the way of it. Either we're stopped dead or we're near overset, and it'll go from one to the other in half a—" He came jolting to a stop, no doubt thinking, as Lyddie was, of another day of too much wind, another oversetting.

"Mr. Gray," Lyddie said, "as it appears we come together to the subject, will you tell me, please, just what happened with my husband?"

Gray looked off, hawked up and spat some phlegm, and never quite looked back at her. "His boat went over, Widow Berry. His boat went over as any boat goes over, the wind, a wave, both together, they knock your stern around and you take a good one broadside and you're over. We saw he was over, and Sam was steersman and he brought us around and we were on them in a heartbeat; we threw over our line and the block and we hauled them up one man at a time, all except your husband, Widow Berry. All except your husband. Sam finally went after him with his oar, at some risk to our own situation, and your husband took hold and Sam brought him close along, but then, I don't know, Widow Berry. I just don't know. It looked like he had him. It looked like he had him good. That Indian's one big, strong ox; he just reached down and took him by the coat and pulled him up out of the water and I saw your husband breathing, I saw his chest heaving, he'd cut his head, Widow Berry, but he was alive. He was breathing. And I turned around to correct our heading and when I turned back your husband was gone, Widow Berry. That's all I can tell you. Gone."

They resumed walking in stiff silence until they reached the Cowett house, where they parted, Jabez Gray continuing into the village and Lyddie turning for the door. The house smelled of mint and sage and disease. She thought of what would happen if the husband died before the wife and decided that very little would change, that she would keep to her task until Rebecca died, an event which could not be far off now. But what if the wife died while the husband lay so ill? She feared that one, because she knew that one in herself, knew the strength of the temptation to give way when you were left with nothing. The Indian had said it himself, she remembered. *I've naught but that woman,* and his saying it had surprised her. Why? Because he was Indian, and a dark skin couldn't grieve like a white one? Or because he was a man, and a man couldn't experience the same dependence that was created and cosseted in women by law and custom? Or was it because he was Sam Cowett and he did as he pleased?

The house lay quiet. She moved softly from door to door and found both beds filled, all eyes closed. She had a scant minute to wonder at her situation, here alone, nursing two people she had lived beside and little known until a month ago, and then Sam Cowett opened his eyes.

"All's well," she said. "Mr. Gray does as he was bid."

"For now."

Lyddie poured out a cup of the herbed tea and brought it to him. She returned to the keeping room and cut up the onions to poultice his feet to draw the fever.

As she sat wrapping his feet he said, "I'll have to pay you double, now."

"A day's nursing is a day's nursing."

"Best take advantage while you can."

"Of your illness? I don't think so, Mr. Cowett."

"Then you're none like your forefathers."

"My forefathers?"

"When you English first came, we believed you carried sickness in your bags and let it loose to destroy us. Then we decided it came with your god, and that he must be more powerful than ours if he could wipe out so many people with so little trouble, just to make way for his own." Cowett set into a long chain of coughing.

When he ceased Lyddie said, "If your forefathers thought all that, why did they go to such trouble to help mine?"

"Because yours had guns and armor. My ancestors thought to use them against the Narragansett. Until they got too many and mine decided to drive yours out. And lost."

"You call them your ancestors, Mr. Cowett, but no Cape Cod Indian warred against the English."

"Because the English had preachers here who told us their god was our god, and as he directed them, so he directed us. As my wife believed. As she believes yet. She would go to English heaven when she dies."

"And you would not?"

"I do as I do. I take what comes or doesn't come. I'll not trouble myself over it."

It made such sense to Lyddie, and yet she trembled at it.

Cowett had finished the tea; Lyddie took the cup from his hand and stood to go, but he stayed her.

"I don't talk of this for naught, Widow Berry. I would ask. If I perish—"

"You'll not perish, Mr. Cowett."

"If I do. Before."

"I'll look after your wife, Mr. Cowett."

He dismissed the sentence with a wave of his hand, as if it were something he knew without asking. "She wished to be buried in the churchyard. You'll see to it?"

"I'll see to it. But I'll take it as an unkind return if you continue to willfully deplete your health for the sole purpose of leaving me with all this trouble at the end. Now go to sleep."

He blinked, and closed his eyes.

Sam Cowett slept and woke, slept and woke, rambling during sleep about his wife, the churchyard, the cousin at the Indian nation. Twice, she heard Edward's name, once shouted violently, once whispered.

But shortly after dawn, when Jabez Gray stopped by on his way to the landing, he was lucid. Gray made a fair job of covering his surprise at Lyddie's presence so early in the morning and hustled into Cowett's room. Lyddie heard fragments of the ebb and flow of Gray's report and Cowett's instructions, and was heartened to hear the Indian's voice so strong.

But his mind remained weak. Or so it seemed to Lyddie when with each trip into the room he moved further back in time, until by noon they were again with their forefathers, a subject that seemed to greatly agitate him. At length, in an effort to move them forward, Lyddie asked what made one Indian remain in the *wetus* by the ponds while another, like himself, went to live in an English frame house in town like a white man.

But Cowett seemed to struggle with the answer to this as well, and after a while Lyddie saw that it was not so much a struggle for an answer for her, it was a struggle for an answer for himself. He began to take apart the town, Indian by Indian, counting up how each had fared in the white world, and as he took it apart he put it together to form a picture Lyddie had never seen. She learned, for example, that Jot's wife, Hassey, was not a slave but an indentured servant, half Negro, half Indian. She learned that the mother of the "white" Mrs. Hale, the grandmother of the "white" Lot Oakley, and the great-grandmother of all those "white" Morrises were, in fact, Indians. Was this, then, another explanation for the slow disappearance of the "Indian" population? But Lyddie noticed that in Cowett's list she found no examples of an Indian man married to an Englishwoman.

The next day Lyddie found Sam Cowett's bedding drenched and the fever broken, his legs strong enough to carry him to his wife's room unassisted. He looked down at her wasting twitching flesh, he watched her strangled breaths, and so many emotions flew across his face Lyddie had some trouble keeping up with them: shock, disgust, relief that she lived, regret that she lived, all of it followed by a hot, black anger. He turned away, pulled out of Lyddie's grasp, lurched into the keeping room, and crashed down at the table.

"Why will your god not take her?" he shouted. "Why did she trouble herself over him if this is all the attention he pays her?"

"I've asked myself the same," Lyddie said. "I know only—"

He whirled on her. "Go home. Leave us be. I've no need of you now. If I'm not well enough to fish I'm well enough to see to her."

Lyddie saw no choice but to obey him.

She went first to the meadow to collect the cow, and then home, through the woods. After two days gone the sight of her house had seldom looked so welcome, even without any smoke from the chimney. She put the cow in the barn and watered her well, opened her back door and looked around.

The house had been emptied.

25

Or nearly emptied. And Lyddie understood at once who had emptied it when she took note of what remained—cooking pot, kettle, iron spider, trivet, knives, spoons, dough tray, salt box, shovel and tongs, pewter plates, earthenware, candlesticks, wooden pails, great wheel, flax wheel, carders, hetchel, workbox, scissors, milk pans, cheese molds, churn, two beds, one bed key, all bedding, one dressing table, one chest—all the things that had come to Edward with her. Now missing were the keeping room table and chairs, hutch, Edward's desk and chair along with pen and inkwell, tea table, candle stand, best room chairs, best room table and chest. Nathan must have had the inventory in hand and gone straight down the list, leaving her her dower and removing every other last item.

Lyddie stood in the keeping room and surveyed the empty floor, marveling at a mind that would take things it had no room for and had not wanted, simply out of spite, but after a minute's quiet thought another possible motivation struck her. Nathan Clarke wanted her out of the house so he could sell it. The quickest way to get her out was to starve her out, and the quickest way to starve her out was to leave her with little or nothing to sell or trade. She looked around. She wasn't there yet, but she was closer.

Lyddie spent the day putting her house to rights as best she could. She salvaged a pair of old barrels from the barn, removed several planks from the loft, and balanced them across for a table. She piled up some old crates for her dishes and upended her washtub for a chair. She stopped at the first mellowing of the light to eat the remains of a pudding, and as she put away the empty bowl a thrill of fear overcame her. If the Indian meant it, if her work for him was over, how long would her few coins hold her? She thought then of Eben Freeman, and his last visit, and if he'd heard about her collecting the cow, and what he might think of it. Very little, she imagined. But what Freeman thought didn't trouble her long. She was both emotionally and physically worn out. She staggered to her room, removed her boots and stockings, dropped her skirt and fell into bed, asleep before she'd conjured up a single worry, white or Indian.

Lyddie slept straight through the birds, past dawn and into the heat, waking in great surprise at the brightness of the light, at the way it rejuvenated her by its presence. Her next thought was of Sam Cowett. She would have to go there, of course, to see how he fared, pay or no, whether he wanted her or no; he might well have relapsed into a state far worse than the one in which she'd left him, leaving his wife untended. As she ate and dressed she tried to think of the softest way to present herself, but as her meal waned her anger waxed. She would go there and make such offer as would be made by any Christian woman, and if Cowett rejected it again she would leave as she had come and the devil take the pair of them.

She knocked on the door with excessive force; he opened it with a face locked shut, and in her determination not to let him intimidate her she came close to shouting at him.

"I've come to see how you are. How she is. Not as nurse but neighbor. Are you going to let me in, or are you done with neighbors, too?"

He stood still, assessing her, which Lyddie determined to stand to the count of three and no longer, but at two he stepped back and waved an arm in his wife's direction. Lyddie moved through the keeping room into the little sickroom and looked down at the bed.

After four children and one husband Lyddie knew what she looked at. She opened her mouth, but Cowett held up a hand. "You may save your words and your prayers. They mean naught to me."

"I was going to ask if you would like me to lay her out."

He nodded. After a minute he said, "Dunne. The churchyard."

"I'll speak to him." She washed and dressed the body alone and left Cowett standing over the corpse, looking down at it as if it were some great puzzle he might put back together simply by examining each of the pieces.

Lyddie found the Reverend Dunne at the back of his barn, digging out a stump. His vest lay on the ground; his shirt had turned translucent with sweat; he saw Lyddie and smiled, no doubt over the chance to lay down his shovel.

"Widow Berry! I'm delighted to see you. I've had in mind to come by for a small chat. A few concerns . . . Now, now, nothing to look such alarm at. Come inside and have some tea."

"I've little time, Mr. Dunne. I'm on an errand for Mr. Cowett. His wife has just died."

The reverend's face fell, but Lyddie felt the change was less over the loss of Rebecca Cowett than the loss of the tea. In no time, though, he'd corralled his features and formed them into the appropriate respect. "Well, then, we must pray for her."

"Her husband desires something else. He wished to honor her beliefs and lay her in the church ground."

"Does he, now? He surprises me. I expect you've had a good influence, Widow Berry."

"I'd naught to do with it. It comes from his great affection for his wife, for his desire to honor her wishes."

The reverend's mouth kilted sideways. "Indeed. Well, then, I would see less affection and more conviction in him."

"He holds great conviction, Mr. Dunne. Not, perhaps, in concert with your own. We may bury Mrs. Cowett tomorrow morning?"

The reverend nodded.

Lyddie began to walk away.

"Widow Berry!"

She turned back.

"I hear things about town. God hears. The Lord is with you while you are with him."

"Perhaps," Lyddie said, "there lies the problem."

Lyddie and Sam Cowett sat through the early part of the night, one on each side of Rebecca Cowett's cleansed body. Lyddie said no prayers, and that, of all her recent lapses, seemed the most horrific.

She tried more than once, even came to move her lips in a preamble of sorts, but then made the mistake of opening her eyes at the sound of a snort from the chair opposite.

"Are you so afraid not to pray?" Cowett asked.

"I'm not afraid."

"You are. I see it in you as if you were lit up with lanterns. Do you think one spineless prayer will save her? Or do you simper at your god on behalf of your own self? Or is it still your husband's soul you fret over?"

Lyddie got up and left the house.

A bright, gibbous moon hung above the woodlot and sped her feet over the road, but as they sped her feet they sped others even faster. In no great stretch of time she heard him behind her.

"Widow Berry."

She wouldn't turn.

"Widow." He came up and caught her arm, his fingers hot against her skin, but she didn't know if she was cold or he was fevered. "I would not anger you," he said. "You least of anyone."

"Let me be, Mr. Cowett."

"If you leave thus you shame me."

"As you shame me."

"I mean no shame to you or anyone. I mean only to free you from your torment."

"You mean to free yourself from yours."

" 'Tis one and the same. And there's what angers you. 'Tis one and the same, and you'd have us different."

"Go back and watch over your wife, Mr. Cowett. 'Tis the last service you may do for her."

"My wife is dead, Widow Berry. I've done my last service for her. And so is your husband dead. They neither of them concern themselves with us now; 'tis time we return them the favor."

He had dropped his voice to the one she had often heard him use with his ailing wife, but the new gentleness ripped through her in a way the harsher words hadn't. Lyddie felt as if she were made of a thin paste that would dissolve with water, the water that had once filled Edward's lungs and now, at last, leaked from her eyes. She rubbed at her face and Cowett turned away to leave her tears private, or so she first supposed, but as he turned, the moonlight caught the liquid gleam in his own eyes.

One and the same?

26

They stood around the grave with bowed heads: Lyddie, Eben Freeman and his sister, the two Grays, a handful of mariners not at sea, a small knot of Indians. The Reverend Dunne rolled out his prayers; the dirt was cast over Rebecca's coffin; the reverend reminded them of their duty to God on the Sabbath day following; they dispersed in twos or threes or fours, Eben Freeman accompanying Lyddie.

"Were you surprised he didn't come?" he asked.

"At first," Lyddie said. "But not after thinking. He held a strong dislike for his wife's religion."

"Yet he put her in the churchyard."

"It was what she wished."

They had reached the road; Lyddie expected Freeman to turn left after his sister, but he turned right with her and kept on walking. She looked her question at him.

"I go there now," he said. "To see him."

"Ah. Then I may leave it to you to tell him she's been seen safe into the ground."

"You may, of course."

They walked a way in silence before he said, "You and he appear to have grown friendly, then."

"We've grown neighborly," she said, but the word seemed to hang before her, empty. False. "And friendly."

"Widow Berry, forgive me. What I'm about to say may be unwarranted, but I know something of the Indian's ways, and as you have no other to advise you—"

"I've been well advised as to his habit of drink, thank you."

"Drink, yes, and . . . other things. I would caution you as to . . . I don't know just the way to say . . . Widow Berry. When a woman calls herself friend to such a man she exposes herself to a certain danger. You must understand my meaning."

"I do. And I thank you for your advice, Mr. Freeman. Otherwise, as you say, I should be left with none but my own."

Freeman stopped dead in the road. "I beg your pardon, Widow Berry, I did not mean to imply—" Again, words abandoned him. They resumed walking in yet another silence. At length he said, "I would have a word with you on another matter, if you're willing."

"Of course."

"I've made progress, Widow Berry."

"In what regard?"

"Yours."

"Mine!"

"Indeed. I've prepared the papers and your son will be delivered a summons shortly."

"I don't understand you. You've prepared papers on my behalf?"

"Indeed."

"But I didn't engage you. I asked you for nothing. I expected nothing."

"I'll get you better than nothing, Widow Berry. I'll bring him before the court for violating the terms of your husband's will, and I'll demand forfeit of his bond if I must, but I daresay when he receives the papers the threat alone shall bring him to comply with the terms of your husband's will."

"Mr. Freeman." They had reached her house. Either their location or the sharpness in her voice brought the lawyer up short again, but as Lyddie had no intention of asking him in to see the depleted condition of her home, they stood face-to-face in the road. "I've not the means for court or any other thing. I can't allow—"

"Rest easy, Widow, please. As I said before, it was your husband engaged me—"

"My husband is dead, Mr. Freeman. 'Tis myself here now. And whatever foolishness you may try on me of being well paid in the past for whatever you may do in the future—"

"I'll not argue who speaks the greater foolishness, Widow Berry; you'll get naught from Clarke without me, and I would no more take whatever little money you've managed to charm out of Cowett—"

Charm? Thick, hot blood swept up into Lyddie's face and neck. She thought of the shit and urine and pus she had cleaned to earn her pay, she thought of the anger and trepidation and desolation she had faced down day after day. She'd worked for her pay and she'd continue to work for it, and if she didn't need Clarke she didn't need Freeman, either. "I thank you for whatever you've done thus far, Mr. Freeman," she said. "But now I ask that you desist henceforth in any effort on my behalf."

"My dear Widow—"

"I dismiss you, Mr. Freeman. I discharge you, whatever the proper term might be. Before it's all around the town that I 'charmed' your services out of you. Good day."

Lyddie covered the remaining distance to her door riding hard on her anger, and she continued to ride it through the remainder of the day, but in the thickest part of the night the fear took hold. She dreamed she was alone at sea in Edward's whaleboat, anchored by lines fore and aft to some unseen rock or pier or possibly another ship, but close enough that she could see a throng waving and calling to her from shore, but whatever they shouted she couldn't hear. She picked up a knife and, one by one, cut the lines. She'd expected to drift to shore with the incoming tide, but a sharp wind came up and overrode the flow of water, carrying her seaward. The people on the shore grew smaller and their cries faded away. Lyddie thought of throwing herself over the side in the hopes of making shore; she knew of people who had taught themselves to swim but knew nothing of it firsthand; she decided to stay on board. In due time another whaleboat set off from shore, and as it drew near she saw Sam Cowett, the steersman, standing in the rear, with Shubael Hopkins, Edward, and the two Grays at the oars. They drew alongside and Edward called to her to jump aboard, but he wouldn't let go of his oar to help her, and just as she had committed to the leap the boat yawed and she fell into the water. The boat drifted away and Sam Cowett reached toward her with an oar, but as she went to grab it he picked it up and brought it down sharp against her skull. She went down, deep down, into a forest of green weeds that wrapped around her legs and pulled at her, and in the middle of them Edward sat, smiling. "I knew you couldn't," he said.

"Couldn't what?" she asked.

"Swim." And he turned into a long, bleached, finned creature, half fish, half eel, that wriggled and beat at the water and disappeared through the gloom.

Lyddie woke with her heart galloping and her lungs pumping, every face and word and look of the dream alive in her mind. She threw back her blanket and sat on the edge of the bed, struggling to command her body's functions, but she knew as long as she still saw the dream in her head her body would not settle. She decided it would help if she moved. She got up, walked through the keeping room to the back door, and stepped out into the yard. The sky was a solid, dull charcoal, punched through with only a few pinprick stars. The air smarted with salt; somewhere too far off to bother her a wolf howled. She felt the cool stones under her feet, stepped off into the bedewed grass, and grew cooler. By now she could make out the dark outline of the woodlot against the less dark skyline, the barn, the cap to the well, and the necessary house. She turned and picked out the square of the house chimney against the slope of the roof, and the solid evidence of her real world comforted her. She stood until the real had replaced the surreal, went back inside, and got into bed.

In the morning the details of the dream had washed away, but the fear still chased her until she remembered the anger that had led to it, and the words that had led to that. So, yes, she was friend to Cowett. And a friend would see how he fared.

Lyddie washed, dressed, and set off, not down the road, but the short way, the friend's way, through the woodlot.

He opened the door to her with shirt hanging loose, hair out of its queue, eyes puffy, but she could make other reasons than brandy for him looking so: he'd lost a wife, she'd come early so as to fit it in before meeting, he'd been ill, he'd not slept through a night in a good long while. And whatever else she saw in his face she saw he was glad, and surprised, to see her.

Lyddie looked around the house and saw that it was greatly out of sorts: a pile of clothes sat on the floor, broken crockery spattered the hearth, dirty plates and bowls covered the table, but she saw no bottle or tankard.

"Are you well?" she asked.

"Near enough to." He turned around and waved her into the room, pushed away the plates and bowls, and sat down heavily, as if he'd just returned from a long trek. He rubbed his temples.

But distemper or drink? Lyddie wondered.

She picked up a plate and bowl and carried them to the bucket.

"You think to work for me yet?" he said.

"Some things are done without pay, Mr. Cowett, neighbor for neighbor."

He watched her. "What say you, then, if I take clean dishes from the neighbor and clean house for one and six?"

Lyddie smiled. "Very well."

He pointed at the clothes on the floor, and this time Lyddie saw they were Rebecca's. "And you may take those, too."

He took his pot down from the shelf, fished out the coins, put them on the table, picked up his canvas sack, and left for the water.

Lyddie first folded the clothes and put them in a pair of tow sacks: two shifts, two petticoats, three aprons, four pairs of stockings, two skirts, and two gowns in flannel, lawn, calico, cambric, a wool shawl, boots, shoes, mittens, gloves, all as English as Lyddie's. She cleared the table and scoured the dishes, swept up the broken crockery and went outside to dump it on the midden. On the top of the pile of shells and bones lay some other detritus of Rebecca's: a near empty tin of some sort of salve, a torn handkerchief, some unmended stockings, the empty laudanum bottle, evidence of the Indian's efforts to clear away all signs of Rebecca; yes, Lyddie thought, he would leave the dead alone.

Lyddie returned to the house to collect her pay, and only at the feel of the coins in her hand did she remember: not only had she missed meeting, but she'd also been working on the Sabbath.

Lyddie picked up the tow sacks and went home. She put Rebecca's clothes away at the bottom of the chest, below her own. She took the coins out of her pocket and marched to the front room, to Edward's desk, and almost got there before she remembered the desk was gone, and with it all the money she'd stashed in its drawer.

27

On the short walk to Nathan's house Lyddie saw nothing of the road or the trees or the houses or the sky; she saw nothing but a gray wall of anger before her eyes until she reached her son's house and rapped on the door. Hassey opened it. Lyddie took only enough time to note what she might have noted anytime before: instead of a mahogany skin an oaken one, instead of a broad, flat nose a narrow, beaked one, instead of a soft brown eye a gleaming black one.

"I would see my son," Lyddie said.

Hassey stepped back without argument.

Lyddie swept in. The family sat in the best room, Nathan reading to them from the Bible. Lyddie stared at Mehitable's swollen womb and could not move her eye along. Nathan clapped the book shut and rose.

"Have I not made myself clear? You're not welcome in this house."

"I'm not looking for welcome. I'm looking for seven and sixpence, taken from me with Edward's desk. It was in the drawer."

"There was naught in the drawer."

"Then allow a sharper pair of eyes to look, as it was most definitely there."

"All right, Mother, I'll look again, if it pleases you." Nathan left the room.

Lyddie addressed her daughter. "Are you well?"

"As you find me." She looked down, and up. "And you, Mother?"

"I am not unhappy. I wish only—"

Nathan returned and handed Lyddie her letter book. "This was all that was found of yours, Mother."

"There were seven and sixpence in that drawer. In a brown leather pouch with a white bead on the cord."

"I'm sorry, I found no money. Perhaps that neighbor of yours—"

" 'Twas the neighbor gave it me. My pay for nursing. You may take the desk and table and hutch as yours; you may not take my pay for nursing."

"An interesting point. I wonder how the law applies it. Your wages would belong to your husband if he were living, but in this instance, if I were charged with feeding and clothing you while you continued to make an independent income of some sort—"

"My husband is dead, Mr. Clarke, and as we all well know, you neither feed nor clothe me. The wages are mine."

"Perhaps Jot—" Mehitable said.

" 'Twas no Jot in this," Lyddie said. "Look at your husband's smile and you will see every penny in it."

"Good evening, Mother," Nathan said. He crossed to his chair, picked the Bible off the seat, and sat down.

"I would not have thought it," Lyddie said. "Truly, I would not have thought it. That you would steal from your wife's mother and smirk about it in front of her and in front of your own children. I'm sorry, indeed, I'm greatly sorry, that another child will be born to a father such as you."

"Oh!" Mehitable cried. "How can you speak so to him?"

"Ladies, please," Nathan said. He turned back the pages of the Bible. "We were at Isaiah, but I think we might now try Paul. 'Let your women keep silent in the churches.' I might add, 'Let them keep silent on the Sabbath as a whole.' "

Lyddie turned to Mehitable. "Daughter, I wish to say this only. I will not lay blame for his actions at your door, and I ask you not to lay his at mine."

She walked out of the room, out the door, and into the road. She heard footsteps behind her and whirled with a single wish, but it was Bethiah who ran toward her. Lyddie caught her up and squeezed her fiercely; the girl squeezed back and melted away as if she'd never come.

The shilling and sixpence sat in a cup in the middle of the plank table. Around it Lyddie collected what items she could spare to sell, totting each up as she set it down: white dish, two shillings; pewter plate, ten shillings; brown mug, one shilling; teapot, one and six . . . Lyddie stopped there. She might sell all her goods, eat off a board and drink out of a boot, but the money would still run out before she did. She would have to make her way in the end, so why not do it now and keep her belongings?

Make her way. She thought of the women she knew who had done so: Widow Baker ran an inn, but Lyddie could imagine Nathan Clarke's response if she usurped his two-thirds of the house toward that end. Widow Crosby at Eastham ran a tavern, but only because her husband had done so, and when he died the selectmen allowed her to continue so doing until some months later she married her best customer, and he took up the deed while she continued the pouring. The Widow Selew, who had been willed life use of her house entire, opened a store in her front room, but in order to open a store, one needed money to stock it. The other single women in town, widow or spinster, lived with their families and earned their keep by spinning, weaving, or nursing, but Mehitable had not required any of this from Lyddie, and with a pound of wool at Sears's store charged at a shilling four pence, Lyddie would have to risk all her funds to card and spin and knit a pair of mittens in hope of selling them at two shillings the pair. She went to bed no further ahead, in fact, a good deal further behind, than she had been that morning.

The salt tang of the flats at low tide woke Lyddie, and her immediate hunger dissolved what little remained of her pride. She put on her most worn skirt, took up her hoe and the tow sack she'd brought Rebecca's clothes home in, and headed shoreward. The sky was barely gray, the beach as empty as she'd hoped to find it. She sat on a drift log, removed her shoes and stockings, pulled her skirt between her legs, and tucked it in her waistband. She waded through the channels and out to the high bar, digging at holes like the poorest Indian, having little idea what hole meant what type of creature, but after twenty minutes she had six clams for her dinner. She straightened her back, and in so doing she realized that the tide had come in fast around the single high bar; now, to reach shore, she'd have to wade through thigh-deep water. She stepped into the current. It caught at the cloth between her legs, tugging it loose, the billowing skirt acting like a drag and pulling her feet from under her. She went down and away, into the cold, the current taking her, numbing her, the water far deeper than she'd imagined. Her clothing pulled harder, like Edward in the weeds; they wanted her down, under. She swallowed water.

She thrashed and shot her mouth clear, but the trade was to sink deeper afterward; she thrashed harder and sank deeper and she saw the end to it, all of it, but after one blink of sheer relief she rejected such an end. She would not die over six clams. She would not exit life before she'd seen her daughter safe in it. She would not leave Nathan Clarke free to do as he pleased with a house that had once been home to her.

She heard a shout from shore. She thrashed harder, and it brought a louder shout, and with it her sense of direction. She rested a minute and as she did she sank, and in sinking, her foot touched bottom. She pushed off, not with the current and not against it but across it; she felt sand again and pushed again, and continued bouncing until she could stand.

Sam Cowett and Jabez Gray were slogging through the water toward her.

" 'Tis the widow!" Cowett said.

"Bloody hell!" Gray said. They each caught her by an arm and half carried her shoreward, to collapse on the same log that had launched her. They wrapped her in some sacking off the boat and pumped her with questions. How long were you in there? Are you numbed through? Are you wet in the lungs? Can you walk?

But neither man asked what she was doing in the water.

Lyddie emerged from her room in flannel gown and wool stockings, her hair streaming down her back like seaweed. Jabez Gray had gone; Sam Cowett sat on the barrel looking over the sparse collection on the table.

She offered him a portion of her dwindling supply of tea and bread, but he refused it. She was hungry, but more exhausted than hungry; he got up and she sat hard on the barrel. Cowett looked around and located the brandy bottle on the upended crate. He tipped the coins out of the cup, poured a stiff measure, and handed it across. Lyddie drank, one sip, then a second.

"If you're thinking I threw myself in after my husband you'd be mistaken," she said. "I was out for clams. I dug out every hole and found but six."

Cowett walked to the fire, picked up her bread peel, smoothed out a patch of ash, and drew a shape that looked something like a keyhole. "That's the hole you're after."

"Thank you. I'll remember next time."

"And the tide. 'Tis at the neap now. Not the time for clamming."

Lyddie took another sip of the medicine. It had just begun to warm the inner parts, but not the outer.

"Do you plan to stay?" she asked.

"Till you've come the right color."

"Then perhaps you'd like to see if there's another barrel in the barn."

He left and was gone some time. When he came back he had a ladder-back chair over each shoulder.

"I've no need of these. What I've need of is a woman to set up a pot and scour me out mornings."

"For the price of two chairs?"

"The chairs are loan. For the other, I'll pay a shilling."

The door rattled. Cowett strode over and tossed it open. Deacon Smalley stepped back, startled.

Cowett turned to her. "What say you, Widow Berry? A shilling a day for setting me right mornings?"

"Yes," Lyddie said.

Cowett left.

The deacon looked after him and back to Lyddie. "So. You work for him still."

"As I would eat, yes."

He looked around the room, spied the brandy bottle on the table, and looked harder at Lyddie. "You're ill?"

"I'm wet. A small mishap at the shore this morning. Sit down, Mr. Smalley. Would you have tea?"

"No, thank you. I've come at the direction of the reverend. You were not at meeting."

"No. I was waylaid."

"You've missed several, Widow Berry."

"Indeed."

"We—the reverend and I and others of the church fathers—have great concerns over your conduct, Widow Berry."

"If your concern is in regard to my missing meeting—"

"It is in regard to meeting, it is in regard to your disrespect of your son, it is in regard to your relation with this Indian."

Lyddie set down her cup, warm enough now, and not from the brandy. "You may tell the church fathers that I'm duly chastised about meeting and will strive to attend better. You may tell them they may take up my disrespect of my son at the same time as they take up his failure to honor his obligation to me. You may tell them nothing of the Indian, as it's not their business. Is there more?"

"There's a good deal more. You put yourself at grave risk, in this life and the next, if you continue without the Lord, if you continue in your willfulness, if you continue in the company of heathens."

"And I see the greater risk in starvation."

"You might return to your son's any time you sign the proper papers, and there you might eat your fill. 'Tis naught but pride keeps you here."

"So, 'tis not the church fathers who send you here, but Mr. Clarke? But of course, you would like my house for your daughter. You should enjoy having her so near at hand, would you not?"

"My dealings with Clarke are not your concern."

"As my dealings with him are not yours. As my dealings with Mr. Cowett are not yours."

"I am deacon of the church. I arrive at an early hour to find him handling your door as if it were his own and you undressed in his company."

Lyddie rose. "I am undressed, as you call it, in your company as well. Best you take yourself off before that's all over town, too."

A rich, bruised color suffused the deacon's face. "You've been warned, Widow Berry."

He left without good-bye.

Lyddie refilled her cup and drank it down.

28

Lyddie set up the Indian with stews and pies and bread, swept out and scoured down, fed the chickens in exchange for eggs, trading some mending for three laying hens, and added one and six to her week's pay whenever she did a washing. The deacon's visit had had a certain perverse effect on her; from that day forth she didn't attend another meeting, but she still observed the Sabbath by not working, until one Saturday Cowett said, "Another two shillings if you come on the morrow." Lyddie worked the Sabbath and felt nothing but richer.

The days passed into weeks, dragging May into June by the heels. The viburnum bloomed. The strawberries reddened. Eben Freeman came. He stood and looked around and sat and looked around and stood and burst out roughly, "Widow Berry, you must know what's said about town."

"What is said, Mr. Freeman?"

"How can you be unaware? You shun your church, you shun your friends and family, you seclude yourself for over a month with this Indian, they think . . . well, good God, what might they think?"

"I'm sure I don't know."

"You and the Indian. A rumor flies. Of him. Here. With you."

"You have this from Deacon Smalley?"

"I have it from all the town! My sister told me of it. The miller told me of it. 'Tis tossed about at the tavern."

"Well, then, it must be true."

"You'd do nothing to help yourself, Widow Berry?"

"What would you like from me, Mr. Freeman? My assurance that I do not lie with the Indian? Then you have it. Will that do?"

He stared at her. "You're greatly changed, Widow Berry. You're very greatly changed. I don't know what to say to you."

"Nor I you. And if you've come from my son with the aim of forcing me to give up my employment with Mr. Cowett—"

"I? Come from your son? This is what you think of me?"

"What should I think of you, Mr. Freeman, having just learned what you think of me?"

He had the sense to fall silent, but soon enough he began again, although in more subdued tone. "I think nothing ill of you, Widow Berry; I never have and I never could do. I've spoken badly. I came with no intent but to warn you of the harm aimed at you."

"But how can they harm me? Unless they drive me away from Mr. Cowett and my sole source of employment?"

"But don't you see? That very employment allows them this weapon against you. There are other means to make your way. If you allow me to help you to regain your keep from Clarke by law—"

"And leave me in debt to you and fighting Clarke every month for my wood and rye? Do you forget? 'Twas you described how it would be."

"You have no other recourse."

"I have my employ with Mr. Cowett. And I'd sooner count on Cowett than Clarke."

"Count on Cowett! You don't begin to know the man; you don't know what moves him. He has grudges to feed, old and new. He's ruled by them."

"And I thought you a friend to him."

"He has no friend in this town."

"Well, then, it makes us two."

"You would say this to me?"

Lyddie didn't answer.

Freeman stood up. "My sister awaits my report on your condition. It will not be a happy one. I see now you have been corrupted by him, if not in one way, then in another equally as damaging. Good-day to you, Widow Berry."

"Good-day, Mr. Freeman."

After he had gone Lyddie sat, half shamed and half angered, the anger fed by the shaming, both warring inside her. It all warred inside her. Was Freeman indeed a friend to her? What poor opinion must he hold of her to say all he had said of Cowett? But what of all his early kindness and defense of her? Even today, he had heard what was said around town and instead of believing and staying away he had come to warn her. Or had he half believed, the half that believed then coming straight to her to hear her denial? But even if that were so, the fact of his coming here spoke to a certain courage no other had possessed, including her daughter. And speaking of her daughter, where did she fall in this? Mehitable had believed her husband over her mother once before; Lyddie could put no faith in her in this matter. And after this last visit, perhaps she would be foolish to put any faith in Eben Freeman. Lyddie was surprised to find that the second thought gave her almost as much pain as the first.

Lyddie returned to Cowett's late in the day to collect the linens she'd left on the grass to bleach; she found the Indian just in from fishing, and she followed him inside to set out his supper. Long, gold rays followed her through the door and across the clean, bleached floorboards; the smell of sassafras but not sassafras was strong and she found it soothed her. Cowett talked of a fine day at sea and his hope for the morrow; once he'd put away his sack he turned and gave her one long look, then another.

"Are you well?"

Lyddie nodded. She set down the meat pie.

Cowett pointed to it. "Will you share?"

Lyddie accepted.

She accepted other suppers. For several weeks she ate, cleaned up the remains, and left immediately after; but one night near the end of June she lingered. They'd been talking of the Indians. She asked him: who were the Indian gods? And his answer had bewitched her. The two biggest were Kiehtan and Hobamock, the first delivering good, the second evil. Kiehtan created the heaven and earth and the sea and all its creatures, all the Indian humanity springing from one man and one woman, as did the Christian's, but the Indian sent his prayers and gifts to Hobamock, to keep on his good side—hence the Christian perception that the Indians worshiped the devil. Hobamock was the more powerful; Hobamock would send or not send their wounds and droughts and diseases. Lyddie asked where these gods dwelled, what version the Indian might have of a heaven or a hell, and Cowett referred to a vague place in the west, where good and bad went together, but from there the bad were sent away to wander. Lyddie asked what sins sent man to wander and Cowett listed among them adultery, but then explained that married or no, Indian men and women were free to leave one mate and try another whenever they wished it.

"Then where lies the sin?" Lyddie asked.

"When the trying comes before the leaving."

Lyddie considered. There were scandals in every Cape Cod village, and Satucket had its share of them: Abigail Gray had been got with child while her husband was at sea; Keziah Doane and Winslow Myrick had each left their spouse to set up housekeeping in Yarmouth; it was rumored, and denied, that the youngest Cobb had got a child on the family Negro, Sarah. But Lyddie believed herself the first Englishwoman in town to be paired with an Indian. She tried to sort the crimes along the Indian rule, but she could only vouch for the last, the one that had never happened, as free of any trying-before-leaving. If one counted dying as leaving.

Lyddie looked up and found Cowett watching her. She flushed. He said, as if he could read color as he read words, "You hear what they say of us."

She nodded.

"It troubles you?"

"Some."

"Enough to stop you coming?"

" 'Tis been said already. What good would stopping now do?"

He nodded.

She said, after a minute, "It doesn't trouble you."

He shrugged. "Naught to lose."

Lyddie considered. And what had she to lose? She had lost her daughter and her last friend. She looked across the table. Her last white friend.

Lyddie got up to go, and Cowett followed her into the yard on his way to the barn. The sun's last glancing blow filled the tops of the trees in the woodlot. Lyddie pointed toward the trees. "Did you divide, then?"

He nodded.

"And do you regret it?"

He came up behind her and put his hands on her shoulders. He turned her to the east. "That way to Namskaket Creek." He turned her south. "There to the Great Long Pond." He turned her west. "And there to the Sauquatuckett, or as you say, Satucket River, or Stony Brook, or Mill Creek." One more turn. "And north to the bay. My great-grandfather sold all of it to the English for fifty-eight pounds. Why trouble over half a woodlot?"

Lyddie made no answer. In fact, she barely breathed. Cowett's hands had stayed on her shoulders, as if he'd forgotten them there, and no doubt he had forgotten himself, thought he was standing in the yard with his wife, as Lyddie could think she was standing so with Edward. But no, she could never take this Indian for Edward. She could sense his great size behind her even if she couldn't see him, she could smell that sassafras smell that she'd never smelled on Edward. He shouldn't be touching her. But of course she shouldn't be letting him touch her. And still she stood there with breath held and knees locked because it had been so long since she'd felt the heat and weight of a man's hands on her, so long since she'd been so physically connected to any living thing, white or Indian.

With great effort of will she stepped out from under the hands. She said, without turning, "But your great-grandfather kept this piece."

"He kept it."

"And gave some to Edward's great-grandfather. Why?"

Cowett made no answer.

"I must go," Lyddie said. She stepped away, deeper into the wood.

He called after her, as if nothing had happened at all, " 'Twas a fine pie."

And Lyddie called back, "Thank you."

Lyddie slept little and arrived late the next day, after Sam Cowett had gone. She put the house to right in a hurry, set him out a cold meat pie, a loaf, and some pickled greens for dinner, and left before he returned.

After she'd finished her own baking she took Edward's ax out of the barn and went into the woodlot to see what she might do on her own about wood for winter. A piece of old fence lay on the ground, and she set to hacking it apart with the ax. When she stopped to get her breath she heard a noise and turned around to see Sam Cowett coming through the trees toward her.

He took the ax from her, cut up the fence with dispatch, took two small, wind-felled trees down to log size, and helped her to stack the lengths on the edge of the woodlot nearest the house.

When they were finished she said, "I've a fresh-baked mince pie by way of thank-you," and stepped toward the house, but he caught her elbow to stop her.

"Some things get done without pay, neighbor for neighbor."

"Yes. Well, then. Thank you."

He continued to hold her arm, and when his thumb slid across the hollow inside her elbow she understood what a fool she'd been to imagine he'd thought nothing had happened in the woods; the whiteness of her skin wouldn't stop him from feeling its heat just as the darkness of his hadn't stopped her. But the thumb slid to the hollow and stopped there, its message clear: it was up to Lyddie which way they went now. If she moved in one direction one thing would happen, and if she moved in another nothing would happen at all. She could smell the Indian's sassafras smell, and she wanted above everything to move into it and let it wrap around her, let those competent hands move over her flesh as they had moved over Rebecca's. What held her? God? Edward? Deacon Smalley and the Reverend Dunne? Not God. The speed with which she could dispense with God shocked her. She'd lost the prayers first, then meeting, then the Sabbath altogether, and if God didn't hold her, what could Deacon Smalley or the Reverend Dunne matter? But what of Edward? No. If

Lyddie's doings on earth mattered anything to Edward now, which she doubted, he would understand this one act above all others. So if Edward didn't hold her now, who did?

Eben Freeman. The name came up by surprise, but once up, it stayed. Lyddie had told him she didn't lie with the Indian, and he had believed her.

Lyddie pulled back. Cowett's hands tightened briefly on her arm, just long enough for the old bolt of fear to find her, and then he released her.

29

Lyddie lay awake, got up and walked the house, lay awake some more. When she finally slept she dreamed. She was fishing for herring in the creek when she heard a cry, the sound carrying over the trees and down the creek on the wind. Mehitable, in labor. Lyddie hurried to the Clarke house, clutching a writhing fish, and found her daughter's bed walled in by the women Nathan had sent for: Cousin Betsey, Patience Clarke, Granny Hall. Lyddie tried to work her way to the bed, but the women stood shoulder to shoulder against her. Mehitable's cries scourged Lyddie's ears, pierced her skin, pressed on her lungs, but when they stopped the silence was more terrible. Lyddie knew that silence, knew the stiff necks of the women looking down at a stillborn child; she elbowed Cousin Betsey aside and leaned over the bed. Mehitable lay white and still; on the sheet between her legs lay a living babe, black-haired and chestnut-colored.

The women pointed at Lyddie. " 'Tis your child. We all know 'tis your child. 'Tis *you* lies with the Indian."

Lyddie scooped up the child. Mehitable rose in a shriek, clutching for the babe; Lyddie bent to hand it to her, but the thing in her hand was fish, not babe; she turned to find Sam Cowett holding the infant, the two of them one face, one color.

"Tell them," Lyddie said. "Tell them we did not do this thing."

"Did you not hear what your reverend told you?" he said. "A sin in the heart is as great as a sin in the flesh."

"Give my daughter back her child," Lyddie said.

"I can't. Your daughter's dead."

Lyddie whirled around and saw that her daughter had indeed gone gray and limp.

Lyddie woke filled with black, whirling fears. She lay still and sweating until she grew angry. She would not live in fear of her own mind. Mehitable was not dead. But Mehitable had not been the only fear floating through the dream. Sam Cowett. Of him, or of herself, or of the near thing between them, it didn't matter which was the true fear; the same thing would get rid of all of them.

Lyddie looked out the window at the pink-gray sun and tried to recollect the tide. She tossed back her sheet, got up and dropped her skirt over her shift, tying the tapes as she searched out her shoes and stockings. She raked up her hair and pinned it on her way to the necessary, not troubling with breakfast.

Cowett opened the door with his feet still bare and his shirt hanging loose over his breeches.

She said, "I can't work for you any longer." She turned around, stepped back through the door, and everything, all of it, was over.

Lyddie now had time to tend to her own household chores that had been let go while she had tended to Cowett's. She collected the corn husks saved in the barn from last fall's husking and restuffed her summer bed tick. She set a barrel of beer to brew. She pickled her cucumbers. She gave the house a top-to-bottom cleaning. She made sure her head stayed full of the next chore and that way she kept it free of Cowett, but that night, in the weakness of near sleep, he took possession, invading her through all her senses. She saw his black eyes reading her, she smelled his sassafras smell, she heard that deep, quiet voice: "Some things get done without pay," she felt his hand on her. But after she'd slept a little she saw that all the wildness in her head only proved that she'd been right to sever ties with him.

The next morning Lyddie sat down with her pot of coins and counted out her earnings: two pounds, four shillings, eight pence. How far would it take her? Through summer with no great trouble, but no great distance into winter. The cow's hay alone would take it all, and although she was owed the hay from Clarke she had as great hope of getting it from him as she did of it raining down from heaven. She would have to make some sort of income.

One idea struck Lyddie when she went out to the buttery to turn and rub her cheeses—she had two of Edward's favorite sage cheeses just ready, and even Betsey admitted Lyddie's superiority when it came to cheese making. She might get a shilling for each cheese. She wrapped one up with care and set off for Sears's store.

The Myrick sisters stood in deep conversation outside the store, as if they lived at either end of town instead of at either end of the same house. When Lyddie came up the elder turned friendly enough eyes on her and asked how she was faring.

"Well enough," Lyddie said. "And yourselves?"

"We're well," said the younger. "And how fares your Indian?"

"My Indian?"

"Oh, now, you know who I mean—that fearsome big thing—Sam, they call him. The one you work for."

"I'm afraid I no longer work for Mr. Cowett."

"Well, now! But I'm not surprised, if I might say so. I don't know how you got on with him. So violent a creature."

"I saw no violence in him."

"Well, in drink—"

"I saw him take but one drink, in distress over his wife. I spoke to him about it, and he desisted."

"You spoke to him!" The sisters changed looks. "Well, you did get on, didn't you? Or should I say 'you do get on'?"

"As he's my neighbor, I certainly hope we continue to get on. Excuse me, I've business with Mr. Sears."

Lyddie stepped past the women into the store.

But Mr. Sears stopped her before she had unwrapped the cheese. "I get my cheese from Winslow. You know how it is, Widow Berry. Can't turn my back on Winslow."

And she was told much the same thing at Smith's store and Bangs's inn.

Lyddie walked home in hard thought. There were, no doubt, some houses in town in need of nurse or housekeeper, but short of knocking on all doors, she had no way of finding them. If she attended meeting, or was still visited by Cousin Betsey, she would have known this information as she knew the day of the week, but as she had spent so long isolated with no one but Sam Cowett to talk to, she knew nothing. Lyddie shifted the weight of the cheese to her other arm. Of course, there was nothing to say that she couldn't visit Betsey; in fact, the case could be made that she yet owed Betsey a cheese.

Lyddie set off down the King's road and covered the three miles to Shubael's house with fair speed. When Betsey opened her door

Aunt Goss lifted her sunken face from her chest, saw who she was, dropped it back, and resumed snoring. Shubael came from the back room, greeted her with a flustered "Cousin! Well, now! How do?" and reversed direction.

Betsey held out longer, but barely. She was so sorry, she was just on her way out, and in a great hurry, too. Lyddie would have to return another day. Although to suggest a free day just now was out of the question. Such a busy time in the village . . .

Lyddie found herself back in the road, but she hadn't got a rod along it when she realized she still held the cheese in her hands. The cheese had now become a point of honor with her; she turned around and heard the raised voices from well outside the Hopkinses' door, beginning with Shubael's.

"I say you might have talked to her, is all I say."

"Oh, do you? 'Tis all how-do-do and out the door with you, but I'm to talk to her!"

"You know my trouble with Cousin Lyddie. If she starts talking about her husband to me—"

"Oh, you and your trouble! Your trouble is you're afraid of that Indian!"

"And why shouldn't I be?"

"Because you're not talking to him, you're talking to Cousin Lyddie. Or you should be. And if you'd talked to her in the first place that Indian wouldn't be in it at all, now would he? She'd have signed that paper instead of disgracing the entire family!"

"Now you don't know for a fact—"

"Oh, you and your facts! You and my brother! A pair of fools, the both of you."

Sturdy heels clacked away. Lyddie retreated to the road with her cheese, her mind swimming in senseless information. Shubael dreading a conversation about Edward? Shubael afraid of the Indian?

Shubael convincing her to sign the paper, to keep away from the Indian?

"Widow Berry!"

Lyddie pulled up and discovered Eben Freeman, dismounted from his horse, standing in her path. "For a minute I thought you might walk right over me."

"I'm sorry. I didn't—"

He held up a hand. "No, I'm sorry. For the manner in which I spoke to you at our last meeting. It preys on me nightly. I'd not be surprised if you did walk over me."

"I won't walk over you, Mr. Freeman. I'll accept your apology and make one of my own. I said something that might lead you to think I don't consider you a friend. Never think I don't know everything you've done for me."

"I, done? I've done nothing. You allow me nothing. When I think what I would like to do—"

Lyddie held out the cheese. "I would allow you to do this, if you're willing. Please give this to your sister. It pays an old debt."

He remembered. He understood. Lyddie watched it work through his features, and a few other things besides. "Did you not just come from there?"

"I did. I forgot to leave it."

"And did you have a pleasant visit?"

"It was . . . hurried."

He flushed. He tucked the cheese under his arm and turned his horse. "Allow me to walk a ways with you."

They stepped out along the road in awkward silence until Lyddie asked, "Are you just come from Barnstable?"

He nodded. "Winslow and Clarke, back in court again. If this goes on as did the last, I shall spend the rest of my life back and forth between villages."

He continued on about the details of the case, but Lyddie barely listened; she had noticed that whenever they passed a walker or rider coming in the other direction Freeman made a point of turning on her some little attention: a hand under the elbow, an agreeable nod, an attentive smile. Was he out to prove her respectable? When they reached the landing road Lyddie said, "You'd best turn back. No doubt your sister waits dinner on your arrival."

"My sister's dinner may wait till it freezes," he said with a passion Lyddie had only heard once before in him. She looked up in surprise.

"Widow Berry," he said. "I must confess to you. I have done a degree of research since our last meeting and I find that my sister appears no great distance behind every rumor concerning you, the only person any closer to it being your own son Nathan Clarke. I've spoken to her; I've suggested she take a different course; if you'd been able to tell me you had a pleasant visit with her just now I would perhaps have been able to sit calmly at her table, but as you cannot—" He waited.

Lyddie said nothing.

"I'll leave you now, Widow Berry. But I'll come by to see you another time, if you're willing."

"Of course."

"Very well. Now, if you'll excuse me, I intend to deny my sister the pleasure of my company and book myself a bed at the tavern."

"Mr. Freeman, if this is on my account—"

"There are a great many things I would do on your account, Widow Berry, but I do this on my sister's account. May I tell you something you perhaps don't know of me? I am, at times, a man of temper. In such mood as I'm in at present, I fear for my treatment of her. I intend to send her a message declining her hospitality on the grounds of some business at the tavern. Shall I include the cheese, with your compliments?"

If that was his definition of "temper" there were few need fear him, Lyddie thought. And then she thought of something else. It hadn't occurred to her to brave the men-only world of the tavern in search of a market for her cheeses, but people ate there as they ate elsewhere.

"You may give the cheese to Mr. Thacher with my compliments. And tell him he may have another at any time, for a shilling."

30

A young Indian woman from the nation began to walk down the road in the direction of Cowett's every morning. Lyddie traveled through town, leaving her name at the shops in case anyone had need of nurse or housekeeper. She even stopped at the tavern to inquire if they were in need of more cheese; she made her trip early in the morning so as to avoid the busiest part of the day and actually found the main room empty, but even so, Elkanah Thacher rushed to meet her at the door in an effort to preserve what might be left of her reputation. When she stated her business he said, "Widow Berry, as much as I'd like to buy my cheese from you, I'll get nothing out of Winslow if he hears I'm doing business with a Clarke."

So there it was in all its black-and-white irony: Lyddie would be shunned by some because she was not with Clarke and shunned by others because she was. Lyddie thanked Thacher and turned to go, but before she'd swung the full way around her eye caught a curious sight: Eben Freeman coming down the stairs trailed by a dun-colored girl with black hair and blue eyes, who took her leave of him by sliding a hand along the seam of his breeches. Lyddie continued out the door, but soon enough she heard him behind her. "Widow Berry!"

She turned. "Good morning, Mr. Freeman."

"Good morning to you. I'm surprised to see you here."

"No doubt. Do you find your accommodation acceptable?"

"Acceptable, yes. Not quite the stuff of home."

"But not as lonely."

He peered at her.

"An old acquaintance, is she?"

"We've met before, yes."

"You must have made a good impression."

"I daresay she's not suffered at my hand."

"I daresay she's not bettered at it, either."

"One might ask what 'better' would be. She's no poorer, surely."

"Ah, yes. And we all have our way to make."

"Perhaps you'd care to choose another subject, Widow Berry."

"I'm afraid I've run out of subjects."

"Very well, then. Good-day to you, Widow Berry."

"Good-day to you, Mr. Freeman."

Freeman came to see her the next afternoon and stepped inside with something akin to sheepishness in his manner. It didn't suit him. He began at once. "Widow Berry, in regard to a recent unseemly conversation I inflicted upon you at the tavern—"

"You forget 'twas I inflicted the conversation on you, Mr. Freeman. I'm afraid I've grown too used to my own company and have lost the knack for polite society."

"No, no, I've always found your conversation most—" He hesitated. "Might I say open?"

"You might better say brazen. But for that you must blame Edward. He nurtured in me a free way of speaking between us that is ill suited to outside company."

"In that case I take it as nothing but compliment that you would speak so with me. May we consider the subject now closed?"

"We may."

After that visit things returned to normal between them, except that Lyddie began to dream strange dreams of blue- and black-eyed Indian children, until the first of July, when Lyddie looked up at the sky and saw the waxing moon and wondered as it rounded if it would pull Mehitable's child from her womb. From then she dreamed of other children, some dead, some alive, some motherless, all white.

On July sixth Lyddie had already put up the cow, bolted her door, and let down her hair when she heard a gentle tapping against the door. The day had begun with a soft southwest wind that had built up into a good breeze, and she thought the shadblow had dropped another limb until she heard the small voice. "Grandmama?"

Lyddie flung back the bolt and wrenched open the door. "Bethiah!"

" 'Tis Mama. She says, would you come? 'Tis her time. She asked Papa to send for Granny Hall, but he said no, he would fetch the doctor."

"The doctor! Why the doctor? What's happened?"

"Nothing's happened. Papa said if a Mrs. Winslow would have the doctor so would a Mrs. Clarke."

Lyddie found her pins, stuck up her hair, and set off with Bethiah, asking what questions she thought the girl might be able to answer.

Was Mama up or in bed? Did she lie still in the bed or did she move about? How long had she been in the bed? Was there anyone with her?

They reached the Clarke house in tandem with Nathan and Dr. Fessey. Dr. Fessey hailed Lyddie with good cheer and hurried inside, but Nathan Clarke stepped square in front of her.

"You may turn right around home, Mother. Have I not made it clear? You're not welcome in my home any longer."

"My daughter asked for me. She sent Bethiah. Excuse me." Lyddie stepped sideways, but he grabbed her by the arm.

"You'll not set foot in my house. Today or any day hereafter." He swung back through the door, dropping the bolt down after him.

Lyddie stood in the darkening air, her mind and body stalled, until a bullfrog in the nearby creek sounded and her mind, at least, went into motion. She considered and discarded any attempt at forced entry on the grounds that such commotion would not be helpful to Mehitable, but should she stay in the yard or should she go? If Lyddie stayed where she was she would at some point find out how her daughter fared; Dr. Fessey would come out and he would tell her. If Lyddie left, she would know nothing until her one visitor, Eben Freeman, arrived, bearing some third- or fourth- or fifth-hand account of the result.

Lyddie stayed where she was. Bethiah had vanished inside with either the doctor or her father, and Lyddie had some hope that the girl might come out to look for Lyddie, but no one came out at all. The dark thickened. The air cooled. Lyddie walked up and down the drive until she stepped into a hole and went down on a knee. Hours passed. Or minutes. The bolt rattled and Dr. Fessey stepped out onto the stoop, leaving Nathan Clarke framed by firelight in the doorway.

"I thank you, sir," Clarke said. "We'll settle the fee when we have something to show for it, shall we?"

The door closed and the dark returned. Lyddie stepped out of the shadow.

"Dr. Fessey."

"Good God! Who's there? What the devil! Widow Berry. You near cost me the last breath in my body. Why do you lurk there?"

"I would know how my daughter fares."

"Oh, yes, yes. An awkward situation, haven't we? Well, let me tell you, we've naught but a false alarm. I've given her some laudanum and she's deep asleep, and if I may say, she'd best make a better job of it when the real time comes. Quite the timid thing, isn't she?"

"She's not had a child."

"No, and she won't, either, if she doesn't put some backbone into it. Say now, are you limping?"

She had walked beside the doctor as he started for the barn, but she hadn't realized until he said it that she was, indeed, limping. He offered her a ride home, and Lyddie accepted. He walked the horse to the block, mounted, and pulled her up behind him. The doctor's coat smelled of the usual smoke and tobacco with none of the Indian's sassafras, Edward's salt, or Freeman's sweat. His hair smelled of camphor. His horse had such a rough gait, even at the walk the doctor had to maintain to keep Lyddie behind him, that by the time she dismounted her limp had worsened.

"Here, now," Fessey said, sliding down after her. "Let me come in and look at that knee."

Lyddie tried to discourage him, not wishing to owe a doctor's fee over nothing but a routine lameness, but he stepped around her into the house, and once he'd spied the Indian's brandy bottle on the homemade shelf he said, "There now, I'll take a dram of that in payment."

Lyddie poured the doctor a dram. She sat on one of the chair's Sam Cowett had brought and Dr. Fessey pulled the other across from her. He lifted her skirt, lowered her stocking, poked the knee, gripped her foot, and turned it in all directions.

He dropped her skirt and patted the knee. "You've done no great damage. Wrap it tight in a flannel soaked in this, and if you give me another dram there'll be no charge for the liniment." He pulled a small jar from his pocket.

Lyddie got up and refilled his glass.

"Now here comes some advice free of charge. Are you ready?"

"I don't think—"

"No, you don't think, Widow Berry. If you did, you would see that your little adventure must come to an end eventually. You can't keep on without support of any kind forever; before long you'll be on the charge of the town and stuffed up in the attics of the lowest bidder. I say, why prolong the inevitable? Now before you say anything else, I know all about you and that Indian, and I tell you I've lived and worked in this village a long time and there's nothing that doesn't get forgotten the minute the next thing comes along. Put it behind you. You've already quit him; now make your confession before the church, sign what you have to sign for Clarke, and get on with what anyone might call a very nice life for a woman in your situation."

Lyddie stood up. "Thank you, Dr. Fessey." She limped to the door and opened it. The doctor set down his glass but remained seated.

"All right, then, Widow Berry, if you won't take the help that's offered you—"

"I would take this. In your journeys through town if you hear of someone in need of nurse or housekeeper—"

The doctor leaned back in his chair and drained his glass. He got up and closed the door, but with himself still inside of it. "Let me tell you something, Widow Berry. There are those in town who take a thing like the Indian in one way, and those who take it in another. Myself, I don't let such details bother me. I'll go to meeting when I can, but if I can't, if someone else's physical need happens to outweigh my own spiritual one, I don't let it trouble my sleep. Now, as it happens, my wife has entered a frail state and I find myself in need of what you might call some housekeeping. You're a fine, strong woman, and me being the sort of man not greatly troubled by a woman's past, being the sort, in fact, who sees some advantage to a certain openness of character, if you take my meaning—"

Lyddie did.

She opened the door. "Good night, Dr. Fessey."

The doctor's face, one minute happily rounded with lust and hope, emptied and lengthened. "Oh, the devil."

He stepped onto the stoop but blocked her closing of the door with his arm. "I'll tell you another thing free of charge, Widow Berry. The person in town who'll want nursing is your daughter. She's not near the stuff of her mother." He walked off.

Lyddie closed the door, the dark, pulsing fear that had dozed in her chest for her daughter now fully wakened. What had Dr. Fessey meant, not the stuff of her mother? It was true, she supposed, that the fate of her children had not been caused by any physical weakness in their mother. She'd suffered long but unremarkable travails in each birthing, entering each childbed with a fierce determination to make the next babe live and breathe. She'd never suffered from fever, she'd been able to return to her kitchen within days of each of the births, but once she'd lost the first living boy, the fear had overtaken her. When the second girl passed her dead brother's age Lyddie took her first clear breath; when the second boy passed the dead sister's mark she knew better. But for the last precious boy to go all the way to five, to run and play with such vigor, to put her mind so near to rest and then to die . . . Was God about to make Lyddie pay for her recent sins with the life of her last child?

If ever Lyddie wished for a prayer she wished it then, but still the words would not come for her.

31

The knee swelled and throbbed all night and throughout the next day, Lyddie's head keeping time with its own pulsing. When Eben Freeman arrived he looked at what must have been a hollowed-out, shadowed face and said, "Widow Berry! Are you ill?"

Lyddie hobbled away from the door.

"Good God, you're injured." He caught her arm and helped her into the chair. "All right, then. What's happened?"

Lyddie told him most, if not all, of her recent adventures, finishing with "And I've not slept in days and I've a great headache as well." She meant the words as explanation of her disinterest in any lengthy visiting, but Freeman appeared to take them as something more pathetic.

"Come," he said. One arm slid behind her back and the other under her elbow; she rose out of the chair with greater ease than she'd done all day; he helped her to the bed and settled her on the coverlet. "This is where you need to be. Leg up, head down."

"I've the cow yet."

"I'll tend the cow." He disappeared and returned with a piece of flannel, dipped, from the smell of it, in vinegar. He began to bathe her temples.

"Mr. Freeman—"

"I think, considering we now share a bed, you'd best call me Eben. But I shouldn't take it amiss if you decided to fall asleep."

She smiled, trying to imagine Sam Cowett, or Dr. Fessey, or anyone, putting her at similar ease in such circumstance. She closed her eyes.

When she opened them he was gone, and so was her headache. She sat up, and he appeared in the door. "Ah! She wakes!"

"Did I sleep long?"

He checked his watch. "Near two hours."

"And you've been here all that time?"

"I made good use of it, relearning how to milk a cow." He pointed to his stained breeches. "And how do you feel, Widow Berry?"

"I feel better. In spirit as well as body."

"Because you slept. There's no greater drain on the spirit than lack of sleep." He came into the room and sat down again on the bed.

"As you're feeling so much better I have a proposal for you. I've reached an age where the vigors of the court circuit are taking more out of my body than they're putting into my wallet. Brother Shubael wants to sell his little sloop and buy a bigger one, to leave whaling for trading; he wants me to take half shares with him. If all happens according to plan, I'll be spending more of my time back here in Satucket—what would you say if I bought this house from Clarke?"

Lyddie stared at him. "And where would you have me go?"

"Well, you'd have two choices before you. You could stay in your third while I occupy the remainder, or you could marry me and we could share the whole together."

He might have put it in another order, thought Lyddie. Or did he think she'd need the house secured before she'd consider the second offer? But, in fact, the minute both halves had been placed side by side on the table a queer sensation overcame her, as if someone had just dosed her with warm brandy, or, perhaps more aptly, bathed her temples in vinegar.

"I see you don't cringe," Freeman said, "but beyond a certain look of surprise, I see nothing more. Can it be you don't know how it is with me? Well, then, perhaps I should put my case another way."

He lifted a hand to her face and brushed back the damp, vinegared hair. He raised the other hand and laced his fingers through to her scalp. He drew her face toward his and kissed her. It was nothing like Edward's first kiss—Edward had begun as if he'd long known all about her; Freeman began as if he understood he had much to discover. But either the dead wife or the tavern girl had taught him well; in no time he'd brought up the heat in her.

He pulled away. "Well, Lydia? Aye or nay?"

It suddenly seemed a very long time since anyone had kissed Lyddie. It seemed longer still since anyone had called her Lydia. Curiously, Lyddie's daughter had never liked her nickname Hitty and in her adulthood had reclaimed her full name of Mehitable. Thanks to Freeman, Lyddie and her daughter might at last share a common trait. And as she thought about it, if she married Freeman, she and Mehitable might share even more. If Lyddie married Freeman, Nathan would get his money for the house and rid himself of his mother-in-law, all in one neat deal. In that case, surely, he would no longer object to Lyddie's presence at her daughter's travail.

But what of Eben Freeman? What of this angular man with the circular mind? What of a self-containment that could not conceal the large heart? What of a man who dared speak of someone like Otis to someone like Clarke?

Whatever Freeman was, Lyddie had come to depend on him in a way she'd depended on no one since Edward's death, not as someone to keep her, but as someone who mattered to her, someone she mattered to in return. To matter. What more in life was needed? But there was more, she must admit it, an eagerness, a quickness, which shot through her whenever he appeared at her door. Lyddie had been either too long widowed or not long enough widowed to be able to trust any name she might put to that last thing, but she knew that it helped her live and breathe and move from day to day. She tried to imagine her day without Freeman's knock on her door, and the thought of it washed her in a paralyzing fatigue, which brought her to another realization. She was tired. Not just a one-day kind of tired, but a months-long kind of tired, a sleepless woman's kind of tired. An image of future nights pressed close against that long, taut body brought first a quickness, but then a restfulness so complete she felt restored by just the dream.

Freeman took her chin in his hand and gave it a gentle shake. "Is this your means of forcing me to reveal all my weaknesses? First my lust and now my impatience? What say you, Lydia Berry? Aye or nay?"

"Aye," Lyddie said.

Freeman jumped up as if she'd shot him, then looked down at the bed with some indecision, perhaps considering the unsanctioned but oft-tolerated custom of bedding-before-banns, but no.

"I must go," he said. "I've a meeting with Winslow and then I must see Clarke, I must publish our names. If I get them up today . . . What falls in a fortnight's time? What say you to a wedding in a fortnight? Or would you stay in this between state longer?"

"No."

Freeman's face cracked open. He bent low and kissed her again.

This time Lyddie was ready and could match him with a similar degree of enthusiasm. He drew back and studied her. "Oh, Lydia Berry," he said, "what a time we're going to have!"

Again, Lyddie couldn't sleep, but this time her head was full of Eben Freeman, of all she did and didn't know of the man. She had now tasted his passion and discovered its effect on her, but she knew better than to trust that effect in and of itself; Sam Cowett, too, had heated her blood, a fact that now troubled her more greatly than it had before. What did it mean to be so moved by two different men? Was she no better than that girl in the tavern? Or did her rejection of Dr. Fessey save her?

But what of all those things she didn't know of Eben Freeman? She knew little of the dead wife, the children, that whole other life at Barnstable. Perhaps it was no bad thing to enter into a marriage with much yet to discover. Lyddie curled toward sleep with her head full of Eben Freeman, but just before she got there, by virtue of a contrariness in her nature that Lyddie had come to know and despise in equal measure, her thoughts left off Freeman and lodged hard against the Indian woman who walked to Cowett's every day. She was a fine thing, fresh into her adulthood, with skin and hair glowing in the sun; the first week she had walked by every morning and back every afternoon as regular as the tide, but for some days now Lyddie had seen her only sporadically coming or going.

Lyddie's thrashing about had set the knee throbbing again. She got up and poured herself a medicinal drop of brandy, returned to her bed, and slept till a steady, persistent knocking woke her.

She went to the door in her shift and threw it open. "Bethiah!"

"Papa sent me. 'Tis the baby coming."

The women stood around as they had in the dream, but this time they parted and allowed Lyddie the bed. Mehitable was the color of the bleached pad of linen under her. She looked up and stretched out her hand. "Mama."

The childish address twisted Lyddie's gut. She took her daughter's hand. "When did you begin?"

Granny Hall answered from behind. "Yesterday dawn."

Lyddie looked around. "No doctor this time?"

"He's been. Still a fair distance between pains. He'll be back."

Mehitable closed her eyes, jerked, whimpered, weakly squeezed Lyddie's hand.

"That's the way, child."

Granny Hall said, "She's worn down."

Mehitable's eyes rounded in fear.

"Nonsense," Lyddie said. "She's just near crushed my hand." She removed her fingers from Mehitable's, smoothed her hair, and patted her cheek. "You rest as you can between. You're doing fine. I'll be back." She left the room.

Nathan Clarke had come in and stood by the window, looking out over the road. Lyddie went up to him and touched his shoulder. He swung around. "How does she go?"

"Slow. As will the first. Mr. Clarke, I wish to thank you for sending for me."

"And why should I not? I've seen Freeman. 'Tis all settled between us. I hereby put aside all differences and trust you to do the same."

But the fact that Clarke then returned at once to the subject of Mehitable went furthest in helping Lyddie put aside their differences. "I've some worry over my wife," he said. "She's not a strong woman."

"Nonsense," Lyddie said a second time.

"The doctor said—"

"The doctor wishes to inflate his own importance so you won't balk at his fee. Pay no attention to the doctor."

"My last wife died not six months after bringing on Bethiah. The poor woman never recovered of her travail. That was also a first child."

"And she was not in health for some time previous."

"I've not been married one year to Mehitable."

"I beg you, Mr. Clarke, don't talk so where my daughter may hear you. She is healthy and strong, and you must have faith in her and in Granny Hall."

But as the day stretched on and the pains increased and Mehitable weakened, Lyddie's own nerve flagged. Granny Hall pulled her aside and said, "Head's too big. It'll be the forceps. I'm sending for Dr. Fessey."

Dr. Fessey returned, examined the patient, and declared the head was, indeed, too large for the passage, that she would need the forceps, but first she needed a good bloodletting to remove the congestion. He opened his bag and laid the contents across the bed: a lancet, a basin, and the rough, tonglike forceps. Mehitable, her face colorless and tight with panic, watched her mother's and appeared to take some comfort from its appearance, which meant that Lyddie had managed to conceal her own fears well. Mehitable was not just worn down but worn out, her hand unable to hold Lyddie's. Lyddie gave the limp fingers a last squeeze and stepped away.

The doctor applied the lancet and drained what seemed like a great quantity of blood into the basin. The women settled Mehitable on her back and secured her limbs, but the girl was too far gone to do anything but moan as Dr. Fessey groped with the forceps for the baby's head and pulled. The head had been squeezed into the shape of a cone, puffed with swelling on top, but the baby breathed and cried. A boy.

"Good," said Granny Hall. "They've enough girls for care of the domestic." Dr. Fessey nodded in happy agreement. He inserted his hand to withdraw the placenta, clapped a cloth quickly over the loin to prevent the dangerous ingress of air, and motioned to Granny Hall to bind Mehitable's knees closed. All the while Mehitable lay as white and immobile as in the dream until Lyddie had to step forward and lay a hand on her daughter's chest to make sure of the weak rise and fall.

32

The child was named Edward. Lyddie moved back into her old room to tend mother and babe, and Jane was sent to tend Lyddie's cow, chickens, and garden. For Lyddie, holding the babe in her arms was both thrilling and excruciating. She could not quite believe in him, she didn't want to believe in him, but she had to believe in him, as his own mother was unable even to support him against her breast as she lay propped in bed; between them they required Lyddie's constant attention.

To Lyddie's surprise, Nathan Clarke appeared not only grateful for her services, but also glad of her company. Lyddie, in turn, found their past differences did indeed fade away in their common concern for mother and child. The problem was Freeman. He came each night after supper, and on Tuesday, after Clarke had been extolling Lyddie's virtues as nurse and housekeeper, he said, "Well, sir, prepare yourself to lose her. I'll be taking her Thursday next."

"Oh, no, we can't spare Mother so soon. Best you put it off for the present."

Freeman turned to Lyddie in surprise. "Surely, in another week—"

"You've been bachelor this long," Nathan said. "I should think you'd last another few weeks. You may have my mother-in-law as soon as my wife recovers."

Freeman forced the old rearrangement on his features, but later that night, as he sat with Lyddie in the front room while she tipped the cradle and mended the spark holes caused by drying the diapers too near the fire, he said, "This postponement. You don't appear to chafe at it."

"Why chafe in vain? I can't leave until my daughter is able to cope alone."

"Alone? She has a Negro and two girls."

"Perhaps better I say until she recovers."

"And how long will this be?"

"I know only that I'm needed here yet."

He watched her through four stitches. "Very well," he said, in a tone meant to say the opposite. He lowered his voice. "I've spoken to Clarke on another matter. I'm happy to report he's joined my effort to correct a previous false impression traveling about town, and my sister does so as well. After all, you'll be double family, now. I believe you may return to meeting with your reputation secured."

Lyddie looked up in surprise. It would, of course, be important to her husband and his position in the community that she be accepted back into the arms of the church, but could she do it? Lyddie looked down at the sleeping babe. If he continued to thrive, if her daughter recovered, could she forgive God? Or was it even a matter of forgiveness now?

"Your son and I settled some other business as well," Freeman continued. "I told him I'd like my house furnished."

It took Lyddie a second to understand which house he meant, and then what furniture he meant. "Do you mean Nathan will return it all?"

"He's done so already. I've paid him cash. And we sign the house papers Friday."

"And I sign, too?"

"Just as before." He smiled. "Or rather, not just as before. This time, I expect, you'll actually sign them." Lyddie smiled back. Freeman stood, rested a hand on the back of her neck, and stooped to kiss her.

A tangle of loud voices erupted from outside the back door. Freeman shot upright. "What the devil? Is that Silas?"

Lyddie shook her head. She had recognized the voice of Sam Cowett, and now Nathan's followed sharply.

"I'll thank you to leave here."

"I'll see the Widow Berry before I do."

"You'll leave, is what you'll do. And smartly, or I'll fetch the constable."

Lyddie jumped up.

Freeman's hand tightened on her shoulder. "Stay here. I'll see to this."

He hurried out.

Lyddie followed. The Indian stood in the dooryard, Nathan on the stoop, but even the height of the door stone didn't bring him eye to eye with the Indian.

Cowett saw Lyddie and spoke. "Good evening, Widow Berry."

Freeman turned in surprise. "Lydia, please get inside. All right, Mr. Cowett, best you go along home, now."

"I've come to talk to the Widow Berry. 'Tis no crime in it."

Young Nate appeared behind his father; Nathan whispered something that sent him out the door and down the drive at a run. Lyddie stepped around Freeman and Nathan and into the yard. As she came close to Cowett she could smell the liquor on him, but his eyes still focused on hers with their same old precision.

"You wished to speak with me, Mr. Cowett?" she said.

"For God's sake, Lydia!" Freeman said. "Get inside!"

" 'Tis all right, Eben," Lyddie said. "What would you say to me, Mr. Cowett?"

Cowett, who had closely watched the exchange between Lyddie and Freeman, turned back to Lyddie. "So. 'Tis true, then. You marry him. If I'd known you were in such need I'd have come sooner." He dug into a pouch at his belt and held out a closed fist. When Lyddie didn't move he took her hand, opened his fist over it, and rained some coins into her palm. "What you're owed."

"She's no need of your money now," Freeman said. "Lydia, give it back." But Lyddie's hand had already closed over the coins, and at that minute they all turned away at the sound of boots on stone. Young Nate and the constable, Elisha Mayo, clattered into the yard.

"Here, Mayo," Nathan said from the stoop, "you may arrest this Indian for disturbing the peace."

Lyddie whipped around. "What are you saying? He's disturbed nothing. He came to speak to me, to settle what I'm owed."

"He's come intoxicated onto my property and disturbed my household."

"You would call this intoxicated? Better you arrest your brother Silas, then." Lyddie turned to Freeman for help, but he stepped off the stoop, took Lyddie by the elbow, and pulled her inside.

They stood face-to-face in front of the cold hearth in her room.

"You surprise me, Lydia," Freeman said. "You surprise and disappoint me in the extreme."

"Indeed."

" 'Indeed'! This is all you have to say to me, 'indeed'?" After disobeying my instruction, after putting yourself into the arms of danger, after speaking against your son and humiliating him in public—"

"In public?"

"You think it will not soon be all over this town that you defied him in defense of a drunken Indian?"

"It would be nowhere at all if my son hadn't called in the constable. But if, as you say, I humiliated my son, it's to do with him and not you."

"You think not? When a woman I've publicly claimed as my own should display such wanton behavior—"

"Wanton!"

"What other word would you have me use, when a man you've already allowed to compromise your reputation shows up at your door, making disrespectful reference to your engagement? And instead of keeping away you rush out to meet him and leap to his defense against your own son!"

"I'll speak against my son if I find him wrong."

"Yes, you will. Excepting, of course, on the postponement of your own marriage. There, it seems, you're happy enough to bend to his will."

"When it's my will as well."

"I see. Perhaps, then, you wish to postpone for all time."

"Or perhaps all this really means is that you do."

They dropped into stiff silence.

Freeman walked to the door. "I've made my feelings known. My wishes remain clear. I make no ultimatum. I leave it to your own inclination to set our marriage."

He left.

Lyddie raised her hand and saw it was shaking. She opened her fist, which had remained clenched around Cowett's coins, and dropped them into her apron pocket.

33

Lyddie got Mehitable dressed and sat her up for several hours the next morning, but the girl was still too weak to do anything but nurse the babe, and even that was achieved only by propping them both with bolsters. Lyddie directed the others in the care of the two houses and herself attended solely to mother and child. In an impressive demonstration of control Nathan Clarke refrained from addressing the subject of Sam Cowett altogether; in a secluded moment Lyddie inquired of Jot if he'd heard news and found that the Indian had been locked up until he'd grown sober, paid his fine, and gone back to his business.

Freeman stayed away. Lyddie thought at first that he meant it as a cooling-down period—she was reminded that in his dealings with his sister, when he felt his temper get the better of him, he chose to remove himself rather than engage in confrontation, and she respected that reasoning—but after one day stretched to two and two to three and Lyddie had had ample time to think through their argument from both ends and each side, she began to think that his staying away might be something more in the way of punishment. After all, what had the argument really been about? Not Sam Cowett, or Nathan Clarke, or Mehitable, but Lyddie's disobedience, first over his request for an early wedding date, next over her going out to meet Sam Cowett. Or perhaps this "cooling down" was in fact cold feet.

She began to remember other things. His shock over the town gossip. His discomfort in their talk at the tavern. The way he'd stood at such a stiff, cold distance in front of the hearth and called her *wanton.* A man who could use such a word to describe his future wife couldn't really be said to believe in her character, no matter how often he defended it around town. But the curious thing for Lyddie was that she couldn't entirely blame Freeman for the word, or the cold feet, if that was indeed what it was. She of all people knew how close she'd come to being that wanton woman, not once, but twice, never mind that one of those times would have been with Freeman himself. And to give Freeman another point, Lyddie didn't believe that Sam Cowett had come to see her merely to pay her wage, which further validated Freeman's concerns over the Indian's motives. But behind all the pluses and minuses lay the total sum: in Lyddie's unmarried state she'd broken no law in disobeying Freeman's instruction, but after their marriage that would change. Freeman would hold total power over her. Could she lay her trust in his character, as he seemed unable to do in hers?

Lyddie thought back over all their dealings, beginning with his early defense of her rights against her son and ending with his purchase of Edward's house. Freeman was not Edward or Sam Cowett; he didn't make his living off the sea and could have little interest in a house along the landing road. He could have chosen a more commodious home on the more prestigious main thoroughfare through town or he could have built a home to his own specification, but instead he'd chosen a house that he knew to be important to Lyddie, in fact as well as principle. And she knew that as long as Eben Freeman should live, which should be longer than any mariner, she could trust him to keep her fed and clothed and warm.

Lyddie had advanced that far in her thinking, and still Freeman didn't come.

Lyddie spent the days taking joy in her daughter's progress as she sat up longer, then walked the chamber, then walked to the front room; by Friday morning Mehitable could bend over and lift the babe from his cradle. By Friday morning Lyddie had so firmly and finally determined cold feet as the cause of Freeman's absence that when he appeared in the doorway to her room she didn't rise to meet him but waited stiffly to hear what he might have to say.

But Freeman crossed purposefully to her chair and pulled her to her feet. "I'm sorry," he said. "I'm sorry to the core for such discord between us."

"As I am sorry. I would say in particular—"

"No. Say nothing more. We know each other well enough that we need not spell out every little word. We'll misstep from time to time, and when we do we'll pay a price in that worst of all miseries, a disconnection between us, but once it's over it's time to move on. Now come, they await us with the papers in the other room."

Too fast, she thought, it was all too fast, and thinking it, she fell back to the last time she'd thought it, standing at the barn with Eben Freeman as he'd pronounced her *widow* before she was quite through with the word *wife*. What did it mean that she would think of that time in the middle of this one? Was she now moving to *wife* before she was quite through with *widow*? Was she mistaking being Edward's widow with being Edward's wife? No. *No*. The former had little to recommend it; the latter was done.

Lyddie stepped into the room ahead of Freeman, but there, too, she found herself falling back to a former time, to the same stiff room, the same grayed and balding men around the table, the same or near-to-same paper and pen awaiting her. But no, she corrected herself: this time all was different. This time there was no need to summon Eben Freeman because he was right there, standing beside her, and she was about to sign a paper that would eventually bind her to the house, not cut her loose from it forever.

Or would it? As flawed as they were, Lyddie's dower rights had given her some control over the disposal of her husband's property; the minute Lyddie signed them away, Eben Freeman would make all decisions regarding the house. Eben Freeman in control was, of course, a better thing than Nathan Clarke in control; Eben held Lyddie's interest at heart, as evidenced by his desire to make the purchase in the first place, but what if an occasion arose where their interests differed? Lyddie had no doubt that Eben Freeman dead would leave her with at least the same rights she was about to lose, but what of Eben Freeman living? What if she had been right about his proclivity to punishment? What if this *price* he talked of in paying for missteps was to be paid by her alone, and in more than just human disconnection? What if he wished to exercise his authority over her by exercising his authority over the house?

Lyddie went back and forth with *he wouldn't, he would, he wouldn't* and then came to the heart of the trouble: whether he would or no, he could. He could, by law, do whatever he chose with the house once she signed the paper, as he could do with her the minute he married her.

Lyddie had barely stepped inside the room; she now stepped back until she was level with Freeman. "Might we speak a moment in private?"

"In private?"

"I have a question about this paper. I apologize for not thinking of it earlier."

She stepped out of the room, leaving Freeman little choice but to follow her to her own chamber.

"What is this, Lydia? We've several gentlemen waiting."

"Yes. And I apologize. Again. But 'tis here I surrender all, and if I do not ask you now—"

"Ask me what? Good heaven."

"I would not surrender all to be less than I was before."

"I don't in the least take your meaning. What do you surrender?"

"My interest in the third of the house. I sign it away today and what do I have tomorrow?"

Freeman appeared to lengthen and straighten. "A husband. Whenever it is you deem yourself able to marry him. I would think, as trade—"

" 'Tis not a question of husband, 'tis a question of house. Nor is it a question of trade. Do you not see? I give away my life interest in a third of the property today in exchange for nothing. I cannot think Mr. Otis, nor, indeed, you, as a man of law, would wish to sign such a document."

"I cannot for one minute comprehend what it is you fuss about. At our marriage you lose all dower rights in the house; 'tis so stated in Edward's will. He well understood that if you remarried you would have no need of such rights. This thing that happens today, then, is only the same thing that would happen a few days hence at our marriage."

"But must it be so?"

"What is it you ask, Lydia? Have it out and let us get on with this business."

Lyddie thought. What was it she asked? "I ask to keep my life interest in the third of the house while you take title from Clarke and continue it thus into our marriage. Cannot such a document be written?"

He stared at her. "Do you know what you ask?" he said finally. "Do you know what insult you do me?"

"I know what I ask. I think it not insult to you, but necessity to me."

"Are you're saying to me that you refuse to sign this paper?"

"I do not wish to sign this paper. I cannot sign this paper. Not as it leaves me now."

Freeman's eyes shrunk to hard, wet pebbles, his jaw lumped and hardened, his skin took on the look of a parchment stained with port wine. Lyddie fixed her eyes on the pebbles, willing them to open, to soften, to see, but they turned away; he turned away. He left her. She heard the study door open and a short, sharp indistinct exchange take place; she heard the study door open and close again and then the outer door open and close. An excited gabble had broken out in the study and the door opened again.

"Mehitable!"

Fast steps, the fastest Lyddie had heard since the birth of little Edward. "What, Nathan? What on earth?"

" 'Tis again! Your mother! 'Tis too much to be borne! Again she refuses to sign the paper!"

"No. You cannot be right in this."

"Can I not? I have it direct from Freeman. Refuses! And now he's gone off to Barnstable and left her on my charge, and here we are, back at the start. Well, she'll not be back where she started, not under this roof."

Lyddie strained her ears to catch Mehitable's response, but it appeared there was none. Lyddie had not expected her daughter would fight her husband for her, but she had hoped for some word that would affirm the recently rewoven thread between Lyddie and her daughter. But, in truth, how strong had that thread ever been? The little girl had rushed to her father's arms at his every return home while Lyddie had stood aside watching—nurturing, yes, and teaching and protecting as she could, but always watching. But watching for what?

Her last child to die, too. The awesome truth struck her like a blow. But she had no time to see the knowledge through to any purpose—heavy heels approached her door. Lyddie picked up the extra skirt and shift she'd brought with her and folded them, anticipating her son's message, but the person who appeared at her door was not Clarke, but Mehitable, her previously bloodless cheeks flushed. She looked at the neat clothes on the bed.

"So. You would leave us and go back to Father's house."

"Have I a choice?"

"Choice! You have every choice! You've always had every choice!"

"You would sign such a paper, then. You would give over all your interest in a property—"

"I would give over the past and look to the future, Mother."

"Do you not see this is what I do? Look to keep some little charge of my future?"

"But why, Mother, when you have a man of scruple who will keep charge for you?"

"Any man may lose his scruple when his interest comes against another's."

"So you speak of my husband now."

"I speak of any man."

"No, you do not. You speak of my husband and the money you say he stole from you. How could you stand in his house and accuse him so?"

"Do you think I would say such a thing if I didn't know it to be true?"

"If indeed that's what you think, you'd best go."

"I'd not leave you, Daughter, nor the babe, in time of need."

"We've no need of you. Go."

34

She'd been gone ten days, and in her absence the peas and cherries had ripened and the honeysuckle and roses had passed their bloom. The house looked better since the furniture had been returned but was stifling hot after being shut up so long; Lyddie propped open the doors and windows and set to work, thinking that the poor house had suffered such a year of off-and-on neglect it must be anxious to get shed of her. She threw out some spoiled milk and the cucumbers she'd laid out to pickle; she turned and reshaped her cheeses, she cleaned a bloody smear off the window glass and carted the dead pigeon that lay below it into the woods; she picked the peas and cherries, weeded the garden, swept and sanded the floor, knocked down the cobwebs, milked the cow, put out her milk pans, ate a supper of the fresh fruit and a crust and dropped into bed like a felled pine. She slept to moonrise and woke, her mind working almost before her body wakened.

She was, as Nathan had said, back at the start. Freeman was finished with her and back at Barnstable; Nathan had again cut her loose; Sam Cowett had . . . Sam Cowett had done nothing, but Lyddie could as little return to work for him as she could stay at Nathan's or chase Freeman to Barnstable. And did she want to chase Freeman to Barnstable? When Lyddie thought of Freeman she saw the unfamiliar, pebbled eyes; she had lost any picture of the other Freeman, the one who had so often quickened her spirits and brightened her mind. How was it that once they'd agreed to wed they'd come at everything from opposite banks, neither one able to find a crossing place? What had changed? Or had they changed? Lyddie thought over each of the boggy spots: Mehitable's travail, Cowett's visit, the paper, and tried to think where she might have done different so as to carry one or the other across the flood. If she had agreed to the early marriage date . . . But how could she, with her daughter unable to feed herself or to sit up? And why should she, when it was clearly nothing but a test of wills? Why should Freeman care so much about marriage one week over marriage the next?

But what of Cowett's visit? Perhaps if Lyddie had stayed inside when Cowett had appeared and saved her son the public humiliation that had so disturbed Freeman . . . but it had not, of course, been her son's humiliation that had disturbed Freeman, it had been his own. He'd ordered Lyddie inside and she'd disobeyed, in front of Nathan, and, more to the point, in front of Cowett, who had come to see Lyddie, who might not have left in peace without seeing Lyddie. But why should he not see Lyddie?

And the paper, too; why should such a small request . . . but no. In fairness, Lyddie knew her request there had been anything but small. In fact, she could well imagine it to be unheard of. It would, of course, be a blow to any man's pride, and especially a man such as Freeman, who prided himself on being fair to all, but why must it be such a blow? Why would a man object to a wife's legal right to live where he intended her to live, unless to demonstrate his mastery over her? And having demonstrated a desire for such mastery, how could he expect her to sign away her solitary counterweight? She might have thought ahead and saved Freeman that humiliation in front of Nathan and Eldred and Griffith, but how to think ahead of a thing you didn't see until you'd looked down at it on the table? So, yes, she'd obstructed Freeman again, and humiliated him again, and minutes later he'd galloped off to Barnstable. But would Freeman be lying in his bed now as she lay in hers, wondering what flaw in him had caused their rift? No. He would be congratulating himself on so near an escape from so unmalleable a wife. But, of course, he had posted their marriage intentions, and therefore he could not legally escape until Lyddie or the court made it legal. Well, then, she would make it legal.

The first thing on rising Lyddie took out her letter book and composed her letter.

Dear Mr. Freeman,

As the circumstances between us would appear to prevent any future domestic harmony, I hereby release you from your bond of engagement.

Yours sincerely, Lydia H. Berry

She hailed Jabez Gray on his way to the landing, and in learning that Seth Cobb was loading clams for Barnstable at the Point of Rock, she set off in that direction, taking the path through the sedge. As the sun heated her and the sweat ran over her she thought of her spring journey in the opposite direction; it seemed she was to spend her life going forward and back, forward and back, never leaving the age-old track that had been prescribed her.

Cobb's ship lay canted on its side in the low channel not far from shore; oxcarts piled with barrels rattled over the sand flats to the ship, where a team of men rolled the barrels out of the carts and tossed them on board. Lyddie tucked up her skirt and trudged over the flats to the boat; Seth Cobb saw her from the deck and swung to the ground.

Lyddie held out the letter. "I understand you sail for Barnstable."

Cobb read the name on the letter and grinned. "Love letter, is it? Never fear, I'll deliver it with my own hand."

"And when do you plan to return to Satucket?"

"We'll be back in Satucket tomorrow, wind and weather complying."

Lyddie wished him fair sailing, thanked him for taking charge of her letter, and retreated across the sand.

Lyddie looked out for Cobb's sail the next day and saw it pull into Robbin's hill at half noon. She waited, and although an assortment of men and carts passed by her house, Seth Cobb himself didn't venture along till near four. She stepped out and met him in the road.

"I trust you had a fair voyage, Mr. Cobb?"

"I did and I thank you. And if you come to inquire on the safe delivery of your letter you may count it done. I put the letter straight in Freeman's hand myself and stood by as he read it, in case there was a return, but he said no. I surmised to him that he'd be taking another trip to Satucket soon, but he said he was quite busy just yet at Barnstable." Here Cobb frowned, as if he'd finally captured the sense of something gone wrong.

"I did offer to wait for a return," he repeated.

"That's quite all right, Mr. Cobb. 'Twas none required."

They said their good-byes and Cobb moved on.

35

August came as it always came: hot and humid at the start, then drying and dropping down until by the end they'd had their first night's chill. Schooners full of blubber began to arrive from Canada and the try yard grew busy, filling the air with the heavy, noxious smell that had always meant prosperity, if not for Lyddie's house now, then at least for the village as a whole. The English hay, salt hay, flax, and rye were harvested. The mill wheel never stopped churning. Lyddie picked her watermelons, took them to Sears to trade for turnip seed, and sowed the seed for a late harvest; at the same time she managed to sell Sears two pair of wool stockings, and her hopes of survival rose, to dash quickly once she returned home and saw her dwindling woodpile. She collected Edward's ax and a tow sack and returned to the woodlot, intent on cutting up the windfall for kindling, but she hadn't been at it more than an hour when she looked up and saw the long, dark shadow moving through the trees as smoothly as warm oil. Lyddie propped the ax against a tree and turned to meet him, her own movements stiff as scorched paper.

He came up and stopped an easy distance from her. "So Freeman puts you to chop his wood?"

"Mr. Freeman's gone back to Barnstable."

"And when do you marry?"

"We do not. He's thought better of the idea."

"And what do you think of it?"

"I don't think at all. I've given it up as bad practice."

He bent over to pick up the ax, but Lyddie stopped him. "Please don't, Mr. Cowett. I wish to say something to you. I wish to express my great remorse over what transpired at our last meeting. My son—"

"Owns no remorse, I'd wager."

"No."

"I see you don't live with him any longer."

"I do not."

"You stay here and make your own way?"

"I attempt it, yes."

Cowett picked up a dry branch, snapped it under his boot, and tossed it into the tow sack. "I'm in want of housekeeping yet."

Lyddie hesitated, the reason she'd given up the job hanging thick in the air between them. She reached for the ax, but he caught her elbow with one hand and removed the ax with the other. She expected him to set off chopping, but he dropped the ax and stood staring down at the part of her sleeve that his fingers still encircled, transfixed. Rebecca's gown, Lyddie realized. She was wearing Rebecca's gown, and of course he would know the gown as he'd known the wife. It took him some time to pull his eyes off the dress and fix them on her face, but the hand stayed as it lay. "You'll come to work?"

"I think—"

"You said you gave up thinking."

"One must think at times."

"One must give it up at times."

If Lyddie hadn't understood the words, she would have understood the hand. It slid upward, over Rebecca's sleeve, familiar and warm, cupping the softer part of her arm. She had stepped away from that hand once and she could step away from it now, or she could stop thinking and take this simple thing that was being offered: the comfort of someone else's living, breathing flesh to knock the dead out of her own. And where lay the sin in it, Indian or English? Neither of them belonged to another. When she thought of Eben Freeman now, she thought of him lying warm and sated in a pair of hired arms at some Barnstable tavern.

Sam Cowett's other hand cupped her other elbow; Lyddie found herself leaning forward until his breath rippled her hair; he slid both hands upward along Rebecca's sleeves until the backs of his fingers brushed against the edges of her breasts, and he turned his hands and caught and lifted them. Lyddie felt as naked as if her clothing lay beside her on the ground, but he didn't attempt to take away the dress, he used it as a pair of handles to push her backward against the rock. His hands slid upward over Rebecca's calico to Lyddie's breasts again and down to Lyddie's thighs; she felt the cold loss in one part as he brought up the heat in another, the desolation when the hands left her altogether, until she realized he'd just reached for his breeches and pushed them down. She clutched at his massive back, his hard buttocks, his long thighs; there was too much of him, not enough of him, over her, around her, in; she lost track of her hands, his hands; the dress balled up between them, but he wouldn't take the time to remove it, Lyddie wouldn't take the time, there was no time, they were finished.

It had seemed so easy: the plunging together and falling apart without any heavy landing; they'd caught their wind leaning on the rock, he'd touched her face, she'd touched his wrist, they'd departed in their separate directions. But as soon as Lyddie regained her own house, in front of the few remaining markers of her old world, Lyddie felt the sting of shame.

She spent a hot, burning, sleepless night, and the next morning she went to see Cowett to tell him that what had once been done could not be done again, but he was waiting for her; he pulled her straight into his damp, distressed sheets, and she went with him, thinking, *once more, just this once more,* but he must have felt it in her, felt her as stiff and awkward as that young girl Edward had lain with in the barn. He pulled back and looked at her.

"What's tied you up?"

Lyddie called up the old list, thinking this time she might find a different answer to each question, but she sailed by all of them without flinching, landing once again at the foot of Eben Freeman, but this time for a different reason. Did she wish to be no more than that girl in the tavern? What now described any difference between that girl and herself, a few coins passed from hand to hand?

Sam Cowett gave her a shake. "Come. What's got you?"

"There's a girl in town makes her way off traveling men," she began.

"So you wish to charge for this now, too, along with the cooking and cleaning?"

Lyddie lifted her face to look at him. She remembered a time when she'd been unable to see inside the black eyes; now they were laughing, mocking her shame, and it blew away like so much wind.

36

The Lyddie who sinned walked about town more comfortably than the Lyddie who hadn't, and perhaps for that reason the new secret stayed secret, aided by the fact that Nathan Clarke had so thoroughly squelched the old rumor once he'd determined to accept her back into his family that to try to circulate the old tale now would have made him, not Lyddie, appear foolish. Lyddie officially returned to work for Sam Cowett, but as this was now old news, the townspeople paid little notice, and she found she could come and go under cover of that employment. Whenever Cowett was in from fishing Lyddie took all her meals with him and often lingered in his bed to be stroked awake at dawn, but she wished to court no trouble; when she traveled from his house to hers at such odd hours she traveled through the wood, not the road, and Cowett never came to her house at all.

During Lyddie's waking hours the person she lay with was always Sam Cowett, their mournful, desperate urge their own, but in those first days she would sometimes come out of her dreams with the Indian's hand between her legs and think it was Edward, or feel the stroke of sure, gentle fingers along her throat and be convinced they were Freeman's. In either case, when she opened her eyes and saw the dark, carved face beside her a wild panic would wash over her, but as the weeks went by both the half-dreams and the panic left her.

Lyddie continued collecting coin for her cooking and cleaning, and bargained separately for Cowett to supply her with wood; she carefully measured out her remaining coins in piles: this for hay, this for meat, this for grain.

Sometimes, as the weeks went by and the days chilled and Lyddie mended Sam Cowett's breeches or emptied his night jar or woke beside him hot and naked, she felt herself as married as she'd ever been to Edward. Sometimes she even thought of him as much like Edward, especially when they came together in that same old rush between his comings and goings, but other times she surprised a look in Sam Cowett that was total stranger, and whenever that happened, she felt a small seed of panic that she had dared to tie her fate to this man in a way she had not dared with Eben Freeman. But whenever such thoughts tried to topple her she reminded herself of the one big difference between the two situations, the one cornerstone of her existence: whatever else she might lose, she still had her own bed, and her own third of a house to keep it in. For the rest, she would manage.

One day at the end of September Lyddie milked the cow and put her to grass and was about to leave for Cowett's when someone knocked violently on her front door. She rushed to open it and found Nathan Clarke on the doorstep.

"Good morning, Mother." He stepped in and minutely surveyed the keeping room, stepped into the southwest chamber and surveyed that as well, then ran nimbly up the stairs and trod around in the attics. Lyddie's first thought was that he'd come to reclaim his furnishings, but when he returned to the keeping room he said, "Very good, Mother. I'm pleased to see you've got things back to rights." He stepped outside and in a minute was back inside, holding a stiff-jawed Silas Clarke by the elbow, a crumpled Patience and the five children trailing behind, carrying or dragging a meager collection of parcels.

"Sad to say, my Brother Clarke has lost his home to debt, but fortunately I was able to offer him accommodation here. Now then, Brother and Sister, you will understand that my mother holds right to a third of the fireplace and that chamber over there, as well as the buttery and pantry and cow space in the barn, but you've the run of the rest. You'll find ample room and a nice collection of assorted beds for the children in the attics, and I'm sure the two of you will be quite comfortable in that southwest chamber. Your rent will be deducted from your pay at the tannery, Brother. I believe that takes care of all our business. Good-day to you both. And good-day to you, Mother."

He left them.

Silas Clarke sat at the keeping room table and began to eat the pie Lyddie had set out to take to Cowett's, while Clarke's wife and children and Lyddie pulled beds out from under the eaves, aired and restuffed ticks, and spread them with the thin bedding Patience Clarke had managed to save from auction. Lyddie could no more afford to feed a family of seven than she could afford to sail to England, but as the five small faces watched in obvious torment as their father devoured the pie, Lyddie set out a loaf and a wedge of cheese and six good-size cups of the milk she had meant to turn into a pudding.

By the time the meal was eaten and the dishes cleared it was midmorning, and Lyddie was unsurprised to hear a second knock or to open the door on Sam Cowett. The five children shrank back at the sight of him, and Lyddie couldn't blame them for it—the Indian's face was as hard and dark as her iron kettle.

"You don't come," he said.

Lyddie waved a hand at the various Clarkes, ranged behind her like a row of tombstones. "My son has just moved in his tenants."

Cowett surveyed the silent Clarkes. The two men gave each other minimal nods. "I thought you sickened. Or dead."

"I'll be along shortly."

"I'll be gone shortly."

"Is there new instruction?"

He surveyed the room again. "No." He left them.

When Lyddie reached his house he was, indeed, gone, but she was not unhappy to find the place empty. Without him catching her up to take her into his bed she was able to complete a good number of tasks that had been let slide and still leave before the house's shadow had stretched as far as the barn.

But when she returned to her own house she found Silas Clarke had already disposed of half her brandy bottle. She moved swiftly across the keeping room and snatched it off the table, went to her room and stowed it under Rebecca's gowns, which had been put back in the bottom of her chest. She took up her new, unused letter book, returned to the keeping room and slapped it on the table.

"This is the tally book. I begin writing in it tomorrow. Any food or drink you take from me will be paid for, Mr. Clarke. Mrs. Clarke, you have the main cupboards for your larder and I'll clear a shelf for you in the cellar; the pantry, however, is mine only."

"Hah!" Silas said. "I've two vultures to live with now, have I?"

"I work to make my way, Mr. Clarke. I feed off nobody."

"You feed off that Indian. 'Tis him pays you, doesn't he? And so he should. So he should. Him who widows you supports you, that's what I say."

"Mr. Clarke," Patience said, "would you care to give me some assistance with an unstable bed leg?"

"I give my assistance where 'tis most needed, and 'tis most needed right here. Widow Berry. Poor fool. Do you not hear what they say?"

"'Tis wobbling terribly, Mr. Clarke," Patience said. "If you wish to sleep in comfort anytime soon—"

"A wobbly bed leg. That's my brother, you may count on it. Never give away a whole when you might give away a part. And at such a rent."

But he got up from the table and worked his way into his new chamber, where nothing was heard resembling repair of a bed leg, but something was heard resembling a poorly governed body falling onto a husk-filled bed tick. Soon afterward a snore that left little to an angry hog filled the house, and Patience Clarke emerged. Her worn-out face and the hollowed-out eyes of the children, still standing stumplike around the walls, pulled at Lyddie's heart.

She spoke quietly to the mother. "Have you any funds?"

"I've kept out a small purse. Brother Clarke has set up my husband with a job at his tannery. Tomorrow I'll go to Sears's store and stock our cupboard, but for tonight, for the children—" She reached into her apron and pulled out the purse.

Lyddie pushed it away. "Tomorrow begins the tally book. Children, come." The children rushed the table and Lyddie set out what seemed a vast part of her store of pickles, cheese, beer, and bread.

Lyddie ate her own meal in her room and retired early.

That night the first real cold and the new dream descended together. Since Edward's death, Lyddie believed she'd not slept two solid nights together; she woke with every creak of pine bough, every shriek of owl, every snap of fire. These abrupt wakings kept her dreams fresh for at least the period of time it took her to fall back asleep; some stayed fresh till morning. Most of her dreams were old stories, peopled with dead husbands or children, and at least initially this new dream seemed no different. It started as many of Lyddie's dreams did: with her daughter Mehitable. Mehitable sat by the fire, sewing on Edward's coat, shortening a sleeve so as to accommodate her husband's lesser stature. Lyddie sat on the other side of the fire, knitting a pile of stockings that grew up so high it nearly hid her daughter from her. But Lyddie could see the coat; she recognized the coat; she spoke to her daughter.

"Why trouble yourself over that hem, Daughter? The coat wants a sleeve."

But there Mehitable held up the coat, intact in every way, Edward's coat, the coat he'd drowned in.

Lyddie woke to a flying pulse, accompanied by a lift of something like hope. The coat was whole. Edward was alive. That was his explosive breath across the passage . . .

But it wasn't. Lyddie sat up. She had long experience with what the night could do to reason; she would not give way to it. She lay back down and cushioned her ears with her bolster.

The Clarkes were up and out early, Patience and the children to Sears's store, Silas to the tannery. Lyddie arrived at Cowett's before he'd set out.

Without hello he began, "Clarke means to keep those people there?"

"He's within his right. He's made the division according to the plan laid out by Mr. Freeman."

"Mr. Freeman." Cowett pushed away his plate and mug and stood up. Lyddie leaned over to clear away the table, but Cowett came up at the rear, hooking her around the waist, burying his face in her neck. "I've no love for that man Freeman," he said. "Or Clarke."

"Which Clarke?"

"Either. But the one you've got under your roof's the greater menace. You'd best watch him."

"I think I'd best watch you," she said, laughing, because he'd already pulled up her skirt, but it was too late, he'd found her damp crevice and begun to work her with his fingers till she quickened, then he pushed into her from behind until she was left knee-less, clutching at the table.

He settled his breeches, shoved the remains of the loaf in his sack, said, "Come tonight," and left her.

But Lyddie didn't go back that night; the house never lay quiet enough for her to feel safe in making her exit. Patience stayed up arranging her pots and trivets around her side of the fire; a bat got in and swooped through the attics; the smallest child was finally gotten to sleep and almost at once woke crying, and, at last, when Patience had given up and gone to bed, Silas came back from the tavern and stood on the stoop, thundering, "Open the door! Open the bloody door, you vile woman! Will you shut me out? I'll lay you open if you try it!"

Lyddie got up and found Patience Clarke hunched in front of the door, unwilling or unable to take the next move to open it.

"We needn't fear a man who can't find a latch and lift it," Lyddie said, and she stepped to the door and opened it.

"Oh, the bloody pair of you. You'd keep me out, would you? Or did you think I was that bloody murdering Indian? You should thank your stars I'm here to protect you."

"The door's not bolted, Mr. Clarke. But as of tomorrow night it will be. See you're in before dark or you may sleep at the tavern."

Lyddie left them in a stunned silence, but until she heard Silas's snore, a signal that he'd trouble them no further, she couldn't fall asleep. And when she finally slept, she dreamed, again, of Edward.

He lay on the keeping room table in Nathan Clarke's house, with the wound in his skull and a terrible grayness in the skin, so absolutely dead that Lyddie could only listen to herself in astonishment as she argued with Mehitable over her husband's clothes.

"No, you can't have the boots for Nate. No, no, Edward needs his coat, he's so greatly cold. Do you not feel his cold? And besides, you see? The coat is torn."

But Mehitable was already easing the coat off the cold body, the dead body, which Lyddie knew full well to be dead, and still she reached out to stop her daughter, slapping away her hands, and Nathan Clarke said, "Mother, don't be silly. You know that coat is mine now, to do with as I please."

And the next minute there was Nathan in an untorn coat and there was Edward naked on the table with the great hole in his head and Sam Cowett looming over him, saying, "You see, Widow Berry? Did I not tell you he was dead?"

But Lyddie knew she shouldn't believe him. She woke knowing it, and it stayed well into daylight, the insane notion that she shouldn't believe Sam Cowett when he told her Edward was dead.

37

Silas didn't go to the tannery the next day. Not trusting him with her pantry, Lyddie waited till Patience and the children had returned with their bundles from Sears's store, and by the time she got to Cowett's, again late, he was gone. He had a good deal of washing she might have caught up on, but instead she tended to his chamber and his meal and his floor and left before he returned.

Silas had got his drink from somewhere and sat at table shouting for his wife and children to bring him his pipe, his knife, his waistcoat, getting up only once to piss in the dooryard. Whenever Lyddie passed near he made some remark about the Indian, sometimes complimentary, such as one remark about the man's skill with an oar, but most times offensive. He called him the black stench, or the heathen slaver, or the keeper of the heathen whores. Altogether it gave Lyddie a headache: she spent the late afternoon working in the garden, and when she returned to the house she found women and children gone, Silas Clarke frozen in his chair at the table, and Sam Cowett leaning over him, speaking low.

"Are you clear on it? 'Tis your own life you'll pay with. You keep off or you'll keep in the ground." He swung around, saw Lyddie, and continued as if he were still talking to Silas. "Come." He walked out the door. Lyddie followed, but he kept walking ahead, down the road.

"Where are you going?"

"Where I can have you alone."

"I can't go there now. Think what these people might say."

He stopped and turned. "What care you what they say?"

"Less than you should, judging by the way you spoke to him just now. Do you wish to pay another fine? Or worse?"

"They can't hold me."

"I'm going back."

He caught her up, but she pulled free. "Will you think what you do? Anyone could come along the road and see."

" 'Tis all been said already. As you said. Come. Come with me now."

"No. Not now."

"Tonight."

"I'll see."

She hurried back down the road.

When Lyddie returned Patience Clarke had set out her family's supper on the table. Lyddie got her own bread and beer from the pantry, ate them in her own chamber and stayed there, listening as the house quieted down. It would have been easy enough to go out the back door, and if seen, declare a need for the necessary house; if unseen, she could continue freely through the woods to Cowett's and either return the same way in the dark or stay through midmorning and feign surprise on her return that no one had heard her leave before dawn.

Lyddie did neither. A general unease filled her. She lay fully clothed on top of her coverlet and reviewed the events of the day, trying to get at its cause, and came first against Sam Cowett's threat to Silas Clarke. Words, she thought, nothing but words, but words spoken against a life. And to what cause? Unease over Lyddie's safety while Silas Clarke remained under her roof? Very well, Lyddie could share the same unease. A drunken man with a kitchen knife might not choose his target with the greatest care, and although Lyddie had no wish to see Patience run through, she had less wish to be run through herself. But Cowett's words gave Lyddie a second cause for unease. They appeared to take his regard for Lyddie a step further than she had so far placed it. Any man making threat against a man's life, but especially an Indian making threat against a white man, put himself in grave danger of the law. Lyddie had no doubt that if Silas Clarke registered a complaint with the constable, Cowett would soon find himself in gaol at Barnstable. She should go to him, she thought. But to do what? Warn him? Thank him? Lie with him?

And still she didn't move, her mind now going back to Silas's words about heathen whores. What had happened to the young Indian woman who had walked back and forth to Cowett's every day, and then had not walked back and forth so very much at all? When Lyddie had first returned to Cowett's house it had seemed well kept, much better kept than Sam Cowett's efforts alone might have accounted for. Was Lyddie nothing but the white replacement of that heathen whore? Or had Silas's heathen whore been Lyddie all along? She'd been long absent from church; she'd believed Nathan Clarke's old rumors to have been squelched by Nathan Clarke, but what rumor was ever completely squelched? Hadn't Silas said the day before, "Do you not hear what they say?" Was everything ever said about Lyddie and Sam Cowett still alive and seething underground?

But what did Lyddie care about a drunken Silas Clarke's ramblings? He'd made little enough sense, his talk ranging from oars to whores. Yet Lyddie did not want to be found in the middle of the road pressed up against Cowett's body, and for him to do such a thing without thought to Lyddie's position took away some of this new idea of the great caring she'd been ready to lay at his door.

She would not go to him. Lyddie took off her skirt and shoes and stockings, got under the sheets, and fell into what she would have called a dreamless sleep, but when she woke it was as if she'd just wakened from the old dream, full of the conviction that she could not believe Sam Cowett.

Lyddie got up and dressed with impatience. There was no room for any doubt of Edward's death; Lyddie had laid out his cold, flaccid body with her own hands; she had watched his coffin go into the ground.

Lyddie breakfasted in her room again, tended her night jar, and left for Cowett's.

This time Cowett had waited for her, his mood no great improvement from the day before.

"What's took you? A half hour and I lose the tide."

"And what need you of a half hour?"

He pulled her into his chamber and would not be put off by her stiff flesh; he stroked her and stroked her till she softened, only easing into her at the last minute and then rushing his clothes so fast he ripped the tape off his shirt and had to find another.

After he'd gone Lyddie sat in his bed among the sheets that smelled of dark and light sweat together and mended Sam Cowett's shirt with Rebecca Cowett's needle. She couldn't have said the minute the old unease of the dream began, but it did begin, and stayed, and grew until at last, looking at the torn cloth, it came to her why she shouldn't believe Sam Cowett, what her dream had really been trying to tell her.

Sam Cowett had told her Edward's coat had torn in the attempted rescue, but she'd seen it herself, in real life and in the dream, over and over: Edward's sturdy work coat had survived whole.

During the day, as Lyddie put Sam Cowett's house in order and then returned to do the same to her own, sidestepping as best she could the many Clarkes, Edward's untorn coat meant only one thing to Lyddie: Sam Cowett had wished an excuse to offer Lyddie for his failure to save her husband, or, put even more simply, he had wished to salvage his pride. But that night, after she'd slid the bolt and thought with some irony that she did nothing but bolt the danger *in,* as Silas Clarke had obeyed her instruction and come back by dark, the matter of the untorn coat returned to disturb her sleep. *The coat tore,* Cowett had said. Could there be another motive for Sam Cowett saying Edward's coat had torn? What might have happened out there on the water that would make Cowett lie about it? Lyddie cast her mind back to every conversation she'd ever had about Edward's death, starting with Shubael's. *'Twas Sam Cowett got there first.* Shubael had had little to say about the drowning, and according to the later overheard conversation that Lyddie had somehow forgotten in all the confusion in her own life, he had feared Lyddie's questions. He had feared the Indian. But why? Because Shubael had seen something that implicated the Indian somehow, and if the Indian knew it, he wouldn't hesitate to protect himself at Shubael's expense? At the expense of Shubael's life?

No, no, no. Lyddie wouldn't think it. But Silas would. Had not Cowett threatened Silas's life the previous night? And what if Lyddie now put another interpretation on the Indian's little speech, put him not attempting to protect Lyddie, but attempting to protect himself? What else might Cowett wish Silas to keep off, if not Lyddie herself? What if the thing he wished Silas to keep off was not Lyddie at all, but the subject of Edward's death? The one man's experience with spirits would have told him what might come out of the other man's mouth. And things had come out of Silas's mouth. His words hammered at Lyddie's head. *Him who widows you supports you . . . Do you not hear what they say? . . . Bloody murdering Indian . . . skill with an oar . . .*

Lyddie threw back her covering and sat up, the bile rising in her chest, thinking of the gash in Edward's head, a gash the shape of an oar's blade. Oh, yes, things had come out of Silas Clarke's mouth, and Lyddie had only half heard them, and what she'd heard she'd dismissed as drunken nonsense, but now, sitting there sick, in the dark, she wondered if she mightn't have dismissed them too quickly. She closed her eyes and tried to remember what Jabez Gray had told her about Edward's drowning: the boat going over, the line and block tossed to the other men to bring them safe aboard, Sam Cowett finally going after Edward himself, with his oar . . . Good God, Jabez Gray had said it himself: Sam Cowett *went after him with his oar.* In that dark, churning water who could say what blow might have been struck with it? Perhaps confident of a fatal blow he'd then gone through the rest of the act, taking hold of Edward's coat and pulling him in, but once he'd seen that Edward breathed, that Edward lived . . . oh, hadn't Jabez Gray said it in just those words? *I saw your husband breathing, I saw his chest heaving . . . he was alive . . .*

But then what? Lyddie didn't know. Jabez Gray had not seen, he'd turned away to tend Shubael's boat, and when he'd turned back Edward was gone. *That's all I can tell you. Gone.*

No, no, no. It was not true. It was another trick of the night. Lyddie would wake in the morning and remember something else someone had said that would make nonsense of all of it. To begin, why would Sam Cowett wish Edward Berry dead? In all their years communing over the woodlot Lyddie had never heard a wrong word between the two men. But even as the forepart of her mind formed that thought, her memory dredged up something else, some words battered about in the wind between the Gray brothers one day after meeting as they discussed Sam Cowett: . . . *I guess I'll not quarrel with him . . . No? Then I guess you're not Edward Berry . . .*

But why would they quarrel? There was nothing, nothing . . . but there was. Of course there was. If Lyddie looked through the window behind her she might stare at it in the moonlight. The land. A valuable piece of land, passing from Cowett hands to Berry hands without a thing given in compensation for it. Lyddie had seen the deed of gift herself and hadn't missed the fact that no Indian who signed with a primitive *V* could have written such formal English. What made her think he would even understand such language? Say, then, that something underhanded had gone on to move the land from Cowett to Berry; say this history had festered over two generations to leave Sam Cowett with an aching grudge. Had not Eben Freeman called him "a man with many grudges to feed, old and new"? Had not Sam Cowett himself referred to God's scales as balancing land with water? Would Sam Cowett take it on himself, when the opportunity presented itself, to right an old theft of land with a death by water?

Lyddie wished to say no, she tried to say no, but interrupting her were more questions of her own role in it. If Sam Cowett had a grudge against Edward, if Edward's death were not enough, what else might he do to hurt the Berrys? He might attempt to stymie the house sale, but once he saw the wife and read a certain rebellion in her, he might have fixed on another path. How easy it had been for him to lure her, first from her faith, and then from her family, and next from her community, in the last gasp putting her at odds with the one man who might right her with all.

But had Sam Cowett really done all that? Lyddie didn't need the clear light of morning to tell her that no, of course, he hadn't. She couldn't blame him for herself. But he had helped. Lyddie had leaned so far toward each of those things that a push by any little feather might have toppled her, and Sam Cowett had been more than a little feather. All that talk of Indian gods and Indian morals, had it all been toward one end, Lyddie disgraced and dependent and his to save or destroy as the spirit moved him?

No, no, no. Lyddie wouldn't believe it. She closed her eyes and thought of his hands on her willing body, but even in that she now saw a manipulation of the flesh that paralleled a manipulation of the mind. How else could Lydia Berry, descended of the very religious elders who had formed the moral laws that ruled the colony, come to such a place where she could find no sin in such acts as she had committed? How had it come to pass that this man of all others had been allowed to strip away her beliefs along with her dress? And there Lyddie remembered something else almost more painful than all the rest. Sam Cowett had stripped away Lyddie's dress many a time, but that first day, that first time, he had made no move to discard Rebecca's. The man who had worked so hard to cut every last thread that bound her to Edward had kept Rebecca's dress between them like a shield.

Morning did not deliver Lyddie her usual reprieve from the night's thoughts, but it did leave them in greater confusion. Where the night before every last piece of information had marched along one behind the other like a neat row of ants, now that line stood broken and scattered as if a hungry bird had dropped down in its midst. While Lyddie wasn't ready to deny outright the night's conclusion, she had some trouble finding her way over the old track.

But where the ants wouldn't line up for her, the stars did; having risen late she was just coming from the necessary when Jabez Gray came by on his way to the landing. Lyddie hurried into the road after him.

"Widow Berry!" he greeted her. "Is all well?"

"An ill night," she said. "Would you be so kind as to tell Mr. Cowett I'll not be there to clean this morning?"

"I'll tell him. What's got you, a stomach? I can tell by looking at you. You've got the color of it. I lost three days to it last month and nothing settled me till I took a good purge and followed it with a tonic of warm wine and skunk cabbage."

"Thank you, Mr. Gray, I'll try that."

"You'll hear them say mint, or gentian, or chamomile, but I tell you, Widow, 'tis the skunk cabbage cures it. Mind you, once you go to bile, you've got to get in something yellow. Gold thread, perhaps, or goldenseal—"

"I thank you, Mr. Gray, for taking my message."

"All right, then, I'm happy to do it. Now is there anything else I might do for you?"

Lyddie paused, considered, leaped. "I do have one thing more. A question that's long been troubling me. If you won't mind going back to the subject."

"No, no, no, we have to keep our health. After that—"

"I don't mean my health, Mr. Gray. I mean my husband, Edward."

"Oh. Aye." His jaw slacked. He stood silent.

"I dream of it yet. Of Edward alive in the water, still breathing."

"Good Lord, I should not have—"

"No, no, I need to know all of it. You said to me, if I remember, that Mr. Cowett had him in his hands while he yet breathed, and then something happened."

"Damnedest thing. I'd just heard this great huzzah from the men because we'd got him. And then I turned around and . . . nothing." He shook his head.

"And Mr. Cowett?"

"What of him?"

"He said nothing? No word of explanation?"

"A few words I'd not tell a lady, if I may say that much to you. A ruddy great streak of them. And something about his coat. His coat tearing out of his hands. But he wouldn't give him up. He kept flailing around in the water with the oar until we almost went over ourselves and we had to put to in a hurry. After that we were too far off the spot. He went back, though. Kept going back. Set me at the stern and stood up in the bow, yelling at us to peel our eyeballs, but we saw nothing. Nothing. I'll tell you this, Widow Berry, no men tried harder, but there comes a time when you say, all right, then, we've lost him. A hard thing to say to yourself, but it comes down to it sometimes: you've got to say to yourself, 'Tis over. We've lost him." He said the words so gently Lyddie couldn't mistake the direction of the message.

She'd taken the coward's way; she was sensible of it and yet didn't regret it for a minute. She needed the day to think. She could see two versions: a Sam Cowett in honest distress over the loss of his friend, shouting out curses, jabbing at the water that hid him long past the point of reason, but what of the coat? The thought of the coat took Lyddie to the second version, in which a Sam Cowett in grudging fury tinged with fear of being caught strikes Edward down with the oar, but as Edward still rises Cowett must pretend a rescue, only letting go when he feels no one is looking, blaming a torn coat, continuing to jab the water to make sure Edward is under, crisscrossing the black water to make sure he hasn't surfaced somewhere farther along.

Lyddie's stomach began to churn for real. She lay down on the bed and pulled up the coverlet. She might actually have slept; she roused to the sound of voices in the keeping room and a strong sense of living an old day over.

Sam Cowett: "I've come to see the Widow Berry."
Patience Clarke: "I'm sorry, sir, she's not well today."
Sam Cowett: "I'll see her."
Patience Clarke: "Sir! Sir!"

But Lyddie had no hope of someone like Patience waylaying someone like Cowett; boots clipped across the floor and Lyddie's chamber door flew open, snapping hard shut behind him. He took a knife out of its sheath and jammed the latch with it.

Lyddie tossed back her coverlet and got up.

"Gray says you're ill."

"I'm a good deal better, thank you."

"I had you dead. Again."

"I'm not dead or anything near it. And you'll give us away with all this visiting, especially behind closed doors. Please, open it."

He didn't move. "You asked Gray about your husband."

"I did, yes. He happened by at a troubled moment."

"What troubled it, Clarke?"

"No one. A dream."

"What of?"

Lyddie stayed silent.

Cowett stepped toward her. Lyddie stepped backward. Cowett stopped still.

"So. You listen to this fool in his drink and are afraid of me now."

"No." But she looked at the door, and he saw her looking. He crossed the room, pulled out the knife, sheathed it, and banged out, one door, two doors. The end of it.

38

A lone sail swept into the bay and moored at the landing. The first time the carts rumbled by Lyddie paid no notice. The second time she noticed but said nothing. The third time she asked the oldest Clarke boy, who stood at the window, "What's all this traffic?"

"Some Indians. With barrels."

The fourth time the boy ran right out into the road, and when he came back in he had a biscuit and the story. Scotto Hallet had landed to take on supplies and crew to make a last trip north after whales, and the big Indian was shipping out with him. They were traveling back and forth with the cart, refitting and provisioning from Bangs's chandlery.

The boy ran up and down the road for two days, happily reporting on progress: the big Indian had replaced some shingles on the roof; the livestock had been carted off to Mrs. Gray's; an Indian woman had picked over the garden; the fire had gone out; and, finally, the sloop had sailed. Lyddie walked down the road past the lifeless house as far as the rise and saw the dirty white triangle of sail just piercing the horizon. She watched until it disappeared, then continued down the road to the landing, thinking to recapture her old habit of walking the shore, but as she stepped onto the flat she saw a fresh-painted sloop in the channel ahead, several men swarming her deck, and Shubael Hopkins standing on the sand talking to Seth Cobb. He saw Lyddie and his hand shot in the air in greeting. Seth Cobb tipped his head in a bow, and Lyddie felt she had little choice but to join them.

Shubael greeted her with, "And what do you think of our vessel, Cousin?"

"She's lovely," Lyddie answered truthfully.

Shubael elbowed Seth Cobb. "You see? All fall in love with her at first sight." He turned back to Lyddie, his old reticence around her forgotten in the glow of this newfound love. "As soon as she's fitted we take our first run to Barnstable. Did I tell you, Cobb, how tight to the wind she sails?"

"Aye, aye, a dozen times now. Widow Berry, I warn you, walk away now or you'll spend the next hour telling your cousin how tight and trim and perfect his vessel looks. Hopkins, you've done well. In truth, I'm quite jealous of you."

He set off.

Alone with Lyddie, Shubael grew solemn, but Lyddie no longer detected any apprehension over her presence. She could understand the change in him; he would have heard Silas Clarke's tavern babble and would know that another had done his dirty work for him; besides, Cowett was no longer at hand to trouble him.

As for Lyddie, she held no grudge against Shubael; one person afraid could not blame another for being so. "She's truly a pretty thing, Cousin," she said. "I fear she'll tempt you away from us too often."

Shubael turned on her eagerly. "And who would not be tempted? Are you not tempted? Have you no business at Barnstable? It would be my great pleasure to carry you there. If we have such wind as—"

"No, no," Lyddie said. "I've no business at Barnstable. But I wish you every success in her. What have you named her?"

He looked down and up. "The *Betsey.*"

"Ah. A fine name."

He beamed at her.

Lyddie spent the rest of the day busying herself in her room, replacing her summer bed tick with the down one, quilting a petticoat, mending stockings, but as busy as she kept, it wasn't long before the feelings she'd run ahead of most of the day caught up with her and ran her down. But how to name what it was that laid her out? Was this deadness in her relief or dread? Were these poundings of her heart fear or anger? And who owned the tears, the Indian? Edward? Eben Freeman? Or were they for some other thing she could only feel without naming?

Silas Clarke carried home all the talk from the tavern. There appeared to be little surprise over the fact that the Indian had left for the north; the surprise was that he'd waited till so late in the season. Some blamed the dead wife; some blamed drink; some blamed the inborn, contrary nature of the Indian. As far as Lyddie could tell, no one, openly at least, factored her into the equation.

But Lyddie had other problems now, or, rather, the same old one. No matter how neatly Patience Clarke kept her shelves, they were seldom full enough for a husband, wife, and five children, and Lyddie's own pantry frequently got raided. Lyddie knew it and even saw it and had no heart to snatch a piece of bread out of a hungry child's hand, but when she caught Silas Clarke ripping open a fresh loaf she shouted so loudly he swung around with the loaf pressed to his chest like a shield.

"Blast you, woman, you war-whoop like some Indian!"

"Mr. Clarke, you will pay for that loaf."

"And what did you think, I was stealing it? Write it in the book and clear out of my way."

"And the beer barrel. I'm marking you down for half."

"Bah! I've not touched your stinking rat piss. Here, step aside or be sorry you didn't."

Lyddie stepped aside. She had as little hope of collecting for the bread as she did for the beer, and if she didn't wish to starve feeding the Clarke family she would have to find some other kind of work, and find it in a hurry.

But the theft of her food was not the only harm Silas Clarke brought down on her. It soon became clear that as he brought home one kind of news from the tavern, he left off another. He hadn't been so blind drunk as to miss the implication of Sam Cowett's several visits, especially the last one, behind a closed bedroom door. Silas Clarke began to look at Lyddie with a certain air of speculation, and soon after that, the Myrick sisters cut off their chatter when Lyddie came into Sears's store and Caleb Sears roughly tossed her change across the counter.

Another week of raids on her stores, another week of nothing but rebuff to all her work inquiries, another good chill descending, and Lyddie found herself where she thought she'd never be again: on Nathan Clarke's doorstep, lifting his knocker.

Hassey opened the door and called behind her in a hoarse whisper, "Madam! 'Tis the widow here!"

Mehitable came into view with the babe on her hip. Hassey backed away. Neither woman spoke, but when Lyddie held out her arms, Mehitable laid the infant in them, a fat, rosy child, fresh-fed and drowsy. "Oh, Daughter," Lyddie said. "It thrives and you thrive. I'll see no happier sight in my lifetime."

Mehitable's eyes teared. Or did it just appear so through the film in Lyddie's? But soon enough Nathan Clarke stuck his head out of his study.

" 'Tis Mother," Mehitable said.

"I need you to tell me that?" Nathan said. "Rather you tell me her business."

"She comes to see her grandchild only."

"She has no grandchild. She's no part of this family. Tell her to be gone."

Lyddie reluctantly handed the babe back to its mother. "In truth, Nathan, my business is with you. It concerns your brother and his family. They invade my stores and strap me beyond my capacity."

"And what do you tell me this for?"

"They're your tenants. You've arranged to extract your rent from Mr. Clarke's pay at the tannery; perhaps you could also extract their board."

He laughed. "You expect me to run your collections for you?"

"Or perhaps if you speak to Mr. Clarke—"

"You speak to him. You seem to have little trouble carping at men. And as we come to that subject, what do you hear from your Mr. Freeman?"

"I hear nothing from Mr. Freeman."

"Hah! Did I not tell you, Wife? You said he would not so easily give over! A lot you know of it. And now, with this latest we hear—" He broke off, even Nathan Clarke not quite able to look at her. It must have been quite the shock to him, to find his own falsehoods come back at him as truth. "All right, then, Mother, does that conclude our business?"

"I came to determine if you would make any effort to remedy an unlivable situation. As you do not, I'll now pursue my own course."

"Your own course! And what might that be? You can't look to Eben Freeman to throw the law after me now."

"Eben Freeman is not the only lawyer of my acquaintance."

Clarke stiffened as if he'd been thrust through. Lyddie had tossed the words out with little thought; indeed, she'd not gone as fast as Nathan to the legal issue, but once Nathan took her there, it began to come together in her mind. Why not find another lawyer and sue Nathan Clarke for her keep and care as Eben Freeman had once suggested? At the time it had seemed a poor choice, but as a last choice, it shone brighter. But how to pay for such legal service?

Lyddie walked home, making a mental list of her personal possessions, taking tally of the sum she might get for this plate or that coverlet, but when she walked into her house she found Silas Clarke rampaging through her room looking for the bottle of brandy. She was forced to drive him out with a pair of scissors held point-first. Once he had gone Lyddie jammed her latch with the scissors and dropped onto the bed, shaking, less from fear than from fury.

To have given up so much in order to secure her small corner and to now have that corner invaded set loose a new thing in Lyddie. Two weeks earlier and it might not have taken her the same way, but now her mind had been eased about daughter and child, and she'd seen Shubael's pretty sloop at anchor in the channel. She took down Edward's picture in its silver frame and carefully removed the canvas. She wrapped the frame in a piece of flannel, set it on top of the chest, and sat down to write a note to Shubael.

39

Lyddie handed out seedcakes to all the children, sending the oldest with the note to Shubael, requesting passage to Barnstable. The child came back with a message from Shubael: they would sail within the week; be ready. Lyddie next sat down and wrote another note to Mehitable, explaining her intended absence. She sent it to Nathan's with Silas's oldest girl. Mehitable sent back no answer.

The message came from Shubael on the following Tuesday: they would sail the next day; be at the landing at half-six in the morning. Lyddie gave Patience Clarke free use of the cow's milk and the hens' eggs if she did the milking and collecting; she took the padlock off the barn door and fixed it to the pantry. She heated a kettle and gave herself a good wash: hair, face, armpits, groin, feet; she packed a bag with a spare gown and slippers, shift and stockings in case of a severe soaking; she laid out one of Rebecca's shorter gowns for shipboard, the better to keep the hem above a sloppy deck. She packed a basket with bread, seedcake, apples, dried salt beef, and her knitting to do on shipboard; that night Shubael sent another message: they would sail Thursday.

Thursday morning Lyddie got dressed, tied her bonnet and buttoned her coat, collected her bag and basket, and said good-bye to Patience and the children. Silas Clarke had at last decided he'd best show up at the tannery, so Lyddie was spared any farewell embrace from him. She set off down the road for the landing, but when she rounded the final turn and saw the bay, she knew they would not be going anywhere soon; not a single ripple marred the water's surface. Shubael stood at the water's edge, directing the loading of the dory with a last-minute collection of boxes and barrels, in between directions staring out across the glassy sea.

As Lyddie came up he turned to her and made some effort to twitch his mouth into a smile. "We'll freshen."

"Of course."

He said the same, off and on at ever-increasing intervals, for the next hour, and then sent Lyddie home. She fussed the house into deathlike neatness until Ned Crowe arrived at two in the afternoon to inform Lyddie that the sail had again been postponed to Friday six.

Friday morning a fine gust lifted Lyddie's hem as she stepped into the road, and by the time she reached the landing a steady breeze scoured the surface of the water. Lyddie and her bag were lifted into the dory, and Ned Crowe rowed them to the *Betsey*.

The wind was stronger than it looked. Lyddie went below to store her bags, and even there she could feel it, pushing at the wooden sides until they creaked with an in-and-out kind of hopeless pleading. In her life Lyddie had taken many sea journeys to Boston in whatever sloop Edward sailed in as master, and she had always stepped onboard with some little consciousness of danger, but at least there she had known full confidence in her captain. Shubael was growing old; it had surprised Lyddie when she'd learned he'd gone out in a small whaleboat after those blackfish in the bay, but she imagined he could manage the less agile task of shipmaster.

The wood creaked again, neither loud enough or soft enough to be ignored; the boards under her feet pitched, and she sat down on the bunk to examine her surroundings: two bunks with narrow table and benches built over lockers in between, topped by a hanging lantern and a slatted hatch for light and air, the remaining few feet packed tight with spare sail. Lyddie wedged her own bag into the nearest locker, left the cabin, and went out on deck.

The wind was out of the southwest and finicky. Shubael brought the *Betsey* to sail, and at once she heeled over hard, causing Lyddie to grab hold of the rail; she found a seat on the leeward bench and Shubael ran her out to the northwest. From there Lyddie lost the hours, her mind flying ahead of the *Betsey*, or behind the *Betsey*, back to other sails, back to Edward. Eventually she heard the call to stand by for sheets, and they came about on a southerly tack, into the harbor. She looked up at the sun and was shocked to see it stood at dead center.

As they approached the wharf at Barnstable Lyddie felt no sense of trepidation; she barely looked at the man standing beside the pile of crates, and her eye only came back to him when it had finished with the rest of the landscape: the marsh, the church spire, the horses and wagons, but as soon as it came back it recognized the height, the clean angles. Of course, she thought. Of course any "business at Barnstable" would involve Shubael's new partner, Eben Freeman. Lyddie went below to keep out of the way while they unloaded; even inside the harbor the wind was considerable, and the banging of the blocks and slatting of the sails competed with the tramp of the crew's feet. The floor under Lyddie's feet pitched and rolled uneasily; Lyddie had a fair pair of seaman's legs while under way, but it was another story altogether at anchor. It soon came to a choice between vomiting into the bilge and going back on deck; as the sounds from above had diminished to nothing Lyddie chose the latter. She climbed up the companionway, saw the sails down and lashed and the deck empty, but the dock wasn't. Shubael and Eben Freeman stood side by side, admiring the *Betsey* together. Shubael saw her and waved. "Come along, Cousin! We're invited to dine with my brother! He's sent for a chaise for us! Is it not delightful?"

Shubael was worse than old, he was a fool; he deserved his foolish wife; he deserved to be shipwrecked or windbound or capsized in the deepest part of the channel. As soon as Lyddie came within speaking distance Eben Freeman walked around to the far side of chaise, stiff-faced and stiff-backed, but Shubael jabbered on blindly.

"All right, Cousin, in you go."

"I wouldn't wish to impose on Mr. Freeman. I'd planned to dine out of my basket on board and attend to my business."

"Dine out of a basket! Don't be silly. Come on now, in you go. We've got a good wind for the return and we don't want to lose time."

But once they were all in the chaise, where Lyddie might have wished Shubael to continue his jabber, he stopped completely. As Freeman still said nothing, Lyddie felt she had no choice but to venture something in his direction.

"This is kind of you," she said.

"Not at all."

"Do you like your new vessel?"

"Indeed."

"Indeed!" Shubael cut in from behind. "Is that the best you say of her? She's the prettiest ship in the harbor."

"She's the only ship in the harbor," Freeman said.

"Not for long, I expect," Shubael answered. "Now with this blow," and silence settled again, lasting until they reached the main road.

It had been several years since Lyddie had visited Barnstable village, and coming from such a backwater as Satucket the bustle of the court town set her spinning. Nathan Clarke owned one of two chaises in Satucket and took it out seldom; here, if Lyddie gazed after one, another was sure to come from the opposite direction, and men and women constantly crisscrossed the road between the shops and taverns. A handful of horses stood tied in front of the courthouse, their tails lifting in the wind, and the sight of them sparked a shower of questions from Shubael: how went the Winslow case? What was being said about Clarke in the village? When did Freeman see it settled for good? All of which Freeman answered with a shrug or a single word.

Freeman lived a short distance from the courthouse along the King's road, in a double-doored saltbox in which he both slept and worked, the working side identified by a professional shingle hung in front of the door. Lyddie passed through the door to the residence in something of a numb state, noting little except a general sense of simplicity and order. She had some recollection of a tender veal roast set out by Freeman's housekeeper, an elderly woman he addressed as "Mrs. Crocker," which did little to explain her life situation. Lyddie spoke when spoken to, mostly by Shubael, but when form required, by tight-voiced courtesy from Freeman; in the main she was left alone as the men talked about the *Betsey*. She looked at Freeman when she could do so unnoticed but found little in his face to describe his thoughts. At length the subject turned to the weather, and as Lyddie had kept an ear on the whistling wind throughout the meal, she was unsurprised when Freeman suggested they might end up windbound. Shubael jumped up at once and charged off for the harbor.

Lyddie stood also. "I must get to my business," she said. "I thank you for your hospitality."

She was nearer the door than the table when Freeman said, "I'd not expected to see you here."

"Nor I you."

"No doubt if you'd known you'd see me you'd not have come."

"I could hardly have expected a welcome."

"I'm sorry, this is the best I'm able."

"I didn't mean—"

Freeman leapt out of his chair. "Blast what you mean and what I mean and what that asinine brother of mine means! What was he thinking to bring you here?"

"I can't think. But I do have business in town. If you would tell Cousin Shubael—"

"Oh, sit down, sit down. Good God, we're not a pair of children."

Lyddie returned to the table and sat down. Freeman remained standing, gripping the back of his chair. "I've had a deal of time to get the better of my anger and I thought I'd done so. I thought I'd most certainly done so. I even thought I might now manage an answer to your letter."

"The one releasing you from our engagement."

He peered at her. "A difficult letter to write."

"Yes, it was."

"I mean to say, my answer to it."

"Allow me, then, to release you from that obligation as well, by acknowledging the offer as accepted. And now may we move on to other subjects?"

"Very well."

They fell into silence. Lyddie dropped her eyes from Freeman's strained face.

At length Freeman said, "Let me begin with inquiring on your business in Barnstable."

"I've come to engage a lawyer."

"A lawyer!"

"I find it necessary after all to sue Mr. Clarke for my keep and care, as well as to deal with a difficult tenant."

"Tenant?"

"Silas Clarke."

"Silas Clarke? He's put Silas Clarke in there?"

"He has."

More silence.

"Perhaps you could recommend a man of law to me," Lyddie said.

"You'll not want Doane, he's Clarke's man. Perhaps Bourne. He's across from the courthouse." He paused, perhaps thinking of fees. "You continue in the employ of Mr. Cowett?"

"I do not."

Another silence. "I believe at one time I spoke in a derogatory way on the subject of Mr. Cowett. I should like to correct what impression I might have given by saying that I have always found him a man of principle."

"I don't believe your concerns about Mr. Cowett were entirely unfounded. You spoke of grudges."

"He holds a few. And not all unwarranted."

"Including one against my husband?"

Freeman's face widened out in surprise. "Your husband?"

"Did not my husband's family acquire his land without paying?"

"Your husband's family was given that land as gift."

"But why? I saw the deed and no reason was given."

"There were too many to put in writing. The Berrys took care of the sachem's ill son; they hired a lawyer to make out a document protecting the sachem's land for his heirs; they aided the son with an English education . . . I can't recall every single instance, but there were many, I assure you. In exchange, the sachem deeded the Berrys a parcel of land, not a large gift by any lights. No, no, Sam Cowett held no grudge against your husband. In fact, he was so distraught at his failure to save him he took it as his job to look out for his widow."

"For *me*?"

"You had asked me what made Cowett change his mind about dividing the woodlot and I didn't know, so later I asked him. He said at first he thought you wished to stay on at the house, so he fouled the sale by refusing to divide. Then he said that you'd spoken to him about your hopes for a speedy sale, so he agreed to the division. In the end he saw the first thinking was correct and that he'd done wrong and he wished to set it right. I don't know whether he did, or what he had planned to do—" Freeman looked at Lyddie and away. "After that we didn't speak the way we used to." He stood up to get more cider, but before he returned to his chair, Shubael entered the room, full of wind and waves and ship, carrying the conversation away from Lyddie. She was just as glad to be left alone, her head too full to be sorted for the purposes of conversation, but too late she came back to it and found that her stupid curse at the dock had taken hold: they were windbound and would not sail till tomorrow. The next thing Lyddie understood was that Freeman had offered them rooms and that Shubael had accepted.

Shubael set off for the dock again to better secure the *Betsey* and Lyddie stood up to hunt out Esquire Bourne, but Freeman stopped her.

"A word, please, before you go. Something that I have on my mind." He made some adjustment to his chair, his mug, his shirt cuff. "We spoke just now of Mr. Cowett, but I don't believe I've said all I should on the subject. I have an apology to offer; I should not have allowed Clarke to arrest him. I was not thinking what was right, I was thinking what was convenient. I insisted on seeing something between you that wasn't; I wanted him away from you; I exhibited poor faith. This is not to say I don't smart yet over your lack of faith in me, of your refusing to trust to my governance; it's more perhaps to say that now I understand what caused it. As you saw my poor governance over the matter of Cowett you were brought to think it might be the same with my governance over you. That is what I wish to say to you and that is what I wish you to accept, if you can."

"If you mean to say you wish me to accept your apology for Mr. Cowett's arrest, that privilege falls to him, not me. I might add, I know of the law that gives you governance over slave, or servant, or wife, but none that gives you governance over free Indian or unmarried woman."

"Married or unmarried, you would not trust to my judgment. You showed it to be so when you refused to sign that paper."

"Can you not understand my reluctance? Can you not think of it as your Mr. Otis would think of it? To have that one small certainty in my life, to know that I, too, will be as secure in my house as any prince in his castle—"

"You would have been so secured with me. You know this. You must know it."

"I do. I do. But—"

"Then why fuss so over it?"

"Then why balk so at it?"

"Even Mercy Warren acknowledges that in every household, for the sake of order, there must be one master."

"I give you master. Can you not give me my one small corner?"

"Do you not see? I would give you more than a small corner, I would give you all, as and when you need it."

"As you would have me need it."

He stared at her. "So you offer nothing and you accept nothing. And you would call that marriage."

Lyddie thought. "I accept this. Today you open your mind and heart in an effort to understand my own, however imperfectly you succeed at it, and that I can and do accept and, indeed, even cherish. I've had few such people in my acquaintance." Lyddie leaned forward. "And I offer this. You now see me as I am and you see I'm not the wife for you, but can we not at least part again in friendship?"

Freeman's features worked. He walked away to the door, returned to the table, and sat down. "Friend. And lawyer, if you wish it. After all, I've had the papers ready some time now."

Lyddie considered and could find no reason against it. She got up, found her bag, and unwrapped the silver frame, and brought it over to him. "I heard talk at my son's of a fee for a will at two pounds fifteen shillings. I've little idea what you might charge for such a case as mine, but you might get four pounds silver from this frame. If you would take it to begin—"

"I will not. Not that or any other thing. There's my condition. And if you truly think me friend, you will accept it."

Lyddie set down the frame.

"Besides, if it goes to court the charge will be set off to Clarke; he'll lose the case and he knows it. But I don't think it will go to court. Once the papers are served I think you'll find your son ready to comply with the will's strictures. The trick will be to keep him in compliance, but I have an idea if he knows I'm in the shadows, with court waiting . . ." Freeman's eyes grew dreamy. "I will say to you, Widow Berry, I should enjoy having Clarke before the bench. And I'll tell you another who would enjoy it: our friend Otis. He'd take your case and sue for life use of house entire, with keep at two hundred pounds of beef—"

"And he'd lose."

Freeman smiled. "And he'd lose. But, by God, he'd enjoy the experiment. And I should enjoy it. But we can't afford any such ride. We won't persuade Clarke to give way with any such madness, and winter comes on. It must be as I said before: he sees the papers and settles."

"And what of the tenant?" Lyddie explained some, but not all, of the difficulty with Silas Clarke.

"You know already what must be done. You said it yourself, to his brother Nathan. If he makes threat against his family or against you, or steals or does damage to any property, you must fetch the constable to arrest him."

Lyddie nodded. She extended a hand across the table, and after a minute Freeman took it and gripped it.

40

Sometime in the night the wind picked up even more speed and the rain came down on the roof like hammers. Lyddie believed she heard every moan and tap and woke thinking they would not sail; but by the time she joined the men at breakfast the wind had veered off to the south and the rain had tempered to a drizzle; Shubael's face was all smiles and happy chatter, Freeman's a paste of shadows and deep, dark crevices.

Freeman disappeared as soon as Mrs. Crocker took away the plates. Shubael set off to the dock to check on the boat. Lyddie went to her room and packed her bag, then waited for the sound of the chaise outside the door before she exited. Shubael handed her in and climbed in after her; Freeman drove them to the dock, and they reversed the process. As Shubael strode toward the ship Lyddie hung back a second to say, "Good-bye, Mr. Freeman," to which he managed to say, in a high, tight voice nothing like his own, "Good-bye, Widow Berry."

At first it appeared that Shubael's luck had turned: the sun came out, a fresh breeze filled mainsail and jib and shot them away from the wharf and out of the harbor, but soon after he rounded the mouth the boat shuddered under Lyddie's feet, heeled over, and stopped, hard aground.

Shubael barked his orders, but the crew were already at the stays; the sails came down and the ship leveled slightly. The tide was on the ebb, another hour yet to low; that meant one hour out and one back and then, what? Another hour again before they'd float? Shubael wanted to take Lyddie into shore in the longboat, but Lyddie refused. She didn't believe she had the stuff for another encounter with a still-fragile Freeman. In the end the crew took the longboat, and Shubael and Lyddie stayed on board. Shubael went below to work on his accounts, but Lyddie fetched her basket with her knitting and stayed above. The wind was brisk, but the sun warm, and it danced across the water, disguising both its shallows and its depths.

Lyddie had already turned the heel on her stocking before Shubael reappeared and gazed out to sea with his glass. Lyddie opened her basket and offered him an apple. He joined her, and they braced their backs against the now severely canted larboard rail.

"It won't be long, now, Cousin," Shubael said. "The tide's now turned; another hour and a half and we'll be clear. I must say, this shoal's filled in since my last run out here. Did Edward ever tell you of the time we ran aground outside New—" He broke off and turned away from her.

Lyddie rested a hand on Shubael's knee. " 'Tis one thing to lose Edward to the sea. 'Tis another to lose him because his cousin can't speak his name to me."

Shubael tossed his core overboard; it plunked like hail into the water. He rounded on Lyddie.

"I've long wished to say his name to you, Cousin, long wished to tell you a thing that will ease me, but not you. I can't keep it to me any longer. I cost you your husband."

Lyddie blinked.

"I was driving a small group of whales into the shore. I heard Sam shout my name and I ignored him. I thought, Hang it, I don't care what he has, I've got these fine, fat fish of my own on the run and I'm going to see they hit ground. I didn't even turn. When I did I saw Sam going like the devil for the overturned boat, but I was closer before, and if I'd turned when he'd called I'd have reached them in good time. When I finally got there Sam had Edward by the belt and he was alive, I could tell because he reached up and grabbed hold of Sam's coat sleeve, but I came shooting in too close and a wave caught me broadside and I ran right into Sam's boat. Sam lost his balance and his hold, but I thought for a minute it was okay, see? 'Cause Edward still hung on to Sam's sleeve, and then the sleeve tore right out of the coat—"

"No. Edward's coat was never torn."

" 'Twas Sam's coat that tore, Cousin. He'd already rent the sleeve, which I suppose is what gave Edward his hold, but then it ripped through, and that was it. Edward was gone. But Sam wouldn't quit. 'Twas all I could do to keep my boat from falling off, going with all hands at the oars, and here's Sam fishing around in the water with one of his, looking for Edward and taking it broadside, until finally Jabez yells to him they're shipping water, they'd have to quit, but it was Sam got there first and gave up last where it should have been me both times. Sam."

Shubael stopped and gulped in air, looking at Lyddie like a hungry dog.

Lyddie got up and half walked, half crawled over the pitched deck to the companionway. She went below and lay down on the leeside bunk. The boat was still locked hard in the mud; she knew this to be true because of the angle and because of the occasional dull nudge of the waves, but it seemed to pitch and rock in time with her staccato breathing. The crisp air funneling through the hatch hit her cheek like a cold wave; she closed her eyes and saw Sam Cowett's drenched, torn coat in place of Edward's whole one, saw a patchwork of words and accounts unravel into a series of incohesive parts. Once Lyddie saw the parts she saw they would not serve to cover her naked, lonely flesh at all. She lay there bare and raw, feeling the boat slowly righting itself, and once she felt herself in balance she got up and went to find Shubael.

He sat on a barrel not far from where she'd left him.

"Cousin," she said. "Do you believe that God rules all?"

He nodded.

"Then 'tis God sent you shoreward instead of seaward after my husband. 'Tis God brought your boat into Mr. Cowett's and tore his coat and left Edward to drown. When we next talk of Edward, let it be Edward live, not Edward dead."

Shubael's wind-scoured face twisted, forcing his tears to zigzag down his cheeks. Lyddie reached up and wiped them away with her sleeve. Shubael caught up her hand and pressed it to his chest. "You were his greatest blessing, Cousin. He once told me so. He said he'd never seen the bottom of your courage and that he took half of his from you. So I teased him. I said, 'She'd need courage, taking up with the like of you,' but he didn't come along with the joke. I don't even think he heard it. He went off on a line of his own. ''Tis the hardest part of life,' he said, 'to be half of something and yet remain whole.' I didn't know the first thing of what he meant and I told him so—I told him he was turning into last winter's squash, but he said his wife knew what he meant and that was all that needed to. Ah, and now I've made you cry, too."

The crew returned, and when the sails were raised they filled with a fine southwest breeze. Lyddie stood on deck facing down the wind and spray, trying to sort through everything Shubael had said but could not get beyond the last thing, could not hear Shubael's words for Edward's. The half. The whole. His voice seemed so clear to her that for a minute she thought he was there beside her on the deck of the ship, but then she realized she was just remembering another time on another deck at Long Wharf in Boston, Edward having just left the ship to do his dealings with the oil merchants, Lyddie preparing to leave to secure them a room. Edward had called back to her from the dock with some instruction, not too near the wharf, or near the wharf, Lyddie couldn't tell. She'd called after him, "What?"

But Edward had turned back and smiled and shouted to her, "Never mind! I leave the whole to you!"

By the time Robbin's hill came into sight the sun had gone and Lyddie was frozen through, but some of those jagged half-edges appeared to have scoured themselves smooth.

She and Shubael made their good-byes and Ned Crowe rowed her ashore. The walk through the dusk as far as Cowett's house seemed long; the walk from there to hers seemed longer. She'd been unsurprised by the lack of smoke from Cowett's chimney, but quite surprised by the lack of it from her own. She pushed open the door and saw first the dirty pot on the cold hearth, then the broken crock on the table. She sniffed. Sour milk. Old sweat. Brandy.

Lyddie worked up the fire, listening for sounds of Clarke children, hearing nothing. Once she had a solid blaze she approached the door to Clarke's chamber and peered around its edge. The bed was unmade and the sour-milk-old-sweat odor was strongest in its near vicinity, but the room sat empty. Lyddie backed away and ran up the stairs. The children's beds had been pushed under the eaves, the room cleared of their few belongings. Lyddie went downstairs, and outside, where she found a distended, protesting cow and a handful of fussing chickens, one with an odd, listing hop, but no Clarkes.

Lyddie tied up the cow, got her stool and pail, and set to the milking. She took an angry hoof in the ankle and a shitty tail in the face, but at length she got the udders emptied and her pail filled. She next removed her stocking, captured the hobbling chicken, drew the stocking over its head, and examined its leg. It had dislocated from its socket. She wrung its neck, removed and replaced her stocking, and hung the chicken in the barn. She carried her pail of milk to the pantry, filled her milk pans, jugged the rest and carried it to the cellar, then collected her kitchen knife and a lantern and returned to the barn, where she plucked and gutted the chicken and returned it to its hook until she was ready to roast it. At last she could go inside and change her salt-crusted, milk-and-blood-spattered clothes.

As Lyddie opened the door to her chamber she looked down and saw a twice-folded paper on the floor. She picked it up, and a pound note in the old inflated paper tenor fluttered from it. She caught the note and unfolded the paper:

Dear Widow Berry,

We've gone to live with my brother in Connecticut. I thank you again and again for your many kindnesses and am most heartily sorry for what trouble we've caused. May God have mercy on your soul.

I am your most humble servant, Patience Clarke

Lyddie changed her dress and returned to the keeping room to address the fire. Some tea inside and a good blaze outside finally chased away the numbness, but under it Lyddie found none of the contentment she'd been expecting if she ever discovered herself back in sole possession of her home. The fact that Nathan Clarke would be unlikely to leave her in peace was part of her difficulty, but not the biggest part. The main thing that set hard on her mind was that dead chimney down the road.

Lyddie had had so little time to think over everything she'd been told by Freeman and Cousin Shubael about Sam Cowett that it came crowding in on her in a disordered jumble, but one thing leaped out of the mess: she wouldn't attempt to deny Sam Cowett's intemperate nature, but she would deny him any crimes against herself or her husband.

Lyddie's fatigue and the comfort of her own bed put her into a deep sleep, so deep she had some trouble coming out of her dream. In it a tall, faceless man, neither black nor white, young nor old, broad nor lean, stood on the far side of the Robbin's landing channel, calling her across, and although she knew he wanted her, he kept calling her by another name. When she opened her eyes she saw the dim shape of the man at the foot of the bed and heard the voice and the name, but still thought it was the dream.

"Come on, Patience. You get back where you belong or you'll see daylight before dawn." And he picked up the foot of the bed and slammed it into the wall.

The jolt catapulted Lyddie into full consciousness. Silas Clarke, drunk, not in Connecticut, but here? But of course he was not in Connecticut. Patience Clarke had done what she'd done before and fled him, this time to her own brother instead of his, and Lyddie might have known if she'd registered what she'd seen: the children's room packed up and tidied, Silas Clarke's used and filthy. If Silas had gone with them, Patience Clarke would certainly have put that other room to rights, too. The question now was, did Silas Clarke know where Patience had gone? Or that she was gone? But Lyddie had learned something about the futility of attempting to communicate with intoxicated persons; she wanted only to get him out of her room.

"I'm not your wife, Mr. Clarke," she said. "I'm the Widow Berry. Now please leave me to my sleep. We'll speak in the morning."

The form at the foot of the bed swayed. "Widow Berry."

"Good night, Mr. Clarke."

"Widow Berry. Did you get your cow?"

"I did, thank you. Good night, now."

"Wife's gone to Connecticut. Found a note when I got home."

"Yes. We'll talk tomorrow. Good night."

He sat down on the floor and began to weep, a ratcheting, coughing, strangling sound.

Lyddie slid out of bed and half pulled, half pushed him to his feet. He smelled of sweat and piss and grease and liquor. She walked him to his room, dropped him onto his foul bed, and shut the door. She returned to her room and jammed the latch down.

41

Silas Clarke appeared full of remorse the next morning, setting off to the tannery determined to leave off drink, earn his pay, save his money, buy back his house, and bring his wife and children home. He even returned from the tannery sober, during which period Lyddie discovered that Silas Clarke sober was little improvement over Silas Clarke drunk. He dropped tuppence on the table in front of Lyddie and demanded to be fed; when he'd finished his food he said, "By the way, Widow, you might care to know, the Indian's got home," and then he left for the tavern.

The Indian's got home. The words made Lyddie's heart race, but not in the old way, not in any kind of way she'd ever known. She didn't look forward to seeing him; she didn't fear seeing him; she knew she must see him, nothing more. She had to take that one step toward him to erase that other step taken away from him; she wouldn't think beyond.

Lyddie waited until sun and water had both fallen so she could be certain Cowett was back from the shore. She ate an early supper and set off down the road. He opened the door when her first shoe touched the stoop, but he didn't stand aside and usher her in; he stood square, with arms folded, shoulders nearly stretching from jamb to jamb.

"Mr. Clarke told me you'd got home."

"Then you listen to him yet."

Very well, Lyddie thought, it will take more than a step. She brought her feet together on the stoop. "I listen to all. I believe some. Among those I believe, Mr. Clarke is not one. I confess to a moment in the first flush of the listening, in a state of confusion over other things, when his one thing added to other things, wrong things—"

Something rustled behind him. Cowett stood away from the jamb, and without taking his eyes from Lyddie he reached back and pulled someone forward, a small, black-haired, cream-colored woman with oval brown eyes and a smooth oval face. She looked from Cowett to Lyddie to Cowett. She pointed to the table, where a fresh-baked meat pie sat steaming, then pointed to a chair as if it were her own. "Sit?" she said. "Eat?"

"No," Lyddie said. "No thank you. I came to say . . . what I've said. I must go home."

Lyddie met up with a stinking, leering Silas in the yard. He pointed down the road in the direction from which she'd just come. "What's the trouble, Widow Berry? A little crowded for you now?"

Of course Silas Clarke would have known about the new woman. Of course the whole town would have known. Lyddie went inside and straight to her room without speaking, lying on her bed with yet another churning mind. Who was this woman? Where had she come from? Was she English or Indian? Had he brought her all the way from Canada or picked her up someplace closer to home? The thought most disturbing to Lyddie was the idea that the woman might be English, that some Englishwoman lived with such courage, but as she pictured the black hair and cream skin and scant words she felt sure the woman was not English. French perhaps, but not English. She'd heard that Frenchmen took up with and even married Indian women with some regularity, but what Frenchwoman would dare take up with an Indian man, and then, if that were not enough, carry her papist ways straight into the heart of this enemy Protestant land? That small, timid thing who had ducked behind Sam Cowett at first opportunity could not have had the courage for anything so bold, but Sam Cowett would, of course, and if Sam Cowett wanted a thing . . . Lyddie of all people could attest to the power of a Sam Cowett.

French, then. Or French and Indian mix, but certainly not all Indian.

That having been decided, Lyddie closed her eyes, and the minute she did so, the other questions swarmed in. Did the heathen Sam Cowett talk to this papist woman about the Indian gods? Did he talk to her about sin? Did they speak of his dead wife? Did they even speak a common language? And what did any of it matter to Lyddie? Well, what mattered to Lyddie was that Sam Cowett was no longer hers to lie with as she pleased, nor would he have need of her cooking and cleaning, or, in fact, any need of her at all.

42

The town called her Indian; it was the best they could do; Lyddie doubted the idea of English had ever been seriously entertained, and to call her French would certainly have confirmed for them every imagined papist evil, but then what to say about Cowett? They may not have liked him or trusted him, but all the men in town had dealt with him at one time or another and would likely do so again. Heathen Indian living with heathen Indian upset no one; Indian with French, and Indian *man* with French*woman,* came perilously close to something else they could scarcely name, never mind condone. Cowett, then, cohabited with an Indian named Marie, and no one's opinion of him changed, up or down.

As for Lyddie, she found little time to think of the pair as she was so busy with Silas Clarke. Sometimes he made it home from the tavern before she bolted the door; sometimes he didn't; when he didn't, he stood outside and banged on the wood until he exhausted himself; once she found him half frozen on the stoop in the morning, but the next time it occurred to him that if wood didn't break, glass would. She heard it in her sleep and thought it was the crack of lightning, until she heard the groan and the thump and the howl. She got up and looked into the keeping room to find Silas Clarke lying in a heap of broken glass, bloody hands curled into his chest. She sat him up, cleaned him off, and helped him into his bed, then dealt with the glass and returned to her own bed.

But there was one thing about Silas Clarke that eased Lyddie's road—the money he dropped on her from time to time to cook or clean or wash—with it she bought ten cords of wood and guaranteed that the first quarter of the winter would be warm.

Lyddie was cutting up apple rings to string and dry by the fire when she heard the knock; it had been so long since anyone had visited her that at first she didn't identify the sound. A woodpecker? A branch blown down? The knock sounded again, this time a clear knuckles-on-wood; she went to the door and tossed it back and Eben Freeman stepped into the room.

He looked older, stiffer, thinner. He cast his eye around the room, and Lyddie followed his gaze, feeling the shame. The window had been inexpertly boarded, the fireplace crane hung loose from one hinge where Silas had wrenched it, the hutch sat bare in defense against his penchant for throwing, two of the chairs wobbled over missing rungs. She'd managed to scrub the blood out of the floor and wash the stink out of his linens, but the air still carried a whiff of soured liquor and rank man.

"I've come by to inform you that papers will this day be served on Mr. Clarke," Freeman said.

"I thank you. I hope you didn't travel all the way to Satucket solely over my business."

"No, I had some other things to attend—business with Cowett, the ship, Aunt Goss. Betsey's run short of patience; Shubael would like her moved along."

"Would you like to trade her for Mr. Clarke?"

Freeman smiled. "In truth, I would. My sister needs to see what a difficult tenant truly is."

Lyddie opened the door wider. "Would you have tea? Cider?"

"Cider, if you please." He came in and sat down by the fire. Lyddie poured him a cider and sat opposite. The silence that seemed to perpetually live and grow between them dropped down.

"I hear Sam Cowett's come home with a woman," Freeman said at last.

"He has."

"You've lost your job, then?"

"I have. But Silas Clarke now pays me for his keep."

More silence.

After a time Freeman said, "I've not had a sound night's sleep since you left me at Barnstable."

"Indeed."

"Indeed. I roll and thrash and knock the bolsters. I think, Lydia Berry, friend? Can we not do better? Are we so far apart in all matters?" He stood up and crossed in front of the fire, casting a long, soft shadow along the floor. She saw the shadow of his hand move before the hand itself, felt it touch her face as softly as the shadow.

She caught his hand and held it. "I cannot—" Think. She wished to say, *think*, but the last time she'd decided not to think she'd ended up an Indian's whore.

"You cannot what, Widow Berry?"

"I don't know."

"Nor I. But can we not go along a little way and see?"

What she might have said to that was postponed by the thunder of another set of knuckles on the door. Lyddie crossed to it and opened it on Nathan Clarke. He saw Freeman at the fire and hopped into the room like a disturbed rooster.

"So I find you here. I might have guessed. Very well, then, Freeman, you may explain this nonsense." He waved a parchment at him.

"I should think it was clear enough."

"Clear! Yes, damn you, it's clear! Eighty cords of wood! One hundred pounds of beef! Ten bushels of rye!"

Lyddie looked to Freeman in surprise. Such figures were far higher than the last she'd heard quoted back in April when the first discussion of keep and care had taken place. But as they argued and she listened she saw Freeman's wisdom; he gave a cord here, a bushel there; he began to give away some twenty pounds of meat and then appeared to remember Silas Clarke; perhaps it were better to settle the numbers high and have the widow feed him out of her keep? In the end it was settled with something less than what Freeman had first asked, but far more than Widow Howland ever got; they agreed to a future date to sign the amended papers and Nathan Clarke got to ride off with a smirk on his face at his fancy dealing while Lyddie got her third the house, a good deal more in wood and foodstuffs than she'd ever imagined, and Freeman's threat of constant monitoring to keep the deliveries on time.

And Silas Clarke.

Once Nathan had gone Lyddie turned to Freeman and thanked him.

"It was all my very great pleasure," he answered with a smile that seemed to stretch all the way to Lyddie's face, and then stretch some more until it seemed the natural thing for her to say, "Would you care to come to dine tomorrow?"

Freeman's smile blinked out so fast Lyddie began to doubt it had ever been. "I cannot. How I would wish I could do, Widow Berry, but I cannot. I'm engaged with Mr. Winslow over the dinner hour and then I must see Cowett. I have a little to do with Cowett, not a great deal, nothing that should take me into the supper hour—"

Lyddie took up the hint. "Perhaps a small supper, then?"

He accepted with a bow.

Lyddie was on the back stoop shaking the tablecloth when she caught a long form in her peripherals, working its way through the woodlot in her direction. She had expected Freeman to come from Cowett's and was not surprised that he'd use the short route through the woods; she swung around to greet him and found herself facing the Indian. In the seconds it took him to reach her she formed and discarded a half-dozen different sentences. He crossed the yard and stopped a body's length away, a rolled paper tucked under his arm.

"I'm told Freeman's here."

"He's not arrived as yet. If you'd care to wait—"

"No. You tell him I've found what he was after."

He swung around.

Lyddie jumped off the stoop. "Wait. Please."

Cowett turned.

"I want—"

"Go tell Freeman your wants. I wager he'll marry you yet."

"I don't want a husband, Mr. Cowett, I want a neighbor. As we were before—" She stopped.

"Can't say it, can you? Can't say 'before I lay on my back with an Indian.' "

The sound was not loud; in fact, Lyddie couldn't have said just what made it—a hurried breath? A creaky boot? A scuffed stone? She had already turned her head away from Cowett and needed only to raise it to see Freeman, who had come around the corner of the house and stopped at roughly the same distance that separated her from the Indian. He looked back and forth between them and then at her. Had he heard? Of course he'd heard. At such a short distance Lyddie could hear him breathing, working the air in and out, a short inhale and exhale, over and over as he struggled to get the best of it, but he could not. What remained in his lungs came out in a sharp blast. He turned on his heel and rounded the corner of the house without speaking to either of them.

43

Lyddie composed her second note to Freeman and discharged it via Jabez Gray. In it she again released Freeman, not from any engagement, but from any obligation to her as lawyer. She expected no return; she was surprised to open her door to him a week later.

He bowed in greeting, entered at her invitation, looked around with new wariness. "You're alone?"

"I am."

He took the chair she offered but leaned forward in it, ready to leap at the first opportunity. He opened the pocketbook he carried under his arm and took out a piece of paper. "Here are your new terms with Clarke. I agree, for the future, it would be best if you found another lawyer."

She nodded.

"I believe I recommended Bourne before."

"Yes. Thank you."

He stood up.

"I should like to say thank you for everything," Lyddie added. "Despite our difficulties—"

"Difficulties! You would call it 'difficulties'?"

"And what would you call it?"

"I would call it a life inside a knot. My mind does nothing this past long week but travel round and round struggling to unravel it." He returned to the chair, sat down, leaned forward again. "I must ask you. I must. What he said . . . Can you make no denial?"

"I cannot."

He leaned back. "And yet right here in your house last spring you made such denial in plain terms."

"Because, at that time, it was the truth."

"And at Barnstable? When I spoke of him at Barnstable?"

"It had reached its end."

He leaned forward. "And where had it begun? Can you not tell me that? When he came after you at Clarke's house, what was between you then? No, you need not tell me. I saw it myself. And then at Barnstable, like a fool, I debased myself before you for my own eyesight. For my lack of trust. Trust!"

"Your trust, such as it was, was not misplaced. You and I had parted before—"

He leapt up. "Enough! I cannot fathom it. You are not any person I know."

"Perhaps it would help if you think of me as yourself."

"Myself!"

"At Thacher's tavern."

"Thacher's . . . Good God! You would compare what takes place at a tavern—"

"It was little different. You were a man alone in want of comfort and you found a place to get it where it harmed no one. That was what you told me. It harmed no one. The only difference between us is that in return you gave her coin where I gave nothing but that same comfort. If your Mr. Otis were here, I believe he would declare our sins equal."

"You may leave off Mr. Otis. God speaks on such behavior in clear terms."

"And you may leave off God. I no longer trouble with him and he no longer troubles me."

"Clearly."

Lyddie stood up. "Mr. Freeman, if you came here to argue God with me—"

"I didn't come here to argue God or Otis or Cowett—"

"Did you not?"

"I did not! I came here because I can make nothing of you, how you think and act, how you would have me think and act! I am a man of reason, a man of noble intention, a man of honesty, and you take and twist me—"

"I take you for all that and more beside, Mr. Freeman, which is why I strive so hard to bring us to understanding. I've said before and I say again that I would keep you as friend. You've gone far beyond any other in aiding me in my situation and I would not give you up over this one small thing."

"Small thing!"

"Very well, not small. I grant you not small."

Silence.

"You've said what kind of man you take me for. What kind of man did you take Cowett for, then?"

"Someone like myself. And not like. What brought it to its end was the unlike thing. I could not cross the gap."

"As I cannot cross this one."

"Very well."

" 'Very well'? You say 'very well'? I'm as far from well as a man may get! You ask too much! I am no more nor less than I am."

"As I am no more nor less than I am."

He stood dumb.

As Lyddie had nothing else to say, she joined him in it.

At length he said, "Good-day to you, Widow Berry."

To which she could answer nothing but "Good-day, Mr. Freeman."

44

Lyddie moved through the days in the steady motion of preparation for winter, making butter, pressing and boiling apples for cider and sauce, preserving currants and plums, storing pumpkins and turnips in the cellar. She worked and waited for the peace to descend, for some sense of victory or vindication, now that she had won her right to her third of the house, but nothing happened. Every other night she was wakened by Silas Clarke, either outside shouting and weeping or inside, snoring and farting, and when she rose one morning and nearly stepped in a slick of vomit she understood that her sense of victory would not come because she'd won nothing. This shabby, bruised house was no more her house now than it had been the week before the agreement; it would never be her house as long as Nathan Clarke controlled its upkeep, controlled who lived there. It would be all delay and neglect with him; Freeman had warned her of it long ago, and now she saw it all ahead, saw it as one long, uneven struggle. And Lyddie was tired. Her legs felt heavy when she pulled them out of the bed; her head ached behind the eyes most of the day; she developed a kink in her hip; she began to lie in bed past dawn most mornings and tumble back in as soon as she'd finished eating supper at night.

But on the first day of November the temperature plummeted as if someone had read it the calendar, and it spurred Lyddie to action. She set out for the sedge ground to pick bayberries to melt down for the winter's candles; by two o'clock she'd harvested six pails and returned to the house to set up the kettle.

Silas Clarke appeared to have given up on the tannery and lay in his room, sleeping. Lyddie fed the fire, and when she'd got a hearty blaze she made her trips to the well, each one pulling at her limbs as if she'd been stretched on a rack. She set her kettle, filled it with water, and as soon as it began to boil she poured the berries across the top, skimming off the wax as fast as it melted, all the while feeding the flames.

A sleep-shout from Silas Clarke startled her; she whirled around, spilling a skimmer full of wax down her skirt; she snatched up her skirt to contain the wax, but she was too close to the fire; the wax dripped into the fire and the fire flamed; a hungry tongue leaped up the wax to the skirt, gobbling wax and cloth. Lyddie beat at the skirt with the skimmer, a foolish thing to do, as the wax remaining in the skimmer just fed the flame and her sleeve caught, too. She grabbed the bucket, but not an ounce of water remained. A thick, black smoke now fumed around Lyddie and she couldn't see; she beat at the seared places and shouted for Silas Clarke; she ran to the peg, caught up her cloak and beat herself with it; the smoke billowed thicker and blacker and she began to choke. She thought: I'm tired. I'm so very tired.

And dropped into nothing.

"The right leg's got the worst of it. And the arms. I've picked away most all the cloth. I can't answer for the lungs. She breathes yet; that's the main thing. She must be kept breathing. Apply this salve morning and night, each time you change the bandages. And give her this tincture in warm wine every third hour."

Lyddie opened her eyes and saw Dr. Fessey peering down at her.

"Ah! Here she comes now. Well, now, Widow Berry, what have you been up to?"

Lyddie looked around. She was back in her old room at Nathan Clarke's; her trunk sat again in the same corner; Mehitable stood just behind Dr. Fessey, Bethiah behind Mehitable and Jane by the door.

"Candles," she said and coughed.

"Candles, she says. Well, and did you have to light them all? Now, then, are you in any pain?"

"Throat. Sore."

"You see? That's the smoke. She says nothing of the burned limbs because the nerves have been deadened." He patted Lyddie on the chest and took himself off, the others following.

Lyddie closed her eyes and listened to the low voices in the other room. At length one spoke closer by.

"Grandmama?"

Lyddie opened her eyes. Bethiah.

"Are you great hurt?"

"No." Saying the one word made her cough, and the coughing made her throat hurt. But after she was through coughing she asked, "Who brought me here?"

"Uncle Silas. He's got cough, too; they're giving him a tonic."

"Is—" Lyddie felt another cough coming on and stopped. It wasn't worth the trouble. Nothing was worth the trouble. She was tired. She closed her eyes.

The next voice she heard was Mehitable's. "Mother?"

Lyddie opened her eyes. Mehitable stood over the bed with a bowl, a spoon, and a napkin.

"I must lift you a very little." She eased Lyddie higher on the bolster, sat on the edge of the bed, and began to spoon a salty, rich broth into her. It felt like fire going down. Lyddie reached up to stop the spoon and saw the clumsy bandage. She lifted the other hand. The same.

"Daughter—"

"Don't worry, Mother. With the proper care, with the proper rest, the wounds will heal. The doctor said so. Are you finished? Very well, perhaps you'd better rest now."

Lyddie closed her eyes.

Rest now.

45

Lyddie slept. It seemed to her she slept through night and day, but she couldn't have done, because she could recount each visitor in her chamber: Mehitable with more broth and warm wine and salve and clean bandages, and Bethiah with more questions, and Dr. Fessey with scissors to cut away the dead flaps of skin and percuss her lungs and announce her good and bad signs to those waiting in the next room. Silas Clarke came, and received her thanks; Cousin Betsey came and chattered at her until she fell asleep; Eben Freeman came and asked how she fared and left almost before she answered. He came again and said something about the house, about tending to the house, but Lyddie was tired; she closed her eyes, and when she opened them he'd gone.

Dr. Fessey came and announced that her legs were healing well, but her lungs were inflamed and the skin on her hands was healing too tight; she needed to breathe deep, drink more wine, use her hands; Mehitable suggested she get up and walk about, but Lyddie was too tired. She needed to rest. Hadn't Dr. Fessey said so?

Freeman came again, and she heard him talking to Clarke in the outer room.

"How does she fare?"

"The burns heal, the throat heals, but she's got the lung fever. If she lives, I don't believe she'll leave here. Best to sell the house now."

"Will she agree?"

"I'd say she will. She's not asked once about it, or her stores, or even the bloody cow or chickens."

"She's made no mention to me, either. Can she use her hands?"

"The doctor says she might eventually, if she worked them. 'Tis an effort."

"Effort! When has effort ever stopped her?"

Now, Lyddie thought. She had no need of effort here. She would sign the paper agreeing to the sale and stay here with her daughter. Mehitable had proved she would take better care of Lyddie than Lyddie would take of herself, and Lyddie would lie and watch the babe grow and prosper . . .

The men had moved on to talk of Silas, flush with pride at his heroic rescue, back at the tannery and, for the moment, sober. Lyddie closed her eyes and slept some more.

When she woke, Freeman was standing in the door, staring down at her as if she were some foreign species of bird blown in on a storm.

"Good morning," she said.

"If you raised your head you might see by your dark window that it's morning no longer." The words carried more bite than the information required and it puzzled Lyddie until she remembered about Sam Cowett. He was still angry about Sam Cowett. In an effort to smooth him she raised her head to the window, but it set her coughing. She lay back down, exhausted.

Freeman approached the bed. He pulled the blanket down to her waist, exposing her untied shift, but it didn't slow him. He gripped her arms high inside the armpits and pulled her forward over her knees. He began to clap her hard on the back. Lyddie began to cough again. He pushed her farther forward, and she spewed big green gobs into a handkerchief, which appeared under her chin at the key moment.

Freeman stopped thumping and laid her back against the bolster. "My wife had lung fever," he said.

"It's taken many in the village."

"It didn't take my wife, and it won't take you, not if you keep spewing." He shoved the soiled handkerchief back in his pocket and left her.

The next time the cough struck, more out of curiosity than anything, Lyddie leaned forward over her napkin and let it shake her. Sure enough, more green gobs came out. They came out green for three more days and then they turned yellow, and Lyddie discovered she breathed easier.

The next morning Bethiah came to see her with her workbox. "Mama says you know the herringbone."

Well, good Lord, of course she knew the herringbone, but she could never work a needle, and Mehitable should know that. But there the girl sat, opening her workbox and taking out a rough piece of tow, threading a needle with scarlet thread. Lyddie lifted her right hand; it had contracted like a claw; she stretched the fingers and felt as if she were breaking them one by one. She reached for the needle and dropped it.

"Another day, child."

The legs were one thing, but the hands were another. The skin stretched shiny and tight across Lyddie's shins, and when she got out of bed to walk to the window it caught her feet up flat so that she hobbled like a duck, but that could be managed. It was the hands that worried her. The skin had healed, not in shiny smooth patches but in hard ridges, and the hands had lain curled inside their bandages so long that the tendons had pulled up tight as well. Lyddie tried to straighten one hand with the other, but the one wouldn't work enough to help the other. She hobbled out of bed and tried flattening them against the wall. That worked better.

After a week she knew she couldn't manage any pretty stitch, but she felt sure she could guide Bethiah's needle. She called the girl into her room and told her about making roofs, one next the other, with a small cross at the top where one might plant the chimney, and two small crosses at the bottom for the eaves. Bethiah held the needle and Lyddie directed, and a wobbly row of red roofs sprung up across the cloth.

The next day Lyddie dressed herself alone and joined the family in the keeping room for breakfast.

The one downside to Lyddie's recovery was her daughter Mehitable. While she'd been charged with nursing her mother the old resentment seemed to have taken a distant seat to a new tenderness; once the nursing ended she retreated to her original edginess, and lately she seemed to actively avoid Lyddie. One morning Lyddie asked Mehitable if she was distressed over something, and Mehitable answered, "Why do you ask that now?"

"Because you're not as you seemed before."

"No one is as they seemed before," and to Lyddie's great surprise Mehitable burst into tears and ran from the room.

Lyddie tried once more to talk to her daughter but got only more stiffness from her.

46

She ran short of wind after four crossings of the room. She dropped as many knitting pins as she dropped stitches. Once she stumbled and fell as she tried to leave her chair in too great a hurry, and she went to bed each night more exhausted than she'd ever been in her life. But when Nathan Clarke called her into his study and she found Eben Freeman waiting with him, an old quickness shot through her system.

Eben Freeman sat quiet, watching her. Nathan Clarke began by complimenting her on her recent progress and then outlining, in detail, her many remaining limitations. "In view of the current state of affairs," he concluded, "we thought it likely you might wish to reconsider our agreement. We thought it likely you might wish to permit the sale that we'd planned originally, and stay here where you're safest."

He spoke kindly. Indeed, through the past weeks he'd treated her with respect and generosity, as had her daughter. If she'd felt any discord at all, it had been between the couple themselves, and for a moment she wondered if they had disagreed over this very offer to return her to the household. But Lyddie knew she could stay where she was in comfort and safety, perhaps as happily as she would stay in her own home with Silas Clarke. Lyddie had learned what a house was and wasn't. But what was she? What might she become if she stayed here? A thing that sat in the corner knitting unwanted stockings, trying to contain her tongue against her son-in-law, and even her own daughter?

"Mother? Come now. You're a woman of good sense. Think of the practicals in the matter. You've great physical limitations; you'll not hire yourself out now to cook and clean; I daresay you'd be hard-pressed to keep your own house in order."

"I would keep my own house in order if there were not your brother in it."

"Hah! You've come to another reason to keep here. So, what say you? We put the house for sale, you live here with every comfort, and you'll have a nice little pot to spend on all your pins and ribbons."

Pins and ribbons. The word shot her backward, to the first time Nathan had thrown them at her during his first attempt to sell Edward's house. If he'd used another set of words, something that didn't immediately cast her back to the place she'd begun, what might she have answered? She would never know. Her words came out the way they had been sown. "I cannot agree to any sale, Nathan."

Nathan threw his hands over his head. "All right, Freeman, you talk to her. I've wasted enough breath on it."

Lyddie looked at Freeman. His mouth had lifted at one corner. "I believe the widow has made her wishes clear. We now return to our original agreement."

Freeman's voice, steady and rich and deep, gave Lyddie courage. She thought of James Otis standing before the chief justice in the town house last winter and her brain seemed to open fully for the first time in weeks. Months. Since Edward. An idea, a bold idea, a fresh breeze of an idea, began to stir among the long-stagnant branches of her mind. She turned to Freeman. He had said *we* and *our,* but she would not presume on it. "We had at one time discussed the necessity of my acquiring another lawyer. I wonder, does your presence here—"

"I am here and at your service as long as you desire me, Widow Berry."

Lyddie turned to Nathan. "You intend to keep your brother in your two-thirds the house?"

"You may damned well count on it, Mother. And if you don't happen to care for it—"

Lyddie faced Freeman again. "Mr. Freeman, have you resolved the matter of Aunt Goss?"

He blinked at her in surprise. "I have not."

"And would you, in principle, have any great objection to my keeping her instead of your sister doing so?"

"I . . . Well, no, I would not."

"Then I would direct you to make my son another offer. He gives me life use of house entire—"

Freeman's eyes flickered briefly and then burned steadily, but Clarke cut her off with a great shout. "Freeman, I suggest you take your *client,* if you would so call her, educate her as to the law, and come back when you've brought her sensible."

"I'm sensible now, Nathan. If you would hear me—"

"If it begins house entire—"

"It does, but it also ends there. No keep and care. You have such objection to this inconvenience and expense, I should think you'd be delighted to get shed of it. If you give me life use of house entire I'll have the means to make my way; I'd take Aunt Goss as boarder at a rate of, say, forty pounds per year, add another long-term boarder in the remaining downstairs chamber or perhaps a few transients up under the eaves, and support us all quite neatly. If nothing else over this past year, I've learned economy."

If nothing else, thought Lyddie, she'd at least stuck Nathan silent. Even Freeman opened his mouth and wordlessly closed it.

"What say you, Nathan?" Lyddie asked. "Would you think it fair exchange? Life use of house entire and you may keep your wood and rye and beef forever? You must remove your brother, of course—"

"And suffer the loss of my own rent."

"I should like to know what you've actually managed to collect in rent from that quarter," Freeman interjected. "As he's at the tavern more than he's at the tannery, I should think it will figure at no great loss. As for my part, I'll send Aunt Goss to the widow at the rate quoted and save twelve pounds a year in the bargain."

"I'd have to consult Doane," Clarke said, but Lyddie thought she could detect a spark of interest in his eye.

Freeman must have seen it, too. He stood. "Consult Esquire Doane at your leisure. When you've made your decision, you may reach me at my brother's house. Good morning." He turned for the door without further look or word for Lyddie.

"I make one further condition," Lyddie said.

Freeman halted as if he'd been shot in the back, and Lyddie felt a moment's pity for him. He turned slowly.

"I would require that the house be returned to the state it was in before the arrival of Mr. Clarke. You'll find a window in need of repair, and a fireplace crane, and several chairs—"

"God in heaven!" Clarke shouted. "Leave off, now! I'll not talk to you longer! When I've made my decision I'll be talking to your lawyer!"

Her lawyer left, and Lyddie followed as soon as she felt sure he'd had time to clear the outer door. She returned to her room and lay down on the bed, her lungs aching, her heart racing, but her brain still working. Nathan Clarke would agree; she was sure he would agree; she held the most valuable bargaining chip of all: he could get shed of her forever.

47

All was settled. Nathan Clarke would give over life use of house entire; he would remove his brother Silas, he would repair the crane and the window, but he declined to do anything with the furniture, as it didn't belong to him, it belonged to Eben Freeman. Lyddie had forgotten that. She offered to return the furniture to Freeman, but he declined to take it. He was still of a mind to purchase a house in Satucket, he said, but until he had the house, he had no place to store the furniture. They agreed that Lyddie would keep it, with its free use paying for whatever she might be entitled to charge for storage. Lyddie well knew the more logical arrangement would have been a charge *to* Lyddie *from* Freeman for use of the furniture, but she didn't argue the point; Freeman seemed in no mood to prolong his dealings with her. They set up the papers and arranged three dates: one when Silas Clarke would exit the premises, one a week later when Lyddie would enter, one more a week after that when Aunt Goss would join her.

That Freeman continued to mind about Cowett was evident when during one of his rare visits Nathan asked if he'd seen "the Indian's whore," and Freeman had stiffened and looked first in Lyddie's direction before he'd answered that he'd yet to have the pleasure.

Lyddie passed the time at her son's house regaining more of the strength in her lungs and legs and hands by taking short walks and by squeezing on balls of yarn as she coached Bethiah with her knitting and sewing. The girl seemed low, and her lowness brought Lyddie down with her; if Lyddie took her own heart for the girl's she would say it was because they were soon to part and Lyddie had no great hope of any visits between the two houses being either encouraged or permitted.

On the eighth of December Silas Clarke moved out of the house and took a room at the tavern. On the fifteenth Lyddie moved in. Jot brought her and her trunk in the wagon, with the cow trailing behind; the cow was Freeman's final contribution to the negotiation, declaring that as the cow was listed separately from "keep and care" in Edward's will, it should be treated separately now and return with Lyddie. Clarke had spouted and fumed, but Lyddie suspected he'd agreed in the end because he'd come to doubt Lyddie's ability to keep herself without it.

Her second day at the house fell on the Sabbath, and Lyddie happened to be spreading Silas Clarke's fresh-washed linens out to dry on the bushes when the Reverend Dunne came by. He would not come in but stood on her grass, staring pointedly at her washing and demanding her reasons for absenting herself from service.

Lyddie considered several different answers, but each would have triggered more argument than she had the strength to counter. She decided instead on a simple "With all due respect, Mr. Dunne, 'tis none of your business."

The next morning Deacon Smalley delivered her notice that she'd been cast out of the church. Lyddie half expected some sort of violence to befall her, or at the very least some tossing and turning and terrible nightmares, but her sleep that night was deep and dreamless.

Lyddie was hobbling from barn and house the next evening when she happened to look down the road and see a small, humped waif coming toward her. Lyddie watched and waited and soon determined that the waif was Aunt Goss, the hump a tow sack she'd tied over her shoulders. She dropped her sheet and hurried down the road.

"Aunt Goss! You were to come next week. Mr. Freeman was to fetch you and bring all your things."

Aunt Goss dropped the sack in the road. "I've come now." She kept walking.

Lyddie picked up the sack and followed; the old woman was nowhere near as disabled as she'd seemed; Lyddie had some trouble, with her weakened lungs and the heavy sack, to keep pace. They reached the house and Aunt Goss led the way in; she went straight to the one chair Lyddie had set up by the fire, collapsed into it, dropped her chin, and fell asleep.

Aunt Goss slept while Lyddie set up a stew, but when the steam came up in the pot the old woman wakened. She pointed a knobbed finger at it and said, "Mutton?"

Lyddie nodded.

Aunt Goss licked her lips.

Lyddie set them each out a bowl, putting a platter of bread between; she poured two mugs of beer and helped Aunt Goss out of her chair. She needed a good boost to start, but once she was upright she trimmed herself well and set off for the table on steady feet. Lyddie made one attempt at conversation, inquiring as to anything else that Aunt Goss might need collected from the Hopkins house, but Aunt Goss held up a flat hand, and Lyddie took the hint. No talking while she ate. And she ate every bite. When she'd wiped the last juices from the bowl with the last piece of bread and drained the last of her beer she licked all around her lips and said, "Good."

She got up, ignored the big southwest room that had held the Clarkes, picked up her sack, carried it into the tiny room off the southeast corner of the keeping room, dropped it on the floor, and looked around. "Needs a night jar."

Lyddie went to the Clarkes' room, collected the night jar, and brought it back. The old woman now sat on the bed, fingering the single blanket. " 'Tis cold."

Lyddie fetched the two heavy blankets she'd folded neatly on the Clarkes' chest. When she returned Aunt Goss had lain down under the one blanket. Lyddie spread the other two on top. The old woman had begun to snore before Lyddie had reached the door.

Freeman arrived a half hour later. The minute Lyddie opened the door and spoke his name the snoring stopped, but Freeman had heard enough of it.

"She's here, then."

"Yes."

"I told Betsey. Next week."

He went into the little room, and Lyddie listened to him inquire after a sore gum, a kinked hip, an aching elbow, and only after the condition of a good number of other bodily parts had been detailed did he return to the keeping room.

"I'll take her back in the morning."

"Please don't trouble, her or yourself, Mr. Freeman. She's all right here, now."

"Very well, then, let me pay you for the month." He fished four pounds sterling out of his pocket.

Lyddie went to the shelf and took down her pot of coins to give him the difference, but he took the pot from her hand and pushed it back. "Forty-eight pounds a year is a fair price, and I still end up with a savings."

"Very well, but if you wish to overpay, you must take something for it. Cider?"

He nodded.

Lyddie went to the pantry for the cider, and when she returned he'd pulled two chairs near the fire. They sat.

"Have you filled your beds?" he asked.

"I haven't. And I've no expectation of it."

"Because you've been cast out?"

"I believe so, yes."

"Did they mention—" He couldn't finish.

"They cited my absence from meeting, and my working on the Sabbath."

Freeman turned to the fire, picked up the poker, and jabbed at it. As if they'd been talking about it all along he said, "You've met this woman he has living there?"

"I have, but briefly. I'm afraid Mr. Cowett and I are not such neighbors as we once were. In time, I hope we might remedy that situation."

He stared at her. "Widow Berry, you're a kind of woman I've never before met."

"And you're a kind of man I've never before met."

He smiled. "I've wished many times I'd missed the pleasure of meeting you."

"Ah. But what's done is done. We have met. In fact, we know each other quite well, I'd think."

"I suppose we do. And yet I sit here and wonder this: now that you have your house, are you content in it?"

"Is that a question we ask ourselves? Do we not do what we must?"

"Yes, but whose *must*?"

"I would follow Mr. Otis; I would obey those dictates written on my heart. As long as I hurt no others."

Freeman occupied himself with the fire in silence for some time. When he looked up he said, "You've yet to answer my question."

"Allow me some time here before you ask it. In the meantime, if you wish, you might answer it yourself. Are you content in your house?"

"At Barnstable, at times, yes. When I'm at a distance, when I'm busy. At my sister's, I believe I'm miserable most every minute."

"Then perhaps you'd like to take a room."

Freeman tossed aside the poker and stood up. "I don't know how you can make such joke of this."

As Lyddie had no answer she said nothing, and as Freeman could have nothing to say to nothing, he left.

48

Except for three seamen off a storm-tossed sloop, directed her way by Jabez Gray, Lyddie received no boarders. The seamen paid down their thirty-five pence for the night's bed and board, drank up all her cider, and left next day for Marblehead.

Soon after, Lyddie packed a tin of honey cakes and a jug of applesauce and walked down the road to Cowett's place. The woman urged her in, but there she appeared to exhaust either her social graces or her English; Lyddie stood awkwardly inside the door and described her return to the house and her hope of greater acquaintance with her neighbor; the woman nodded and smiled and shut the door behind Lyddie with what must have been great relief. Lyddie saw nothing of Sam Cowett but a half-mended pair of breeches tossed over a chair by the fire.

But as Lyddie walked home she was almost dropped with a sudden rush of grief, a grief she had somehow lost amid all the rest of it.

She missed Rebecca. Or perhaps more truthfully, she missed the lost opportunity, all that time living next to the stranger when with very little trouble she might have discovered the neighbor.

Within a month Lyddie had put up her winter stores, dipped two hundred candles, boiled up a vat of soap, and purchased five barrels of wool from Winslow's farm in preparation for the winter's spinning. She got Aunt Goss to keep awake till dinner by giving her the task of sorting the fleece, picking out any pitch or matted bits, which Lyddie then greased and returned to Aunt Goss to card into fine straight bundles, which Lyddie then combed into rolls. By the first week in January the walking wheel was in place a safe distance from the fire. Lyddie tried out her hands and found them slow and awkward at feeding the wool; Aunt Goss watched, sucking her gums together, but remaining silent.

Lyddie worked at the wheel a short two hours the first day; the second day her hands cramped up after an hour; the third day she decided to give them a rest.

A light tap on the door the morning of the fourth day brought both women eagerly around; they'd had no visitors since Freeman's the previous month. Lyddie opened the door and found Mehitable on the stoop; her surprise was so great she stepped backward, which made Mehitable do likewise. Lyddie had to take three steps ahead to catch Mehitable's hand and attempt to pull her into the house, but Mehitable hung back. "I mustn't. He returns at any minute and will inquire on my absence. I only wished to give you this."

She thrust a clenched hand at Lyddie; Lyddie reached out, and a leather pouch with a white bead dropped into her palm, soft and heavy. Lyddie opened it and spilled out its contents: seven shillings sixpence. She looked up at her daughter. "Come into the house."

"I cannot."

"Then tell me how you fare."

"I fare well." She looked down at Lyddie's fingers, which were struggling to pick up the coins and return them to the purse. "And yourself, Mother? Are you able to manage your house?"

"All but my wheel. In time, I hope to get the better of it. The children are well?"

"The babe has cough." Mehitable paused. "I see you do not ask after my husband."

"With what I hold in my hand, can you be surprised?"

"I found your purse while you were still with us and couldn't think what to do. I didn't know what to think. At last I concluded you must have the money back, no matter the consequence to me. But I further concluded my husband meant you no harm. He wished only to persuade you of what was best for you to do. He was wrong to take what belonged to you, but now you have it back. Can you not forgive him as I have done?"

Lyddie stood silent. It seemed a short time, two seconds or perhaps three as Lyddie measured out each coin in grief and toil and apprehension. Mehitable burst out weeping and stumbled down the stoop. Lyddie wished to call her back, but beyond her daughter's name she had no other words to offer.

49

February 1, 1762

Eben Freeman dismounted in front of the barn and walked his horse inside, tying him a safe distance from the cow; he'd experienced firsthand the cow's tendency to raise a hoof whenever she sensed something solid behind her. He removed the saddle, grabbed a rough sack, and rubbed the horse down; he'd no intention of staying long, but they'd just come through heavy snow, and a wet horse steaming in a cold barn always led to trouble. Freeman fought the wind for the barn door and finally bolted it behind him, pushing through the drifts that had blown up between barn and house; when he reached the house door he lifted his knuckles, hesitated, then dropped them against the wood with some violence. While he waited he looked up at the sky; pewter gray and not through with them yet, but bad weather at Candlemas meant winter's back was broken, or so the old women said.

The door opened. Freeman carried a picture of her in his mind wherever he went, and yet every time he saw her she looked nothing like it. Harder, he thought. More determined. He would soften her where he could. And he wouldn't.

"Mr. Freeman," she said and held the door wide, looking pleased enough to see him, but nothing beyond it. Which, he reminded himself, was how he'd wanted it. He might ask himself why he came through a storm to see such a look, but he might ask himself many things, some time when he had the stomach for it.

He stepped into the welcoming heat and looked around with approval. He couldn't say what in the house had changed, but she'd reclaimed it, despite Aunt Goss carding wool by the fire, despite the girl Bethiah at the spinning wheel, her feet moving awkwardly forward and back. He'd heard from Betsey that Mehitable had sent the girl to her grandmother to learn spinning; he'd been glad of it and not glad. Another pair of eyes and ears. Not that he had anything so private to say. But the Widow Berry was glad to have the girl there, that much was apparent; she hurried over to set the tangled feet right by providing a demonstration, and the pretty dance brought Aunt Goss to attention. It brought Freeman to attention. Very well, then, he could live with it.

Oh, the things he could and couldn't live with!

Freeman went to Aunt Goss and kissed her on the cheek; she lifted her head and looked up at him with more alertness than he'd seen in her at his sister's. He wondered what these women talked about, alone with each other night after night.

The widow left the girl and came to Freeman's side. He handed her the four pounds sterling, Aunt Goss's board for the month, and she pocketed it. He could have paid the year in one, he could have paid via his brother Shubael, but instead he put himself through this monthly visit.

What he could and couldn't live with.

"Stay to tea?" Lyddie asked.

He nodded.

She knew by now that tea for him meant cider. She went to the jug and poured his tankard before she set up the kettle for herself and the others. While he waited, Freeman watched the girl twist the wool between her fingers and walk the wheel, backward first, then forward, lose the rhythm and stop and start, stop and start. She'd walk five miles before she'd fill the spool, he wagered.

Once the tea had steeped, the widow set Freeman's tankard and her cup together at the table, putting a fair distance between them and the aunt and the girl, and Freeman wondered if she'd set them apart on purpose. Could it be she had something private to say to him? He doubted it. And as he had but one thing of interest to say to her, he hated to exhaust it too early.

A grubby-looking journal sat open beside Freeman on the table, and he'd have given a good deal to be able to read just one of its pages, but the widow reached over and flipped it closed before he'd caught more than the date and the usual notation on the weather. All right then, best to drink his cider, say what he had to say, and get home to his sister's; she wouldn't be pleased if she had to set out two suppers.

"Do you happen to recall a conversation over a year ago where I mentioned a case before the court in which Mr. Otis attacked the legality of the Writs of Assistance?"

"I do, and vividly."

"Then you might be interested to learn that the verdict has come in. Mr. Otis has lost his case."

She gazed at him with the unfocused eyes of a person in deep thought and then nodded. "This comes as no great surprise to you," she said.

"It surprises no one, least of all Mr. Otis. But although the Writs are declared legal, there seems little interest in their enforcement."

"So. 'Tis the end of it."

" 'Tis the end of nothing."

She studied him again, nodded again. "I would hope—" She left it there.

Very well, Freeman thought. He might not know what she wrote in her journal or talked of with Aunt Goss, but he thought he knew what she hoped of.

And without planning it, barely even thinking it, he fished in his pocket and brought out an assortment of coins. "How much for a bed?" he asked.

She looked straight at him and never faltered. "Without board?"

"With."

"Up under the eaves, with such company as might wash in, or full room below?"

"Full room below."

"Below room with meals, three shillings."

"And what for a fortnight?"

Again, not a flinch. "Two pounds."

"Well, then, at a savings of two shillings, best make it the fortnight."

He flipped his hand upside down, spreading the coins over the table. He pulled out two pounds sterling and pushed them at her.

"Thank you," she said.

He nodded, and they fell into their usual silence, like two birds after dark.

"Would you like to see your accommodation now?" she asked at length.

He nodded. She stood up, and he followed the gently swishing skirt into the northwest chamber. The minute he stepped into it he thought of that other room in the opposite corner, and that night in Barnstable, when he'd walked the floor in his own room while she'd lain in the one opposite. He wouldn't sleep a minute in this house, he was certain of it, but what did it matter? He'd not slept a great many minutes down the road, either.

She pointed out each piece of furniture as if he had no eyes, as if in fact he didn't own them. She talked about linens and breakfast and dinner and supper; when she ran out of things to list she gave a little shrug and a smile and led him back to the keeping room fire. She reached for a fresh log, but Freeman got there first and dropped it onto the hot cinders. The flames shot up and turned her face bright gold, erasing the lines, making her appear the very opposite of himself, all rest and contentment. But was she? She barely limped now, the hands were marred but functional, her flesh had filled out some, but more than one of the old shadows still danced across her face as the flames withered.

"Will you answer my question now, Widow Berry?" he asked. "Are you content in your house?"

She had that way of looking off in thought as if she'd just been carried bodily out of the room. He'd been trying to decide if she'd been carried off to sea or only down the road when her eyes came back and fixed on him.

"I intend to be, Mr. Freeman."

Historical Notes

In 1761 Massachusetts:

- James Otis, a lawyer from Barnstable, Massachusetts, had just resigned his lucrative position as advocate for the Crown rather than defend some trade acts that authorized, in his view, illegal search and seizure. Instead he accepted, without fee, the task of challenging the legality of the Writs, and in his challenge he shifted the argument from one concerning technical rules of trade to one concerning fundamental liberties and natural rights of man, principles on which future revolutionary activity was grounded. (As John Adams later claimed, "Then and there the child Independence was born.")

- So many Cape Cod men died at sea that one heard reference to its "towns full of widows."
- One in two hundred women and one in four children died during the birth process. The greatest cause of accidental death for a woman was fire.
- John Sequattom, the last full-blooded Sauquatuckett Indian "recognized as such," had been dead eighteen years.
- A married woman could not own property or sign contracts. A widow was legally entitled to life use of one-third her husband's real estate, actual title to the property customarily passing to the nearest living male heir.
- Punishable crimes included working on the Sabbath, nonattendance at church, profanity, and any white woman seducing an Indian.
- Slavery had been legal for a hundred and twenty years and would remain legal for twenty more, although the term "servant" was commonly used in place of "slave."
- Only males who attended church and possessed an estate valued above twenty pounds could vote.
- The Cape Cod town known today as Brewster was the north parish of another Cape town, Harwich, and was commonly called Satucket Village, after the Satucket River (today Stony Brook), whose fertile banks and powerful stream first drew settlers, Indian and English, to the area. The river in its turn was named after the Sauquatuckett Indians who first peopled the area. Route 6A, which runs the length of Cape Cod, was called the King's road and was laid out by the English over the original Indian trail. In Satucket it ran along

much the same path as it does today, with the exception of the piece between the two ends of Stony Brook Road. That section didn't exist, because the gristmill on Stony Brook Road was one of two main centers of town (the other being on Main Street around First Parish Church) and the King's road took the more frequently traveled route past the mill. Modern-day visitors may still travel the King's road past the site of the original church onto Stony Brook Road to a nineteenth-century working version of the old mill, which was built diagonally across the road from the site of the original. The mill wheel still grinds corn, the herring still run upstream each spring to spawn, and traces of the old Sauquatuckett Indian path can still be found along the millpond.

Bibliographical Notes

The following primary sources from the Massachusetts Historical Society were most useful in researching this book: John Adams's diaries; Isaac Backus's book of accounts; diary of Experience (Wight) Richardson; Josiah Thacher's diary; and Peter Verstille's account book. One additional source was so invaluable that it deserves separate mention. Benjamin Bangs, one of Brewster's leading coastal traders, whalers, merchants, and farmers, kept a diary from 1742 through 1765, in which he logged everything from wind direction to religious musings to local scandal to the politics of the day, and Lyddie Berry's Satucket would not have come to life without it.

The following books or periodicals were also most informative: Alice Brown's *Mercy Warren;* Joy Day Buel and Richard Buel Jr.'s *The Way of Duty—A Woman and Her Family in Revolutionary America;* Delores Bird Carpenter's *Early Encounters—Native Americans and Europeans in New England—from the Papers of W. Sears Nickerson;* Culpepper's *Complete Herbal;* Simeon Deyo's *History of Barnstable County, Massachusetts;* Doris Doane's *A Book of Cape Cod Houses;* Joan Druett's *Hen Frigates—Passion and Peril, Nineteenth Century Women at Sea;* Alice Morse Earle's *Home Life in Colonial Days;* Frederick Freeman's *The Annals of Barnstable County and of Its Several Towns;* Alexander Keysarr's *Widowhood in Eighteenth-Century Massachusetts: A Problem in the History of the Family;* Henry Kitteredge's *Cape Cod—Its People and Their History;* Haynes R. Mahoney's *Yarmouth's Proud Packets;* Daniel R. Mandell's *Behind the Frontier—Indians in Eighteenth Century Eastern Massachusetts;* Mary Beth Norton's *Liberty's Daughters—The Revolutionary Experience of American Women, 1750–1800;* Jane C. Nylander's *Our Own Snug Fireside—Images of the New England Home 1760–1860;* Josiah Paine's *A History of Harwich;* Nancy Thacher Reid's *Dennis, Cape Cod, from First Comers to Newcomers 1639–1993;* Charles Swift's *Cape Cod, the Right Arm of Massachusetts: An Historical Narrative* and *History of Old Yarmouth;* William Tudor's *The Life of James Otis of Massachusetts;* Laura Thatcher Ulrich's *A Midwife's Tale* and *The Age of Homespun;* John Waters Jr.'s *The Otis Family in Provincial and Revolutionary Massachusetts;* Rosemarie Zagarri's *A Woman's Dilemma: Mercy Otis Warren and the American Revolution;* and Michael Zuckerman's *Peaceable Kingdoms—New England Towns in the Eighteenth Century.*